AIR:
Sylphs, Spirits,
& Swan Maidens

Edited by
Rhonda Parrish

AIR:
Sylphs, Spirits,
& Swan Maidens

Edited by
Rhonda Parrish

TYCHE BOOKS LTD.

Air: Sylphs, Spirits, & Swan Maidens
Edited by Rhonda Parrish
Copyright © 2020

Published by Tyche Books Ltd.
Calgary, Alberta, Canada
www.TycheBooks.com

Cover Art by Ashley Walters
Cover Layout by Indigo Chick Design
Interior Layout by Ryah Deines
Editorial by Rhonda Parrish

First Tyche Books Ltd Edition 2020
Print ISBN: 978-1-989407-20-2
Ebook ISBN: 978-1-989407-19-6

This book was funded in part by a grant from the Alberta Media Fund.

Alberta
Government

Dedicated to Jo.
Always.

Contents

Introduction

Rhonda Parrish

To PARAPHRASE MARGARET Curelas when I told her what the Table of Contents for this anthology looked like, "Air is definitely a thing all its own." Despite being book three in a four book anthology series, *Air: Sylphs, Spirits, and Swan Maidens* absolutely has a distinct flavour all its own. It stands out as something which belongs in this series, but doesn't blend into it. Something which is difficult to describe or pin down.

Which, honestly, seems appropriate given the subject matter.

Air is the first anthology in this series to contain a significant amount of poetry content, for one thing. That also seems appropriate for the element. Small, powerful bursts of story (not unlike gusts of wind that come up out of nowhere) that just happen to be in the form of poetry, not prose. I used to deal a lot with poetry but it's been a while, so it was refreshing (like a spring breeze!) to be able to jump into that again.

Working on *Air* also made me aware of how closely tied to some other elements it is—water in particular. This Table of Contents doesn't accurately depict the number of air/water hybrid stories I saw in my submissions—far more were submitted than were accepted—but even so, some stories could have easily found their home in a water anthology as an air one.

1

Conversely, some stories may not, on the surface, feel like they rely very heavily on any element at all but they definitely checked one of the "Sylph, Spirit, or Swan Maid" boxes.

I like that. It helps keep the anthology from feeling homogenous while still staying true to the theme. The intent.

A couple things about this anthology surprised me. One was the vast amounts of mythology from all over the world referenced in the works in my submissions, as well as those I eventually chose to include. And fairy lore too.

Another pleasant surprise was the variety of birds that made an appearance. I ought not have been surprised because birds and air are a natural combination, but I'd expected most of the bird stories to be about swans. I was excited to see other varieties such as cranes and ravens and geese (oh my!) as well.

The result of all this is an anthology I'm very proud of and a worthy addition to this series, I think. I knew going in that air was going to be the trickiest element to try and anthologize but I did my best and I'm pleased with the results.

Rhonda
Edmonton
4/21/20

The Snow Wife

Rose Strickman

THE SNOW WHIPPED in white curtains around Nathaniel. Sawhorse snorted warm air down his neck, and he patted his old gelding while blinking through the developing blizzard, desperately trying to find the road again. But there was nothing: just the bare New England winter forest, dark and menacing through the weird white light of the evening snowstorm.

For the thousandth time, he cursed his foolishness in setting out to see Martha at such a time. She might be his fiancée, but what a lot of good that would do them if he died of exposure on his way to her house. But this blizzard had come out of nowhere. One moment it had been a clear winter day, the forests spiced like Christmas, and then the skies had darkened, the clouds crowding in, and the wind whistled down with a fluting shriek, bringing the first stinging blast of snowflakes. He'd lost the road in short order, and now wandered the forest, leading his horse, growing colder by the minute, and trying not to think of what fate might await him tonight.

The wind swirled around him, whipping through the trees. For a moment, it sounded like a woman's laughter. Something fluttered in the corner of his eye—a white sleeve? He whipped his head around but saw no sign of a sleeve, or a person.

3

But he *did* see— "Come on, Sawhorse, I think we're saved!" He led Sawhorse forward, toward the dim, flickering light.

They stepped out of the forest onto a path and made good time to the snow-decked wrought-iron gate set in the stone wall. Nathaniel wiped snow from his eyes, blinking at the gate and the great house beyond. He'd thought he knew all of the worthy houses in this region—his own family had lived here for generations, wealthy and well respected—but this place was a mystery to him: a tall mansion in the woods, laced with snow and gemmed with lit windows.

The woman's laughter—no, it was just the wind—whistled again behind him, and he started forward, pushing the unlocked, icy gate open. It didn't matter who owned this house. He couldn't stay out here.

He fought his way to the front door, the wind pushing him one way and then the other. He kept thinking he heard laughter, and a singing cry. But he didn't stop, crossing the frozen yard to tie Sawhorse to a relatively sheltered post and then staggering to the icy front steps, mounting them to the tall dark door. He knocked on it, loud and clear.

It seemed an eternity passed before it opened. When it did, it let out a blast of light, and an old man, a butler, peered out nearsightedly.

"The missus?" The butler's old voice came out sharp. "Have you seen the missus?"

Nathaniel blinked. "The—missus? Ah, no. I was caught in the storm, and hoped I could ask for shelter—"

"Let him in, Hamilton." Another man glided into the front hall behind Hamilton, hair grey, back straight. His ice-grey eyes travelled over Nathaniel. "He hasn't seen the missus. He's just lost."

"Thank you, sir!" Nathaniel stepped inside as Hamilton shuffled aside with an audible sniff. "There's my horse too, outside—"

"Hamilton, see that his horse is taken to the stables and given food and a rub-down," ordered the master. "And then bring us hot wine in the library."

Hamilton bowed and ghosted away as Nathaniel peeled off his icy cloak, gloves, and hat. A footman appeared to take them away. "Thank you again, sir," Nathaniel said fervently.

"Not at all," said the master, a bit more warmly. "This way, young sir." The master led Nathaniel through the house. It was clean but cold, and there were no signs of any festive Christmas decorations, despite the season. "Might I ask your name? And how you got lost on a night like this?"

"I'm Nathaniel. Nathaniel Greene. We live down near Ayleton. I'm up from Harvard for the holidays. I was . . . well, I was going to see my fiancée, Miss Martha Dumfries, but the storm came up and I got lost."

The master gave an odd, sardonic laugh as he opened the door to a cigar-scented room lined with books. "Of course you did."

Nathaniel decided not to address that strange response. "May I ask *your* name, sir?"

"Crowell," said the master after a moment. "John Crowell." He went to the cold fireplace and began to lay out logs himself.

Nathaniel, hurrying to help, stopped dead. "John Crowell?" He gaped. "*The* John Crowell? The explorer? The one who went to Asia? My God, sir, we all thought you must be dead! I mean," he stammered as Crowell looked up and raised a sardonic eyebrow, "that is . . . No one's heard from you in a while . . ."

"It's all right. I have lived a rather retired life since my return to America." The fire flared up and Crowell stepped back. In its light, he was a craggy man, with deep lines on his face, well into his middle years, but still vigorous. "And I'm hardly an explorer anymore. Come, Mr. Greene, warm yourself."

Nathaniel hurried to stand by the fire, holding out his hands with a sigh of bliss. Outside, the storm rapped at the windows.

Nathaniel looked at his companion, mind whirling with a hundred questions. He asked the first that came to mind. "Do you live here alone, sir?"

"I have the servants." Crowell paused. "And my wife."

At that moment, Hamilton came in with a tray of wine and cakes. He set it on the table nearest the fire and turned away, the light glimmering in his eyes, to leave the room before Nathaniel could thank him.

He poured himself a glass and took a slice. "Ah—when I was at the door, Hamilton asked me if I'd seen the missus. I hope your wife isn't . . . ?"

"Oh, no," said Crowell. "She's perfectly fine." Outside, it was

5

almost completely dark.

"Will she be joining us tonight, sir?" Nathaniel cast his mind back; he'd heard something strange about the explorer's wife, long ago. That she was Chinese, or Japanese, or some similar outlandish thing, but no one was sure. No one had ever properly seen her since the day she'd stepped off the train with her new husband, to travel to his remote house and, apparently, never leave it again.

Crowell gave his odd, joyless laugh. "Not tonight." He gestured with his wineglass out at the raging storm.

"You must live quite a quiet life here, sir," said Nathaniel, when it became clear Crowell wasn't going to elaborate. "Does it suit your wife?"

"Down to the ground," said Crowell. "I prefer it, too."

"Really, sir? After all your travels?"

"One gets tired." The light caught Crowell's icy eyes as he shrugged, like sunlight off glaciers. "How are you enjoying Harvard, Mr. Greene? Studying for the bar?"

They discussed Harvard and other commonplace matters a while longer, while outside the storm intensified and Nathaniel's words slowed as his exhaustion caught up with him. At last, Crowell called an end to the evening.

"You'll have to spend the night, I'm afraid," he said. "I'll have Hamilton lay a fire in one of the guestrooms and bring you wash water and a nightshirt."

"Thank you," Nathaniel said fervently. "You're very kind."

Crowell gave a slight smile. His face really was very pale, Nathaniel thought, with an odd sheen to it. "It's the least I can do."

THE NEXT MORNING, Nathaniel woke to a knock on the door. "Mr. Greene?" Hamilton called. "I hope I'm not disturbing you, sir."

"Oh—no, no." Nathaniel tried to orient himself. The guestroom was filled with a bright, cold snow-light: it was clearly mid-morning. The storm had ceased sometime during the night, but the world outside was smothered in snow. The fire had gone out and the room was cold. "Please come in."

Hamilton came in, shaving equipment at the ready, followed by a maid carrying logs. "I apologize for the fire going out, sir," he said. "Mr. Crowell said we were to let you sleep, and I fear we do not usually need to lay fires in the guestrooms."

"Quite all right." Nathaniel remained in bed while the maid laid the fire anew. He glanced out the window. His heart sank. The house grounds were covered in a thick white layer, the forest beyond an impassable wilderness.

"Mrs. Crowell is back," said Hamilton suddenly. He was watching Nathaniel with those penetrating green eyes. "She's in the house now. But there might be another storm tonight."

"I hope not," said Nathaniel fervently. "I need to get home. My parents must be so worried."

"You'll have to discuss that with Mr. Crowell." The maid left the room, and Hamilton went to the fire to heat up Nathaniel's shaving water. "Let me dress you, sir."

Nathaniel let himself be dressed and shaved. Feeling marginally better once he was clean, he went downstairs, where Hamilton said breakfast was being served.

Apparently they woke late in this house. Mr. Crowell was still in the dining room when Nathaniel came in, sitting by the cold fireplace and reading a newspaper. The woman sitting beside him looked up at Nathaniel's approach.

Nathaniel came to a halt, blinking. He'd seen Chinese men, dockworkers in New York City, but he'd never seen an Asian woman before, let alone one so striking. Her hair glossed black over her long white dress, her pale face was a perfect oval, her frame delicate and petite. Her most marvellous feature, however, was the colour of her almond-shaped eyes: a vivid, arresting violet shade that pierced the dim room.

"Ah, Mr. Greene." Crowell put down his newspaper with a rustle. "Allow me to introduce my wife, Mrs. Rumiko Crowell. Rumiko, this is the young man who got lost in last night's storm, Nathaniel Greene."

"How do you do, ma'am?" Nathaniel bowed politely to Rumiko. She smiled slightly, inclining her head.

"It is good to see you up and about, Mr. Greene." She spoke with a slight, unfamiliar accent, but her tone was warm. "I trust you slept well?"

"Yes, ma'am." Nathaniel surreptitiously rubbed his hands together as he approached the table. Why didn't they have a fire laid, on a morning like this? "Thank you for your hospitality."

He sat down and began helping himself from the covered trays. At least the food was hot.

He turned to Crowell. "I was wondering if I could get a message to my family in Ayleton. They must be wondering where I am."

"I'm not sure." Crowell glanced out the window. "The snow's very thick."

"And there may be another storm tonight." Rumiko smiled.

Crowell gave her a strange, sour glance. "Perhaps not."

Nathaniel decided to ignore this. "Well, maybe later, then." His heart squeezed, thinking of what his family must be going through, but he thrust it aside. They would soon learn that he was safe and sound—he hoped.

He turned to Rumiko. "Do you enjoy living out here, Mrs. Crowell?"

"Very much." She smiled at him, and his heart caught. She really was very beautiful. "I've been married to Mr. Crowell for ten years now, and we've lived here the whole while."

"We met in Japan." Crowell toyed with his napkin, glowering at the polished surface of the table.

"Really? It must seem very different here for you, Mrs. Crowell."

"In some ways, yes." She turned a dreamy smile out the window at the wintry scene. "But in other ways it is much the same. The important ways."

"Love's always the most important thing, of course," Nathaniel said warmly. "I'm due to be married this summer, you know, to Miss Martha Dumfries."

"Summer." Rumiko's lip curled. "I'm not so fond of summer." Her plate was perfectly empty, Nathaniel noticed suddenly, without even the smallest crumb.

"No," said Crowell, tone slightly venomous. "*You* like a snowstorm best."

She laughed at this, a surprisingly loud, bell-like sound. "True!" She turned her smile on Nathaniel. "Still, every happiness to you and your intended, Mr. Greene."

"Perhaps you could come to the wedding," said Nathaniel politely. "You and your husband."

"Thank you." Crowell sipped coffee. "We'll see."

Outside, the clouds grew thicker, lowering grey over the

winter world.

AFTER BREAKFAST, NATHANIEL went out to visit Sawhorse. He was relieved to find his gelding warm and happy in the stable with several other horses, eating hay and oats, wrapped in a horse blanket and snorting cheerfully at Nathaniel's approach. At least the Crowells had good stable hands. Nathaniel borrowed a brush and curry comb and gave Sawhorse a good, thorough grooming before heading out again into the snowy yard.

Outside, the wind bit him through his coat, ruffling his hair. The sky was a vast, undifferentiated grey, the forest unbroken stillness. Nathaniel picked his way out of the stable yard and across the snowy gardens, thinking he should go find Crowell again, when a high, melodious laugh rang out.

He turned to see Rumiko skipping across the snow. Almost literally skipping: she didn't seem to fall through the crust at all. She wore a long white cloak, lined with white fur, the hood pushed back so her hair, escaping from its pins, flowed jet-black. Her cheeks were flushed, her violet eyes bright. She laughed again and let out a long, high-pitched whistle.

The wind picked up, hissing around the house and spitting snow into Nathaniel's eyes. He stepped back in a crunch of snow, and Rumiko turned to look at him, her whistle ceasing.

The wind died away almost immediately, but Rumiko remained, smiling at him. "Hello, Mr. Greene!" she called. "I didn't see you there."

"Hello, Mrs. Crowell." Nathaniel bowed. "Are you taking a walk?"

"Oh, yes," she said happily. "It's a beautiful morning."

"That it is." And it *was* beautiful, he had to admit: beautiful with an icy white serenity that seemed to cut off the outside world. "Did you often have snowy days like this in, ah, Japan?"

"Of course," she laughed. "Especially where I lived."

Nathaniel crunched toward her. "Do you ever miss Japan?" he asked curiously. "It must be so different here."

"Sometimes," she shrugged. Up close she was more beautiful than ever, lips parted, astonishing eyes brilliant. The wind waved tendrils of her hair, and an odd, cold scent wafted off her. "But, like I said, the most important things are still the same here."

"Like what?" Nathaniel knew he was prying, but in that moment his curiosity was stronger than his sense of propriety.

In response, she pursed her lips together and blew another whistle, high and whining. The wind kicked up again, whipping around the pair. Snow swirled around their shoes, stung Nathaniel's face. He felt another dagger of cold, stabbing deep under his clothes. A part of him shrank from it, wanting to run, but another part seemed to open to the chill, unfurling like an icy flower.

Her brow knit. She let her whistle die, and the wind vanished again. She tilted her head at him quizzically. "Interesting," she said at last, softly.

"Rumiko!" Crowell was standing on the porch without a coat, glaring at them. "Rumiko, come inside."

Rumiko tossed her head with a merry laugh. "Yes, dear. Coming." She wafted lightly back across the snow, with one last look behind at Nathaniel.

Crowell remained after she'd gone inside, arms folded as he stared at Nathaniel. "Hamilton's laid a fire in the library," he said at last, tone almost curt. "You're welcome to come warm yourself. And perhaps we could discuss getting a message to your family."

"Yes, sir. Thank you, sir." Nathaniel began floundering toward the porch, thinking glumly that his stay here was likely to become even less enjoyable if Crowell thought he had designs on his wife.

Around the house, the wind picked up again.

"RUMIKO, LEAVE THE boy alone!"

Nathaniel started awake at the raised voices wafting down the chimney. The fire had gone out again and he huddled under a pile of blankets. Outside, another storm wailed, snow lashing the windows loudly, but not loudly enough to drown out the argument now raging right above Nathaniel's room.

Nathaniel's first reaction was one of sleepy resentment. It had been a long, strange day. He'd spent most of it with Crowell, playing billiards in the library and discussing getting a message out on horseback or sending Nathaniel home in the Crowells' sleigh. Even while they talked, however, the wind picked up, and it became obvious that another heavy snowstorm was on its way. Crowell had watched the first snowflakes falling, his mouth going thin and tight, and excused himself abruptly, leaving the library on some unnamed purpose. Left alone, Nathaniel had tried to read, then examined the various foreign ornaments on display, and finally gone in search of his host. But he couldn't find him, or Rumiko. Around him the domestic work of the house went silently on, Hamilton smiling sarcastically at Nathaniel while supervising the few, mouse-like servants, who hurried past without looking at him. The afternoon dragged on, until dinner came at last. That, at least, had been somewhat enjoyable, even with Crowell silent and tense. Rumiko had more than made up for her husband's lack of conversation, asking Nathaniel many questions about himself, his family, his studies and his fiancée, and cheerfully answering his own questions about her homeland.

Still, Nathaniel had been glad to get away and go to bed. And now he wasn't even able to sleep while the Crowells fought.

Then he realized what they were fighting *about* and came completely awake, blinking up at the ceiling.

Rumiko said something inaudible, which earned Crowell's contemptuous laughter. "Don't try that. I know you. The boy is a guest in my house. You don't touch him."

"I haven't touched him." Rumiko's voice, quieter than Crowell's, didn't sound afraid. On the contrary, she sounded slightly amused. "Quite the opposite, in fact."

There was a pause. When Crowell spoke again, he sounded almost panicked. "Rumiko, please . . . Don't do to him what you did to me!"

"Oh? And what did I do that was so dreadful?" Rumiko laughed mockingly, and the wind rose, chuckling around the house. "You feel no cold, my John; you stride untouched through blizzards. Winter has had no power over you since you married me, the ice and snow cannot hinder you, and your eyes proclaim your allegiance. Many would envy you."

"And would they envy the frozen bodies you leave in the woods?"

Nathaniel's heart pounded. He must not be hearing this right. He buried his head beneath his pillow, piling up his blankets, but somehow he still made out Rumiko's response:

"The boy stays, John."

"IT LOOKS LIKE you'll be trapped here again today, sir," said
Hamilton the next morning as he helped Nathaniel dress.
Outside, the snow whirled against the windows. "I am very
sorry."

"It's all right, Hamilton." Nathaniel hoped Hamilton couldn't
tell how hard he tried to avoid the butler's chill, dry touch. "I
only hope I'm not too much trouble to you, in addition to your
usual work."

"Oh," said Hamilton with an odd smile. "No trouble at all,
sir." He straightened Nathaniel's collar and made a sweeping
gesture toward the door. "The master and missus await you."

Nathaniel went, trying not to feel like he was marching to his
doom. There was no need for such dread, he scolded himself as
he descended the stairs: the Crowells might be an odd couple,
but they had been nothing but welcoming toward him. He
pushed last night's overheard quarrel out of his mind: he must
have been dreaming.

Rumiko was all smiles as he entered the dining room. "Good
morning, Mr. Greene! Did you sleep well?" At the head of the
table, Crowell glowered.

"Very well, thanks." Nathaniel shivered as he went to sit
down; *why* was there no fire in here? "Though it looks like I'll
have to impose on your hospitality a little longer."

"Oh, it is no imposition!" Rumiko leaned forward. "We quite
enjoy having you here, don't we, John?"

"Oh, yes." But Crowell didn't look at Nathaniel as he said so.
He glared murderously at Rumiko, who gave him a seraphic
smile. "Of course."

"I'm glad," said Nathaniel after a pause. He clapped his
hands together. It really was chilly in here. "If I may ask," he
said tentatively, "why is there no fire in here?"

"Rumiko doesn't like them," said Crowell, glaring at his wife.
"Do you, darling?"

"Not much," she said with a gentle smile. She toyed with a
fork. "Though, you know, John dear, I don't mind fire nearly as
much as I used to. Before we married."

Crowell barked his sardonic laugh. "I'll bet you don't."

Nathaniel gulped. If he hadn't been hollow with hunger, he

would have bolted from the room. As it was, he ate as quickly as he could before excusing himself.

He went to care for Sawhorse again, rubbing him down and exercising him by walking him up and down the stables, ignoring the ostler's offer to do so. He tried not to let his eyes stray to the dark hulk of the sleigh in the corner, or wonder if he could get it hitched by himself, in the middle of the night, without his hosts noticing.

Outside, he was not really surprised to encounter Rumiko again, gliding over the snow in her white fur cloak, her hands demurely hidden in a white fur muff. "Good day, Mrs. Crowell."

"Good day, Mr. Greene." She smiled at him, and again, despite himself, his breath caught at her beauty. "How is Sawhorse?"

"He's fine, thank you. Getting restless, though."

"Well, he can't go anywhere until it stops snowing." Rumiko extracted a slim white hand to gesture at the still-falling snow, gentle now that the wind had died. "And it looks as though it'll be a while."

Nathaniel sighed, breath frosting out. "You've been very kind," he said. "But I wish I could go. My parents must be so worried."

"These things happen." She was so near now, snowflakes glinting on the embroidery of her wealthy dress, breath invisible between those soft lips. "You'll see them again, I think. And your lovely Miss Martha Dumfries."

Nathaniel frowned at her. "What—"

Rumiko let out a piercing blast.

Her whistle tore straight through him, leaving an empty chasm of ice in its wake. Cold, cold: the world was nothing but cold and snow and icy, howling wind. Nathaniel staggered back, numbness climbing his limbs as the gale wrapped around him, sucking at him, frost spreading over his skin. Cold, *cold*— Nathaniel screamed silently, ice scraping his throat, even as he felt something open deep inside him, pulling that cold in. Inviting the gale. Letting it seep deep within him.

The last thing he was aware of, as the darkness took hold and he lost consciousness, was Rumiko Crowell's triumphant laughter.

THE CHILL BREEZE was soft, caressing. Nathaniel lay, weak and floating, enjoying its touch. The cold felt so good.

An arm levered him up, and the rim of a cup pressed against his lips. "Here, boy," said Crowell, sounding far gentler than Nathaniel had ever heard him. "Try drinking this."

Nathaniel drank—and immediately spat out the scalding liquid, coughing and choking. This stuff *burned*. Blearily, he opened his eyes, to stare up into Crowell's concerned face, and, beyond him, the dim library, lit only by lamps. There was a strong smell of oil.

"Ah." Crowell put aside the hot coffee. "That's what I thought." He looked at Nathaniel with a strange pity.

"I—what—" Nathaniel looked around. He was lying on the sofa in the library. It was night, and there was no fire laid. The open window let in a chilly breeze. At least the snow had stopped and the storm cleared away, Nathaniel thought dazedly, seeing the blistering stars above the treetops outside.

"I've sent the servants away," said Crowell quietly. "Even Hamilton. They all went out on the sleigh. They took your horse—they'll return him to your parents."

"Sawhorse . . . ? The sleigh . . ." Nathaniel half-sat up, earning a wave of dizziness. "But you said—"

"I lied," said Crowell casually. "Rumiko insisted on it, said you had to stay." He pushed Nathaniel back gently. "Lie still. Let your strength come back." He paused. "You won't need a sleigh or a horse to get home now, boy. Not as long as there's snow on the ground."

Nathaniel stared at Crowell. The older man's eyes gleamed that steely ice-grey, and his breath did not mist out in the freezing cold library. He stood in his dinner jacket, showing no sign of discomfort. Just as Nathaniel felt no discomfort, in his thin clothes, in this winter room without a fire . . .

"Where's Mrs. Crowell?" he asked in a small voice.

"She's out," Crowell said eventually. "I don't think I'll be seeing her again." He gave a small smile.

"How did you two meet?" Nathaniel asked after a long pause.

"Ah." Crowell sat down in the armchair near the sofa. "Now that's a story and a half, young Mr. Greene.

"It was in Japan, ten years ago. I was traveling with several companions, friends from my college days. We'd travelled together before and thought we knew what we were doing. The locals warned us not to take the mountain pass—they said that storms could come from nowhere up there, and more than animals lived in the mountains—but we thought we could make it. And of course we paid no credence to local legends of monsters who lived in the snows and summoned storms.

"Well, a storm came up all right. We pitched tents and prepared to wait it out. We were so cold . . . We huddled around the fire, in the midst of that gale. Then we saw something.

"It was a human figure, out there in the storm. A woman, dressed in a kimono, after the Japanese style. A young, beautiful woman, just beyond our firelight, looking at us with lovely violet eyes.

"One of my friends—James he was, James Prescott—stood up, asked her who she was and what she was doing there. She just smiled. Then she whistled."

"Whistled . . . ?" Nathaniel's voice was faint.

"Yes." Crowell smiled grimly. "She whistled, and the gale wrapped around us. I watched while ice blasted over all my friends, frost over their eyes, freezing to death in seconds. The ice crawled over me too, but I didn't die. Instead, something in me opened to that cold, that wind, invited it in, made it one with me—"

Nathaniel cried out, lurching to his feet, room spinning around him. Crowell's chilly hands took hold of him, pushed him back onto the sofa. "Listen, boy," he hissed. "There are things you must know. I lost consciousness, there in the snow. When I awoke, I was weak, but the cold no longer touched me. The wind blew, but it couldn't weaken me. The snow couldn't freeze me. And the *yuki-onna* stood there still, among the frozen bodies of my friends, waiting for me to wake."

"The *yuki* . . . ?"

"*Yuki-onna.* The snow woman. They are creatures of cold and wind and snow, immortal beings: they live in the forests and mountains, and feed by blasting human men with their icy breaths, eating their lives as they freeze to death. But some men—some very few men—do not die when the *yuki-onna* blasts them. Instead, they take in her power, their souls attuning to the winter magic. These men become immune to the winter, to cold and snow and wind. But there's a price for this." Crowell smiled, a slow and terrible smile. "The *yuki-onna* has

15

power over the men who survive her breath. They have to marry her, bring her into the human world, where she can hunt beyond the forests and mountains, impervious to the warmth that is as deadly to her kind as the cold is to ours. Even flames lose their power—"

"No!" Nathaniel's vision blurred. "No, it's not true—"

"It *is* true." Crowell's voice pursued him through the dark. "I had to marry Rumiko and bring her with me back to America; I had no choice. She's had power over me, and over those under my command, for ten years now. She's killed so many with her icy breath, out there in the forest—but not you. You're like me— you accepted the winter into your heart, and now she is no longer my wife. She's yours."

Outside, in the clear cold night, Nathaniel heard a high, sweet voice singing out a single name: *"Nathaniel . . ."*

A scream ripped itself from Nathaniel's throat. He lunged forward, dodging Crowell, lurching toward the window. He half-fell through the opening, into an intense cold that had no power to touch him, onto snow that did not collapse under his weight, but bore him up, letting him stand easily as he beheld the figure awaiting him in the yard.

She stood on top of the snow as he did, more beautiful than ever now that she had set aside her illusion of mortality, beautiful with the deadly loveliness of snow and ice. Her loose black hair whipped in the wind that played around her, stirring the long white kimono she wore, violet eyes bright as stars as she took him in.

"Nathaniel," she sighed again. Her lips curved. "Husband."

"*No!*" Nathaniel screamed, and there came a sudden roar behind him.

He whirled around to see the library window engulfed in flames. Crowell must have soaked the curtains and furnishings in oil while Nathaniel slept, for the entire library went up in seconds, infernal orange light blazing from the windows, the heat beating Nathaniel back as the fire spread. Smoke poured upward, the whole house whining and moaning as the flames began to devour it, and Nathaniel could hear the screams and squeals of the horses as they fled from the stable, the doors left open just for this purpose.

From Crowell, however, trapped inside the house, there was no scream. Instead, Nathaniel thought he could hear a sardonic laugh. Coughing, Nathaniel backed away, feet leaving no prints in the snow, away from the heat back toward the loving, life-giving cold. A small hand fell on his sleeve.

"Nathaniel." Rumiko smiled up at him. "Come. We have far to travel, to get to your own home." Her grin turned vulpine. "I'm looking forward to meeting your parents."

"No!" He recoiled.

"Too late for that, Nathaniel." She leaned in close, cold breasts against his arm. "You're my husband now."

An eviscerating horror ripped through Nathaniel. He lashed out, taking hold of Rumiko, her flesh so cold (but of course cold had no power over him now, not even hers) and, with a strength he'd never known he had, he threw her backward into the flames.

Her shriek kicked up a wind such as he'd never felt. He crouched down, face hidden, as the gale screeched and whirled around him, snow skating harmlessly over his flesh, the trees moaning and blowing backward under the gale. Even the flames blew low under the wind's force. But Nathaniel fought his way up—he got to his feet—and he ran, ran as he'd never run before, over the top of the snow, into the trees, away from the burning house and the *yuki-onna* who burned within it.

NATHANIEL'S PARENTS, WHEN he returned home, were as overjoyed and dumbfounded as he'd expected. They were also puzzled and concerned: where had he been? Why had that Hamilton fellow dropped off Sawhorse without him? Nathaniel fended off their questions with vague answers, implying, without too much difficulty, that he'd been ill and couldn't remember much. Too relieved at his return to question him overmuch, his parents let the subject drop.

He did not try to go see Martha Dumfries again, but she came to see him the day after Christmas, hurriedly climbing down from her sleigh and clutching his hands, brown eyes bright with anxiety. Nathaniel let her love and relief wash over him and tried not to think about how her warm flesh made his skin crawl, as all heat now sickened him.

Her visit went well, Martha and the Greenes revelling in each other's company and Nathaniel's safe return. It was only when it came time to hand her back into her sleigh that Nathaniel froze, eyes on the coachman.

Martha's gaze followed his. "Oh! That's Hamilton, our new butler. He's standing in for Tom, who's still with his family over Christmas. He's quite good with horses, aren't you, Hamilton?"

"Thank you, miss." Hamilton inclined his head to her and slid his green gaze over the stock-still Nathaniel. His mouth curved slightly. "Not too cold, I trust, Mr. Greene?"

Nathaniel found voice. "Not at all," he croaked. And, indeed, the cold did not touch him, nor the winter wind. "Goodbye, Miss Dumfries. Take care of her, Hamilton."

Hamilton nodded, still smiling, and lashed the horses into motion, bearing Martha home. Nathaniel stood and watched as they disappeared up the road.

He returned to Harvard in due time and suffered silently as the winter melted away, giving way to a long, stickily warm spring. Summer approached unstoppably, the heat unrelenting, a vile sensation on his skin, sapping Nathaniel's strength, but he refused to long for winter. He refused to think of Rumiko's cold, perfect flesh, or the dreams that tormented him, night after night, as he returned home and his wedding to Martha Dumfries approached.

The wedding day dawned, and the ceremony took place, attended by both families, in the little church near Nathaniel's home. Nathaniel stood and sweated by the altar, but felt all his discomfort, all his worries, disappear at Martha's approach, shy and smiling under her white lace veil, on her father's arm.

Yes, Nathaniel thought after the ceremony as he took Martha's arm, processing back down the aisle under the smiles and gazes of their friends and families. Yes, this was who he was meant to marry. Her flesh didn't even burn his anymore; indeed, it was pleasantly cool.

The wedding feast lasted long into the night, and then it came time for the couple to go to bed, in the house their families had built for them. Beforehand, however, Nathaniel's father took him aside, closing the door behind them.

"Son," he said, beaming. "I'm so proud of you." He kissed Nathaniel on the forehead, and he tried not to flinch at how it burned. "You know what to do, right?" He cuffed Nathaniel playfully.

"Of course, Father," Nathaniel grinned. "No worries there."

"Good, good. But there's something you should know . . ." His father leaned in, then checked, frowning. "Were your eyes always that colour, son?"

"What colour?"

"A sort of pale grey. Like ice." His father craned around, still staring. "Must be the light," he shrugged. "Anyway, Nathaniel, what I meant to tell you is that you've had some unexpected good luck."

Dread built in Nathaniel's stomach. "Good luck?"

"Remember that old explorer fellow who lived out in the woods? John Crowell? Well, he's left you a fortune!"

Nathaniel recoiled. "What?"

"Yes, I've just heard from the solicitors," his father beamed. "Apparently he took quite a shine to you when you were staying with him over the winter. Tragic about his and his wife's deaths, of course, but he's left you all his money! You're a wealthy man, Nathaniel."

Nathaniel couldn't speak, but only choke.

"So go in and please your wife." His father gave him a manly embrace. "You two will have no financial worries. Your marriage is off to a wonderful start!"

Dazed, Nathaniel let his father lead him from the room. The wedding guests all raised glasses in one last toast as he headed numbly upstairs to the flower-hung bridal chamber.

He was not entirely surprised to see Hamilton there, setting up the final touches to the decorations while the summer moon beamed in through the open window. "I don't suppose," said Nathaniel at last, "that Crowell left you to me as well?"

Hamilton looked up, emerald eyes agleam. "Oh, no, sir. I came with my mistress." And, with a bow, he opened the door to the dressing room to let in Nathaniel's bride.

She stepped in through the door, graceful as a snowflake, flesh as white as frosted ice, hair—now that she had dispensed with the illusion of Martha Dumfries—shining black and flowing over her lacy nightgown. Rumiko's violet eyes shone as she smiled lovingly at Nathaniel. "My dear husband," she said softly. "Husband who gave me the power to survive the flames. Let us to bed."

Outside, the wind whistled through the trees.

Into Thick Air

Davian Aw

they work within the haze in the self-same way
other creatures prefer the darkness of shadows;
the only importance the fading away of features,
identities blurring in smoke. they whisper
soft secrets to the ears of children cast away
on green fields of isolation, gazing at the streets
with their rushing masked figures hurrying
past schools full of naked faces.

smoke-pale hands outstretch in the murk,
gesturing invitations to another plane
cajoling young feet onto clouds of grey
into another realm.

P.E. teachers idly turn their way
to squint towards the empty patch of grass
eyes stinging, seeing nothing more
than white upon the green.

Faery Dust

Mark Bruce

"I'M A FAERIE," his client said through the iron grill of the custody room.

Martin looked at the woman—a girl, really—and considered her small delicate features, her mischievous green eyes, her short red hair.

"These days it's okay to call yourself a lesbian," Martin said.

"You don't understand," she said sadly. "I'm a real Faerie. Like Titania. Or the Faerie Queen, Gloriana."

"Oh," Martin said, wondering if he was going to have to declare a doubt as to the client's sanity, "you mean like Tinkerbell."

"She's a Pixie," the girl said, wrinkling her nose. "They're all tramps."

"Okay," Martin said neutrally. "Well, I'm a Public Defender. Some people think we are imaginary creatures, too."

"Sir Defender of Public, you must release me from this awful place," the girl said, staring at him through the grill with green eyes which reminded him of a leafy tree in the forest.

Martin nodded. Faerie, Pixie, or normal woman, no one really wanted to stay in custody. He felt rather than looked at the long concrete walls around him, the metal table that ran the length of the room, the small booths with wire grills through which he talked to his clients. He had been on a tour of the cells, so he knew how dark they were, how hopelessness seemed to have seeped into the yellow paint of the walls.

"Seems as if we're going to have a problem doing that," Martin said. "You have no identification."

"Where I come from we all know one another by sight. No need for papers that tell who we are." The girl seemed offended by the idea.

"Well, here in Victorville, the cops need something to verify who you are," Martin said, somewhat apologetically. He knew better than to provoke a mentally ill person, even one as pretty as this one. He looked at her file on his iPad: Miranda Morningstar. *Of course.* She couldn't be Shirley Jones or even Lequisha Anderson. He sighed to himself again.

"Do you have family I can contact?" Martin asked her.

"Not around here," the girl said. "I belong in the enchanted forest with my brothers and sisters."

"Your elven family," Martin said.

"No, not elves. Elves are trash. Faeries. I'm a Faerie." She folded her arms and glared at him.

"Sorry," Martin mumbled. He was apologizing again. He was apologizing to a faerie. He should just go tell the judge the girl was wacky and have done with it. But there was something special about her. It wasn't a sexual thing—Martin was well into his fifties and this girl couldn't be more than eighteen. No, it was more of a . . . well, a magical thing.

"So, no family locally," Martin said.

"No," she said. "Is that bad?"

"If you had family, I could ask the judge to release you to them. You'd have an address where the court could track you down if you didn't show up for court."

"Once I get out of here," the girl said, gritting her little pearly teeth, "I am never going to get within a league of this ugly place."

"Then they'll issue a bench warrant and you'll be back in jail all over again," Martin said. "Let's try this again. You are Miranda Morningstar. You are a Faerie. And you're being accused of breaking into a candy store and gorging yourself on chocolate." The police report said she had been found sleeping against the storefront in the morning with chocolate smeared on her face. But the alarms in the shop had not gone off.

"Is that what that wonderful food was?" Miranda said dreamily. "I've never had its like. Do you think I could get some to bring back to the Faerie Queen?"

"Of course," Martin said. "So long as you pay for it. I don't suppose you have any money?"

"Money?" her face squinched up into a thoughtful frown. Then the clouds cleared. "Oh, you mean gold. No, to touch gold or any kind of metal is poison for a Faerie."

Again with the Tolkien, Martin thought. He tried another approach.

"Where do you come from?" he asked. He needed something to tell the judge for his O.R. pitch.

"Faeries are a woodland people," she said. "Do you have any woodland around here?"

"In the desert?" Martin smiled. "Only a sad little tree sitting in the backyard of the place I rent. I've never seen it flower. It looks like it needs water. I feel badly for it sometimes."

The girl's face saddened.

"Poor thing. Neglected and thirsty. It pains my heart to hear of this." She wiped away a tear.

Martin looked down at his file. The break-in at the candy store was the least of the girl's problems.

"The big thing we gotta talk about," he said, putting on his most serious tone, "Is the methamphetamine they found on you. Several grams."

"Meta what?" she said innocently.

"The granulated substance in your pocket," he said sternly.

"Oh," she laughed merrily. "You mean the Faerie dust."

"The . . ." Martin clenched his teeth to be sure he had heard what she'd said.

"Faerie dust. We use it to make magic," Miranda Morningstar said, as if that cleared everything up.

"The cops think it's meth," Martin said.

"I don't know what that is," Miranda said.

"I guess we'll find out when they test it," Martin said.

"Test?"

"They have a reagent test that will determine the nature of the substance."

"How do they . . . I don't understand," she said, her pretty face crinkling up again.

"They have chemicals that they mix with the stuff that tells them . . ."

"Oh, no!" Suddenly Miranda Morningstar was laughing hysterically. "They will mix my Faerie dust with . . . Oh, I wish I could be there."

"What do you think will happen?" Martin asked, concerned.

"Probably a little *boom* and all my Faerie dust will disappear," she said. "No one will be hurt but they'll be plenty surprised."

"Is it some kind of explosive?" Martin asked. He was sure possession of explosive powder was a much heavier charge.

"No, but when Faerie dust mixes with human dust . . ." she laughed again.

"I have to tell you they want state prison out of you," Martin said when her laughter had finally subsided. "They think you're a big-time drug dealer with all that . . . uh, Faerie Dust."

"I don't understand. I am a Faerie. I don't deal anything. Gold is poison to me, as I told you."

Martin nodded. He could declare a doubt and have the girl examined by the psychiatrists. But that would take months. He had looked at her police report and he thought there might be a good suppression motion in the case.

"Mr. Berry, good sir," the Faerie said, her face now sombre, "please, please release me from this horrible place. It has iron inside its walls and on its windows. My magic can't overcome the iron and it's making me ill. Please. I need to be back in the woodland with my friends and family."

Martin nodded.

"I am going to try to help you. I am going to file a motion to suppress the evidence they found on you. I don't believe they had a right to search you. According to the report, they put you in handcuffs right away, began searching you, looked in your satchel, all before they had any idea any criminal activity was afoot."

She listened to him with the expression of a puppy having the Theory of Relativity explained to it. Finally she shook her head.

"I cannot understand your strange speech," she said. "But I

will make an oath to you: If you release me from this awful place, I will bring magic into your life."

Martin looked at her sideways. Was she coming on to him? Sometimes clients did that, thinking if they offered sexual favours it would motivate the lawyer, but he did not play the game like that.

"I will do my best for you," he said.

"Swear you will get me out of here," she said.

"I swear I will do my utmost," he said.

"Good enough," she said. "It is an unbreakable oath."

He suddenly felt a weird light burn through him. His body jolted as if he had French kissed a live wire. He lost consciousness for a second, then regained his bearings, though the world had a weird pale green tint for a minute or so.

He swayed on the metal bench. He blinked. She was gone.

"I sent your client to court," the bailiff told him. "They were calling for her. Are you okay?"

Martin took a deep breath.

"Yeah," he lied. "I'm fine."

THE JUDGE WOULD not release Miranda Morningstar despite Martin's impassioned pleading. He reminded the judge that this was a non-violent crime and that his client did not have a record.

"Your client is a cipher," the judge said. "She doesn't seem to exist in the official records. Which leads me to believe she's using an alias."

Miranda's sad face was almost more than Martin could bear.

"I know you have fought gallantly for me, Sir Defender of Public," she said. "I shall not forget your kindness."

"This isn't over," Martin said. "We still have a prelim next week. We didn't waive time, so they've got to go forward or release you."

She didn't seem to understand a word of what he said.

That night he went home, feeling more drained than usual. As he drove up to the little duplex he rented in Victorville, the sad tree in the back yard drooped in the heat. Its leaves were wilted and dull. Its branches sagged. The tree seemed to be moaning in the heat.

Martin realized that he had no idea of what kind of tree it

was. He had never seen it flower. It had always seemed dried out and half dead.

He went into the duplex and changed his clothes. He turned on the television but could not concentrate on what Rachel Maddow was trying to tell him. He kept thinking about how thirsty the tree must be.

Finally he went outside and found, rolled up against the side of the duplex, the ratty old garden hose for the house. He screwed the hose onto the outdoor faucet and turned it on. Only a few little leaks sprung out of the hose and a trickle of water emerged from the snout. He stood under the tree and watered it deeply, hoping the roots were catching some of the moisture. In the desert it was hard to tell.

"I met a friend of yours today," he told the tree. "Miranda Morningstar. You know her?"

It was probably just the late afternoon wind, but the tree seemed to nod.

"She was very concerned about you. I guess I haven't taken care of you like I should. So I'll be better about giving you water in the future."

Great, Martin thought. Now I'm talking to trees. Never mind declaring a doubt about his client; he might have to go in to his supervisor and declare a doubt about his own sanity.

ON THE DAY set for Miranda Morningstar's prelim, Martin walked into Department 10 hoping the DA on the case would be willing to give him a misdemeanour and credit time served. For the last week Martin had been wandering lost through haunting dreams about dark forests. Weird creatures lived just beyond the ridges of his consciousness. Miranda would appear from time to time but he could never seem to catch up to her. She would smile sadly and disappear into the bark of a tree.

"A misdemeanour? Are you kidding?" Janet Chang said. She was a tall thin woman with long dark hair and predatory dark eyes. "You know how much meth this girl had on her?"

"I know that the cops usually weigh the meth with packaging, which could add lots of grams to the total if they didn't take it out of the leather pouch," Martin said. "Come on, this girl's never been in trouble before."

"That we know of," Janet said coldly. "The officers think

she's some kind of drug mule from another country."

"Ridiculous," Martin said.

"And she's been causing trouble in lockup," Janet said.

"Trouble?" Martin said sickly. Oh, no. Please don't let her pick up more charges.

In response Janet handed Martin a two-page incident report from the jail:

Inmate Morningstar seemed to be obsessed with the chocolate pudding at mess. She ate her own, then took the pudding of two other inmates, causing a disturbance. When the other women—both of whom were larger than Morningstar—tried to take their pudding back, inmate Morningstar threw them against the wall.

Inmate Morningstar appeared to be intoxicated. She continued to yell that she was a lady in waiting to the Dairy Queen and would not be "trifled with."

It was decided not to request new filings against Inmate Morningstar because the other inmates physically attacked her and she was defending herself. However, Inmate Morningstar was the cause of the incident and has been placed in solitary confinement.

Solitary! Martin's heart went heavy. For a forest creature to be crammed into a small cell by herself was cruel.

He stopped himself. Jesus, he thought. Now I really believe she's a Faerie.

He went to see her in lockup. He had to wait for the special visiting booth for inmates in protective custody. Miranda slogged in wearing the special bright red jumpsuit of a "special" prisoner as if she were walking in tar.

"Sir Defender," she said listlessly.

"I hear you've had some issues with the pudding," Martin said, trying to make her smile.

"The pudding," she said bitterly. "No one told me it was made with milk."

"Um . . ." Martin paused. "Yes, usually pudding is made with milk."

"Milk makes Faerie folk drunk," she said.

"Milk?" Martin said. "You mean drunk like alcohol?"

Miranda nodded. "Yes. Just as men are made stupid by ale and mead, milk makes Faerie folk giddy."

"So we'll keep you away from milk. I'll tell the jail you are allergic."

She nodded her pretty little head.

"Can you get me released from this dungeon?" she said, desperate and weary.

"I'm doing my best, Miranda," he said. "I tried to get the DA to offer you a misdemeanour but she thinks you're part of an international drug cartel."

"DA?"

"Janet Chang," Martin said.

"Oh, the tall one with the angry face. She has no mercy or grace within her."

"I'll tell her you said so," Martin said.

Miranda sighed.

"How much longer must I be in here? Sir Defender, you made an oath to release me."

"I filed the suppression motion," Martin said. "We're having the prelim today. I'm trying to move this case as fast as I can. But, as you see, I am not the guy in charge around here."

Miranda sighed heavily.

"Much longer and I will dwindle to nothing."

"Come now," Martin said, alarmed at the finality of her tone, "that's no way for a young girl like yourself to talk."

"Young girl?" Miranda looked at him in surprise. "How old do you think I am?"

"Nineteen?" Martin hazarded a guess.

Suddenly, Miranda laughed.

"Oh, thank you, dear sir. You have made me laugh in this horrible place. Nineteen? You mean nineteen years?" She wiped a tear of laughter from her green eyes.

"Well, yes . . ." Martin said.

"Dear sir," she said, "Faerie folk have been on this earth for thousands of years. Long before the race of men even walked upright. I am so old I can no longer remember my birth. It was many, many thousands of years ago."

"Okay," Martin said. He again thought it was time to declare a doubt and have the girl sent to the State Hospital. He hesitated because putting her on the Incompetency train would delay her case for months and, if anything, the State Hospital would have an even worse effect on her. Better to try the suppression motion. If he lost that, he would talk to his supervisor.

"Well, then," Martin said, playing along, "if you've been around so long, this ugly little time in your life will just be a blip."

"A what? Sir, you talk strangely. But then, you always talk strangely." Tears welled into her lovely green eyes. "I miss my home!" she cried.

He let her cry—he had been doing this job long enough to know that you just had to let a client cry sometimes—and waited for her tears to abate.

"I am still fighting for you," he said. "Never lose hope."

"Oh, sir," she said, her eyes shining through the tears, "I am most grateful for your assistance. This will not be forgotten."

THEY WERE SENT out to Judge Kita. Judge Kita was as hard on the prosecution as he was on the defence. He was smart, he knew the law—and he was a former prosecutor who couldn't help but instruct the Deputy DA about how to better handle a case.

He and Martin played Hearts every Wednesday in his chambers, but Martin was smart enough to know that a game of hearts would not make Judge Kita his ally in court.

The patrol officer who had arrested Miranda, a young blond man named Sampson, was testifying:

"And I came upon the defendant loitering around the entrance of the business known as *Chocolate Dreams*. She had chocolate on her face and seemed to be sleepy."

"Did she have permission to be there?" Janet Chang said in her snottiest manner. Miranda looked at her and stuck her tongue out. Thankfully, Janet didn't notice.

"I contacted the business owner after we had arrested the defendant," the officer said. "She indicated that she did not know the defendant, did not give her permission to be there."

"And after you arrested her, what happened?"

"She would not give us consent to search her leather pouch on her belt, which made me suspicious that she was hiding something. So, pursuant to arrest, I searched the pouch." The officer testified in a choirboy manner about this casual breach of the Fourth Amendment.

"What did you find in there?"

"A dark crystalline substance suspected to be methamphetamine."

"Objection, foundation," Martin said.

"Overruled for now," Judge Kita said. "You can question him on his qualifications on cross."

Martin shrugged. The cops always got in their opinion as to the identity of the substance anyway.

"How much meth was in there?" Chang asked.

"Objection . . ."

"Sustained," Judge Kita said. "The officer testified it was suspected meth. Remember that, counsel."

Janet Chang gave a brief, tight smile, and looked down at her notes. She didn't like Judge Kita at all.

"How much did the *suspected* meth weigh?" Chang asked.

"Twelve grams," the choirboy sang. It was his high note.

"I don't know what they mean, *grams,*" Miranda whispered to him.

"It's a weight. Like pounds."

"There were not twelve pounds of Faerie Dust in my pouch," she said.

"A gram is a smaller increment . . . I'll explain it later." Martin said. It was always annoying when the client insisted on having a conversation in the middle of testimony. Sure enough, Chang had seen his distraction and had slipped in the question of Miranda's identity.

"I think she might be a drug mule, which is why she has no ID," Officer Sampson said.

"Objection," Martin said.

"Too late," Judge Kita said, giving Martin a smile. "It's irrelevant anyway, but I'll let it in."

"No more questions," Janet Chang said. She sat down and purred.

"So, officer, when you came upon my client, you had not been called to the scene by dispatch, correct?" Martin began. Might as well sail right into the suppression motion.

"I had noticed your client and thought it was suspicious she was sitting near the business at that time of day," he said primly.

"So, no dispatch, correct?"

"Correct."

"And," Martin continued, "you had no information that any criminal activity was afoot, correct?"

"Well, trespassing," the officer said.

Martin pulled out a photo of the business. He'd had an investigator go out and take photos of the scene last week.

"This is what the place looked like that morning, right?" Martin said.

"Yes," Officer Choirboy said uncertainly.

"Look carefully," Martin said. "Is there anything missing?"

"No," the officer said. He looked under his brows at Martin.

"For instance," Martin continued, "there are no signs saying it is illegal to loiter there?"

The officer studied the photo as if it were an icon.

"Look all you want, officer," Martin said. "There are no signs. Am I right?"

"Right," the officer said.

"And there are no signs saying 'No Trespassing,' correct?"

"There don't have to be signs if the owner tells me that they don't want someone there," the officer said triumphantly.

"Ah, but you didn't know this until *after* you put the handcuffs on Ms. Morningstar, correct?"

There was a long silence. The officer finally nodded.

"Does that mean yes?" Judge Kita cut in harshly.

"Yes," the officer said reluctantly.

"And you didn't talk to the owner of the business until *after* you had searched my client's leather pouch, correct?"

"Yes," the officer said in a small voice.

"So when you put the handcuffs on Ms. Morningstar, you had no information whatsoever that she had committed any crime, right?" Martin said.

"No," the officer admitted. "But I thought it was suspicious that she was sitting out in front of the business with chocolate on her face."

"You hadn't been called out to any alarm, right?" Martin said.

"No."

Judge Kita sat back in his chair. Martin knew that the judge hated to grant suppression motions—as did most judges. The case wasn't won yet.

"Let's talk about the weighing of the suspected substance,"

Martin said. "When you weighed it, did you take it out of the leather pouch?"

"No," the officer said. "We always first weigh the substance in its container."

"So the outrageous amount of grams the substance weighed was in part due to the leather pouch?" Martin asked.

"Objection," Janet Chang said.

"The word 'outrageous' will be stricken," Judge Kita said, smiling at Martin.

"The weight included the pouch," the officer said.

"And did you perform the standard reagent test on the substance?" Martin asked. Local police had a chemical test which could tell them whether what they seized was meth or baking powder. You add the reagent chemical to the suspected substance and look for it to change colour. It was so easy, any patrol cop could do it, then testify at prelim like an expert.

Officer Sampson, however, shifted uneasily in his seat.

"We did the test," he said. And nothing else. Which raised Martin's antennae.

"You did the reagent test, and what happened?" Martin asked, remembering what Miranda had told him earlier.

"It, uh . . ." Officer Sampson was actually turning red. "The suspected substance . . . it sort of vanished."

"It *what?*" Judge Kita was almost out of his chair.

"I can't explain it, judge," Officer Sampson said. "When we added the reagent chemical, all of the meth—the suspected substance—disappeared in a puff of smoke. Even the portion we weren't testing."

Judge Kita was completely out of his chair now.

"Are you telling me that you have destroyed the evidence?" he bellowed.

This was fun, Martin thought.

The officer shrugged.

"Counsel," Judge Kita turned on Janet Chang, "were you aware of this?"

"Um, I'm not sure," she said, trying to hide her face behind her notes.

"You're not . . . ?" Judge Kita's face was fire engine red. Martin worried that he might stroke out on the bench. The judge sat down again, trying to control his anger. He failed.

"You've brought a preliminary hearing into my court, you've held this young lady in custody for the last ten days, and you *knew* the evidence had been destroyed?" Judge Kita's tone was incredulity mixed with fury. Janet Chang said nothing.

"Unbelievable!" Judge Kita said, looking at Martin. Martin shook his head and tried not to smile.

"This case is dismissed and the defendant is ordered released immediately!" The judge stalked off the bench.

"What is happening?" Miranda said, terror in her voice. "He seems very angry! Am I in trouble?"

"Far from it," Martin said gallantly. "You are to be released today. The case is dismissed."

"Released?" she said, wonder in her voice. "You mean that I can leave this awful place?"

"Back to the woodland with you, girl," Martin said.

Miranda threw her arms around Martin's neck and kissed his cheek. She whispered in his ear, "You have fulfilled your oath honourably. I will do magic for you, Sir Defender."

THAT NIGHT WHEN he parked at home and got out of the car he was greeted by a pungent sweet aroma of vegetation. He walked into the back yard to tell the tree that Miranda was free, and then dropped his briefcase in astonishment.

The tree was vibrant, green, straight and tall. Small white and blue flowers budded on its branches. It seemed to nod at him amiably as he went to touch its trunk in disbelief.

"Well, old fellow," he said to the tree, "looks like Miranda left a little magic here for both of us."

Of White Cranes and Blue Stars

Alexandra Seidel

SHE HAS CLAD herself in feathers. They are white. A long, long time ago, she appeared as the bird-woman, the Horus-mother, but no more. She wants no more stories sung about herself, doesn't want her feathers drawn on coffins any longer.

So she wraps herself in the shape of a crane, and her white feathers echo forward a shadow of death to those who see her.

From the distance and invisible, a red fox watches her.

MARYNA CYCLES PAST a budding field under the first sun of spring. A thermos with lavender tea rattles softly in her bicycle's basket, but Maryna barely notices the small sound. Sun-glazed leaves hold her attention, the magic of change sweeping over the earth.

Maryna can smell the soil thaw, can feel the brightness warm her winter-pale skin. A gust of wind makes her turn her head, and she sees a white crane she's not supposed to see.

From the distance and invisible, a red archer clad in fur rattles his ribs in a fox laugh.

THE SOUND OF air caressing one's feathers is the sound of being alive. The bird-woman flies off, and while there is not blood,

37

while her feathers are a perfect white, it looks almost as if her heart was struck by a feather-fletched arrow. She leaves the field beneath her wings, and wonders what just happened; was she there too early or too late, did a trickster mark her shadow and confuse her sense of time?

She is precise, has always been precise. It is her nature, the knowledge of when to migrate, of when to flee from a storm, of how to move in a flock.

She was not meant to kill that woman.

THE SIGHT OF the crane remains with Maryna. She looked over her shoulder to get a second glimpse, but the beautiful creature was already gone.

All day, the image is with her. She hears birdsong all around her, but attributes this to the coming of spring.

All day, the birds sing, and only once night falls do they fall quiet.

Maryna dies in her sleep not long after. Her heart simply stops as if an arrow, fletched with feathers, had pierced it.

THE BIRD-WOMAN has donned everything she could find between blue and green; shimmering turquoise, muted celadon, a sprinkling of lime amongst the aquamarine. Her forest-tinted talons grab the branch of a leafless tree, grab it more tightly than is necessary.

Those colours of sky and leaf, the bird-woman gleaned, were Maryna's favourite colours. The name she also gleaned; it is that bird sense of hers that lets her know, the same way she knew the right words to say to the Horus-father amongst the reeds, so many years ago.

The shade stumbles into view through the high grass that marks the entrance of the Underworld.

The bird-woman rustles her emerald feathers. "Hello," she says, in a voice like wind.

The shade lifts her head to the sound. "Hello," Maryna says, all of her alive-ness stolen off her face by Death's choking veil. "Do I know you?"

"Yes," the bird-woman says, and rustles all her plumage to buy time. When she took a raven's dark form, the guiding home of the shades was so much easier. Things were simple then, and so very clear. "Yes, Maryna. You have seen me before."

From some distance, vulpine eyes watch them. It is almost the same careful distance he chose from the bird-woman and her lover-to-be, back in the reeds.

BEING A SHADE means being on a journey. The bird-woman knows this, but hasn't bothered to explain it to any of the shades in a long time, because even if told, they don't understand. They have to walk their path, and realizing this for themselves is part of the journey also.

But Maryna was not supposed to walk with her, not yet.

"You were the crane in the field," Maryna says.

This surprises her. She is rarely recognized. "I was."

"What is this place?" Maryna looks around, but the landscape shies away from close inspection. It will reveal itself in the occasional tree or rock, but prefers to be dominated by grass, in rare cases by hot desert sand. In rarer cases still, by rustling reeds.

"It's not my domain. It's part of the Underworld, and it shapes itself into whatever it needs to be." The bird-woman punctuates this with a high chirp from her teal beak.

"Oh; this is Death then . . . why am I dead?"

Driven by a need she doesn't understand, she flies onto Maryna's shoulder. The shade doesn't shy away from her. There is a long moment in which their gazes meet, entwine, crumble apart again.

The bird-woman could tell Maryna that seeing her is what brought her here, it would push the conversation into something circular. Instead: "You are here because I made a mistake."

THERE IS A long silence among the grass. The sky here usually appears overcast, but now, something shifts and stars appear.

"You killed me?"

"I did."

"But you were just a bird?"

"I was never just a bird."

"That doesn't make any sense!"

"Whenever did Death bother to make any sense?"

The bird-woman leaves Maryna's shoulder, settles down

again on the bare tree; maybe this way Maryna won't hear her thrushing heart.

"You are telling me I'm not actually supposed to be here, is that it?"

The bird-woman has ages of experience in how to avoid giving uncomfortable answers to unwanted questions. She resists the impulse to use this experience. "I am telling you that you are here now, no matter how. I am telling you that there is no way back from here. The moment you turned your head to look at a white crane in a field there was no way not to come here, and I am sorry."

Maryna is a creature of silent anger. She walks off, turning her back on the blue bird.

When they first met in the reeds, the bird-woman recalls he, too, stormed off. That was how his journey began.

MARYNA WALKS SILENTLY for a long time.

The bird-woman considers shedding her cerulean feathers to wrap her human shape in the black winged coat of the Morrigan, but that wouldn't do. She would lose her voice of blooming violets then, take instead the raven's harvest voice.

She tries song instead of words. She serenades Maryna with all the melodies of all the birds while the shade keeps putting one foot in front of the other.

"Will you stop?" Maryna says. It's been ages since they first met, it's been seconds. Time has become an unnecessity.

"I might stop if you stopped walking for a moment and let us talk." The bird-woman is not supposed to do this. She is supposed to encourage them to keep on walking.

Maryna stops, turns around to face her.

The bird-woman alights on a tree that is just there, and once more, their eyes meet in a current of blue electricity.

"Talk then."

"I am sorry. It's not adequate, not helpful, but I am."

"Put me back then, or find someone who can."

At this, the bird-woman lets out a song, a long wailing melody once sung by a blackbird who grieved for her chicks. "There is no way, no way back for you at all. Death never gives anyone back what they lost, I told you."

"There are stories though . . ."

"The story of the minstrel, yes, stories of other resurrections, yes; they are lies, nothing like that ever happens."

Maryna eats silence once more, the chewing of it can be felt between them.

"Maryna. I can help you now. It's not nearly enough to repay what I took, but I can help you."

"With what?" The silence is still sticky on her lips, but Maryna forces out the words.

"With finding where you are supposed to go. It is what I do."

But is it really? In truth, the bird-woman has been wondering for a long time.

WHEN MARYNA WAS a girl, the wallpaper in her room was sprinkled with midnight blue stars.

Maryna has told the bird-woman this while one of them was walking, one flying.

They have talked about many more things since, but the bird-woman cannot get the image of blue stars out of her head. Maybe as a result, her plumage has washed to darker hues, the greens among it almost gone.

"Your eyes were blue," the bird-woman says.

It is true, though as a shade, Maryna has lost that detail, along with all her hard-won wrinkles and crow's feet.

"That's right! Did you notice when we first met?"

"I did."

Maryna stops. They both stop. There is something between them that blooms like a shooting star, sparks on kindling. They find each other's eyes and hide in the high grass, hide for days like she and Osiris once did. But this is not the same. There is no more need for another god in the world, all that is needed is what they can have, now.

Death's wind rustles the grass. The sound is drowned in their kisses.

From a distance, the archer hidden behind fox eyes watches, then turns and leaves. His arrows always fly true, no doubt, but he likes to make very sure when the one that gave him fletching feathers is involved.

THE BIRD-WOMAN knows, through instinct, that Maryna will complete her journey soon after they get up from their nest in the grass. Consequently, she tries to make seconds last forever, something that is contrary to her avian nature.

"Tell me about the stars again," the bird-woman says for the hundredth time.

"They were midnight blue and painted by my parents before I was born."

The bird-woman has made star shapes appear on her feathers. Maryna follows the shape of one of them with her finger now, caresses each of the five points. "They looked like the stars in your feathers."

A shade may never sleep, and to steal more time, the bird-woman shifts her beak to lips, chirps another kiss into Maryna's mouth.

But no matter what she might try, their time is running low.

IT SEEMS LIKE dawn when Maryna gets up and leaves their nest even though the Underworld knows no mornings. "I feel like I should keep moving," is all Maryna says.

The bird-woman makes a noise that hovers between agreement and sigh. They leave their place in the grass behind, leave the warmth of it to cool, leave the stars drawn there to be forgotten.

They share a long silence peacefully.

"I think I should say that I forgive you," says Maryna, breaking something. "I forgave you a long time ago."

"I've known for a long time," the bird-woman says, "but I was hoping not to hear you say it for a little longer."

Maryna smiles at her. She is growing less and less in substance, is thinning out as the end of her journey nears. "What's next?" she asks.

"I don't know," says the bird-woman. "I've never gone that far."

This, for some reason, makes Maryna laugh out loud, a happy noise that blooms like a rare fruit among Death's fields.

"Perhaps I can meet you when you decide to make the journey? Like you met me?"

"I would love that," the bird-woman says, and feels the string of promise binding to her right leg.

Maryna, without another word, dissolves to elsewhere, or nowhere.

The bird-woman's chest aches as if an arrow had shot through her heart, an arrow brighter and hotter than a shooting star.

THE BIRD-WOMAN will no longer clothe herself in crane, not for fear of repeating an error that she has come to suspect wasn't really an error, but because she doesn't want to remember the day she first met Maryna.

Instead, she takes a blue jay's feathers these days. She can rush past the people she is supposed to call, make them look astounded with her skill of flight; in this shape, after all, she looks like a shooting star of deep blue, something you might paint on the wall of a child's bedroom to help her fall asleep, to guide her softly in her dreams.

The archer with his fox eyes watches the bird-woman in her blue guise sometimes. He knows she will not herald death forever, knows one day soon, she will let go of her feathers so that she can fly.

Dead Man's Hustle

Damascus Mincemeyer

"YO, ZEKE, GOT room for one more?" DeShawn asked, approaching my table. His voice shook, and through the bar's haze I noticed him sweating though it was cold as a murdered hooker's tit outside.

Here comes trouble, I thought, looking at my half-empty glass of Honey Jack; Bryson's is a hole-in-the-wall joint even by Dexter-Linwood standards, but I dug its quiet, laid-back atmosphere. Everyone there knew my name and the rumours, but I could still be just another face in the crowd.

Yet now DeShawn was pissing all over that. He was the neighbourhood twitcher, eaten up by crack years before, but somehow managed to reach thirty without overdosing or biting a bullet, a feat I envied. I leaned forward, wincing at the pain in my right knee. "What the hell y'all gotten yourself into now? You rip off those Chaldeans down on Cortland again?"

DeShawn's movements were herky-jerky as he sat. "Nah, ain't like that. Got you a case to work. A bone-a-fied haunter file for you, man."

I shook my head. "I don't do that sorta shit no more. Only ghosts I wanna see these days are at the bottom of a glass."

"I feel you," DeShawn's twitchiness increased. "But this is no

45

bullshit. Gotta desperate mothafucka wit' me."

"Wait, you brought someone wit' y'all?" A flush of anger rose in me. "Who put you up to this?"

DeShawn smiled, baring his grill of gold teeth. "Nobody. Dude was askin' 'round for you, an' I remembered where Martina use'ta say you hung your hat. That's all."

"Martina?" It'd been a long time since I'd heard the name, and it brought a flood of memories—most good, some bad, but all painful in one form or another. "Fine. I'll listen to whatever fool you got with you. But I ain't makin' no promises."

DeShawn grinned, disappeared through the bar's crowd, and when he returned, I swore. I hadn't been able to see who he'd been sitting with at his corner table, but now there was a sleaze of a dealer beside him named Tyrell who fancied himself sultan of the streets but in reality was just another 'hood rat. I'd cleared out the spirits of a few murdered Crips from his crack den back in the old days and had hoped to never see him again, but here he came, shady as ever as he sauntered over to the table.

"That's the man himself," DeShawn told him. "Got my hook-up?"

Tyrell took a small plastic baggie from a pocket, and DeShawn snatched it, vulture-like, from his fingers. Enamoured with the white crystals the baggie held, he flashed that grill again and slapped Tyrell on the back. "Now y'all just tell Zeke 'bout your haunter problem and he'll fix y'up."

With that DeShawn shuffled outside, leaving Tyrell and me alone at the table. He bared his own set of gold teeth and sat, grabbing my glass. "Ezekiel Deveroux," he said, taking a swig. "You's one hard cat to find, y'know that?"

"I like it that way. But now you've found me, tell me what's what."

Tyrell glanced uncomfortably around the bar. "You ever heard of Poppa Nario?"

I shrugged, fakin' dumb, but I knew. Nario was a major player in Detroit, in any game you wanted to name. Dope. Whores. Guns. Bribes. He was so high up on the food chain, though, he was practically a ghost, known only in whispers on the streets and little else. I'd never seen him, and doubted anyone beyond his inner circle had in a long time.

"I heard the name. What 'bout him?"

"Got himself iced."

"Someone did Poppa Nario? How?"

"Drive-by. Weird shit, too. Poppa was cagey 'bout where he went and who went with him, what time he left a joint. Always hadda dozen dude's 'round him, too, but three nights back I was pickin' up the week's brick when this Escalade rolls up just as we was leavin' and sprays down some serious lead. Bitches got off a lucky shot, and now Poppa's got some real estate down at the morgue." He looked me over with bloodshot eyes. "But word is you can rectify the situation, know what I'm sayin'? I mean, way DeShawn tells it, you can make Poppa an up-and-comer again."

"DeShawn likes runnin' his mouth."

"True. But I remember what you did for me back in the day." Tyrell paused, leaned in closer, then whispered: "You's a necromanc—"

"*Don't* say it," I snapped, my irritation finally edged into anger. "I don't *do* that shit no more." I glared at Tyrell. "And if you meanin' what I think you mean 'bout Poppa, *forget* it. Clearin' out haunters is one thing. Raisin' someone's dead fool ass ain't as easy."

Tyrell smiled again, but this time his grill seemed sharper. "But it *can* be done?"

"Not without a price, and not without almost killin' me. So put this on a bullet and put it in your brain: I. Ain't. Interested."

"But DeShawn said you've tried it before. Down at . . ."

He let the sentence hang, and my mind tightened the noose: *Fenkell Avenue.* I closed my eyes, saw it all again—that worm-rotted apartment, Vernell's gut-ripped corpse lying in a corner, Martina screaming my name while the demon clutched her with blackened fingers, the sizzling-shit stench of sulphur from the open gateway thick in my nose.

Make your choice, ghost-eater, the demon taunted. *Make your choice.*

I shook the images. "What dice you got in all this? Why you care if Poppa's worm meat or not?"

Tyrell polished off my whiskey. "Poppa's powerful, but he done got lazy over the years, an' his crew split in two 'cause of it. I run most of the dope show, but this other cat, Levonte, he takes care of the other hustles, bitches an' guns an' all that. Problem is, with Poppa toe-taggin' it, Levonte thinks he's got rights to take over the throne, an' a lotta people gonna go down if he does." He tapped a gold-ringed finger on the empty glass. "But if Poppa ain't *dead* . . ."

I groaned. "Look, I don't know what DeShawn done fed you 'bout me, but I don't do this kinda thing no more. No haunters. No resurrectin'. *None* of it." I grabbed my cane from where I'd leaned it against the table and stood, knee aching worse than ever. "Be seein' you."

"Damn, didn't you hear nothin' I just said?" Tyrell asked. "The whole damn 'hood's gonna bleed out ugly."

"Ain't my fault. Ain't my problem, either."

"You's a cold-hearted bastard, you know that?"

I opened the door and a chill rush of December air cascaded into the bar; before I stepped out, Tyrell turned in his chair, asking, "What's it like, Deveroux? Talkin' to haunters, I mean."

Shit, I thought. *Here it comes.* I'd heard all there is about what I do, the jokes about Casper and rattling chains, but to the dude's credit Tyrell acted serious, so I glanced down and said, "It's cold. Suffocatin'. Like static worms crawlin' 'round your brain. Like you gonna be soon dead yourself." I gave him one final glare before going outside. "*Don't* come lookin' for me again."

DETROIT'S FULL'A GHOSTS, and not just from dead folks. It's the abandoned buildings and burned-out lots, the dope and despair. Dexter-Linwood ain't no different; the entire 'hood's one sad spectre after another: liquor store on every corner, Arab-run markets, crumbling homes on trash-filled streets, every stairwell and alley claimed by thugs. But as I made my way home from Bryson's that night nobody made a move to touch me; even those hanging out in front of my own building only stared and whispered when I went up the steps.

I lived on the third floor. The elevator hadn't worked in the five years I'd been there and the climb up was hell on my leg. That night was noisy: music blared from behind the closed door of one apartment, an arguing couple in another.

My pad didn't have much going for it besides mojo-marks painted around every windowsill and doorway, boxes of old LPs, empty whiskey bottles, and a ratty green recliner that I collapsed into. Ever since DeShawn swaggered into the bar it felt like something was pressing on the back of my brain, and I took a small, rusty coffee tin from the bookshelf, rattling it before scattering out the handful of animal bones it contained onto the tabletop. I usually ain't one for divination, and wasn't reassured by the upside down horseshoe configuration the bones assumed. It meant spiritual blockage, a harbinger of ill fortune, and after seeing it I swore, reached for a bottle of Hennessy, and finished what had been interrupted at the bar.

The sound of breaking glass woke me just past three. I'd been having another nightmare and thought I was still asleep until I heard voices in the back room. My bad knee buckled getting up too fast from the recliner, and I went down, dropping the whiskey bottle and knocking a stack of records from the table. The voices silenced then, and shapes emerged from the hall, lit just enough from the street's neon for me to see a pair of hoodie-wearing, piece-toting thugs step into the room.

I ain't carried since Fenkell, and for the first time regretted it. One of the thugs, bigger than the other, spotted me trying to stand and sent me back to the floor with repeated kicks until his partner pulled him back, saying, "Yo, Ruffie, quit tenderizin' an' Wesson this cat already."

When I heard his gun cock I knew then it wasn't some robbery or shake-down: this was a hit, pure and simple, and I rolled just as a shot plugged through the recliner. On the floor I fumbled through the records and bottles, snatched my cane from the edge of the chair, and unsheathed the hidden foot-long blade attached to the handle, slashing just as my would-be assassin lunged again. One of my stabs cut deep into his calf, and he fell howling to the hardwood.

"Mothafucka!" the second thug yelled, but by then I was up and charging. I'm a big dude, broad-shouldered and heavy, and if not for the streets and haunters would've made varsity for sure as a kid. Ignoring my pain, I tackled the little guy and slammed his gun-hand until the piece bounced across the floor. I stayed on top, railing the bastard's face with the cane handle, but the larger thug limped over and kicked me again, only this time something broke and I doubled over into a screaming ball.

The thug I'd clobbered scrambled upright then, babbling like a loon as he searched in the dark under the recliner for his lost revolver.

"Yo, G-Don, this is *stupid*, man!" he snapped, growing more erratic every second. "I done told Levonte this cat's cursed! We shouldn't even be here!"

The pair started arguing, and I seized the lull, grabbing the coffee tin from the table. Pain made me clumsy; the tin clattered to the floor, spilling the bone contents everywhere, but I snatched the closest one, gripped it firm and closed my eyes. Words I'd thought buried five years earlier slipped effortlessly over my tongue:

"*Invoco te, spiritus mortuorum, veni in mundum iterum Pilatus foras . . .*"

There was a sharp, icy pain in my head that spread down my spine and through raw, shrieking nerves to the fingers clasping the bone. From the corner of the room came a low, steady growl and I opened my eyes to see the quivering, incorporeal form of a pit bull melt from the shadows, snapping and barking as it approached the thugs.

"The *fuck?*" one of them cried, staggering backwards just as the dog lunged. He opened up with a flurry of shots, but the bullets passed through the animal, striking the drywall behind, and the dude's shock dissolved into panic.

"S'a *ghost*, G!" he yelled.

The phantom stood its ground between them and me, and their distress only increased when a piercing, shrill hiss filled the room. Around us the whole apartment seemed to come alive—things fell off shelves, the windowpanes rattled, and the dishes in the cupboards shook. At first I didn't know what was happening until the mojo-marks nearest me started to writhe snake-like on the wall, and I realized the hissing was theirs.

"Son of a *bitch*," I said; the symbols had been intended as protection against haunters invading my crib, but evoking the dog's spirit awakened the magickal barrier like an immune system trying to purge some disease. They crawled from the wall and devoured the living room, overwhelming us like a cloud of squirming flies.

"To *hell* wit' this!" one of the thugs screamed as he fled into the hall. His terrified partner quickly followed, going out the window and down the fire escape the way they'd come.

Even with my attackers gone, the black miasma came at me. I choked, gagged, clawed desperately to get away, but the soul-smothering suffocation was relentless. I pulled free just long enough to make for the door, work the deadbolts, and dive into the hall. When I chanced a look back the entire apartment seethed with otherworldly energy, but being over the threshold put me beyond its reach, and a moment later the door slammed shut, everything starkly quiet again.

I crumpled to the floor, and soon the spirit dog appeared beside me, its tongue happily flapping side-to-side, tail wagging as it licked my face; a cold sensation brushed across my cheek, and I smiled at the ghost, glad it had escaped the barrier's wrath.

"Good boy." Still grasping the animal's bone, I whispered, *"Spiritus mortuorum, et recedat hoc mundo ad inferna."*

Immediately the pit bull's shape blurred to fog, slithered along the floor, and disappeared into the hall's dark corner. Afterwards I slowly stood and sheathed the cane's blade. It took all I had to stagger down those three flights of stairs; once on the ground floor I slipped out the back, and in the alleyway my legs finally gave out. Laying there, I felt my life fading and knew I needed help, so I waited for the strength to stand then stumbled to the street, set for the only place I could think to go.

BACK IN THE day there was four in my crew. I was the ghost-speaker. Martina was the empath. Vernell was our bookworm and Vernell's older brother Big Bertrand DeBaptiste was our magick man. He ran a barbershop on Livernois, but that was just a front for the voodoo-hustlin' operation he kept in back. It wasn't something he did for everyone, just some of the Haitians who believed and had the scratch for it—a protection amulet here, a hex there—but his hoodoo knowledge was unsurpassed. It'd been him who taught me bone-castin' and tagged my joint with mojo-marks. *Sealin' that shit airtight against the haunters,* he'd say.

Dawn broke when I reached his apartment in the back of his shop, and when he let me in, it was like five years hadn't passed. Everything was in the same place—furniture, appliances, decorations—and the whole joint still smelled like shaving soap, Old Spice, and blood.

Bert was true to his name. Dude was six-nine and built like a tank, with a permanent smile that only expanded when he spotted me.

"Always knew *you* saw ghosts, Zeke, but never thought *I* would 'til now." He yawned. "Y'know what time it is?"

I tried laughing, but coughed bloody phlegm onto his floor instead. Bert's grin vanished as he guided me to a chair and poured a glass of rum. "What the hell your ass get into now? Haunters? Demons?" He offered me the glass, but when I waved it away Bert shrugged and downed it himself. "Sigils in your apartment holdin' up?"

"They *was* good. 'Til tonight."

I told him everything, 'bout Nario, Tyrell's visit, being attacked. Bert listened patiently, then got a first aid kit from a drawer, some flour and foul-smelling herbs outta the pantry, and began boiling water. "I'll do a poultice for your ribs. Take some of the pain out."

"I appreciate this, Bert. I wasn't sure you'd help me after what went down between us."

Bert shrugged. "Well, you *did* just show up on my doorstep lookin' like you'd been chewed up by every critter at the zoo. But you an' me go way back, even if I ain't heard shit from your ass in five damn years. We're riders, Zeke. Through Heaven and Hell."

I did laugh then. "I think Hell's done finally caught me."

Bert shook his head. "Nah. But let me tell you—them punks tryin' to kill you tonight weren't just some 'hood rats lookin' to run your shit. Way I hear it, a cat named Levonte wants you spilled in a major way."

"*Levonte* . . ." One of the thugs spoke the name in my apartment. "You knew 'bout him gunnin' for me?"

"I run a barbershop. I know everything."

"An' you didn't warn me?"

"Damn, Zeke, you made it pretty clear you didn't want *nothin'* to do wit' me after Fenkell."

"I couldn't . . . It was too damn painful knowin' you lost your brother 'cause of *me.*"

Bert smiled again, pulling up a gold chain from around his neck, a shining cylindrical pendant sliding out from beneath his collar.

"I still got Vernell," he held the jewellery in one huge hand. "Saved one'a his finger bones. Had to have a part of him near me, Zeke. *Had* to, you feel me?"

Bert finished his poultice and I grimaced as he applied the herbal paste to my torso. It smelled rank, but after a few minutes the pain subsided and I asked, "What you know 'bout this Levonte?"

"Not much. Thinks he's king shit, but he's just a thug like all the others. Someone told him Tyrell asked you to raise Poppa off the slab, an' he don't like that. If Poppa's up again, Tyrell's one dead mothafucka."

"How's that?"

Bert shrugged again. "Word is he's the one who put the hit on Nario in the first place, which means if Poppa comes back it ain't gonna be pretty. Retribution's the biggest bitch on the block, and believe me, Nario's worse than Levonte and Tyrell put together. A hundred dudes is six feet under 'cause of him. Tyrell might think raisin' him'll stop some killin', but it ain't gonna do shit except stack up the bodies."

"I won't do it, Bert," I said. "Not after what went down before. I ain't raisin' *nobody* again."

I slept the rest of the day while Bert tended the shop, but at eight that night I woke to him shaking me by the arm. Just by his expression I knew something was wrong.

"We got ourselves a problem." He held up a thick manila envelope; DEVEROUX was written on the front in thick, bold letters. "Cat came in 'round closin' time, dropped this off with one of my employees, told 'em to give it to their boss."

"Who knows I'm here?"

"I ain't said shit to nobody. But these streets got eyes big as lions, Zeke. We both know that."

I opened the envelope; six gold teeth tumbled to the tabletop, a DVD with the words WATCH ME scrawled in marker along the top sliding out right behind. Next to me, Bert wryly chuckled.

"Hell, ain't Christmas for two weeks yet. Looks like Santa done came early this year."

The video quality was clear but the room being filmed was dark; there was a row of thugs standing there, faces covered with bandanas, but a dude closest to the camera was unmasked, and the moment I saw that shady swagger and shifty grilled grin, I knew the worst was still ahead.

"S'up, Deveroux?" Tyrell said, staring into the lens like he was looking right at me. "Wanted our little conversation the other night to go my way, thought after what you did for me back in the day you'd be interested in helpin' a dawg, but turns out you's just a bitch who don't care 'bout nobody's ass but your own. So now it's time for real talk."

He snapped his fingers and the row of thugs parted, what they'd been shielding from view coming into focus: a person sat bound ankle and wrist with duct tape to a chair, black garbage bag tight over their head. From the frightened whimpers, I knew the hostage lived, but Tyrell's predatory grin didn't give much hope they would be long.

"I figured you need some motivatin' to see things my way, an' there ain't no motivatin' better than watchin' some fool bleed out, is there?" Like some sinister stage magician he yanked the bag from the captive, and there DeShawn was in all his stupid-ass, twitchy-nerved anguish, eyes bulging with terror, a dirty sock in his mouth muffling any cries. Tyrell ran his fingers through DeShawn's hair, slapped him on the cheek, then looked at the camera again. "Y'know how easy it was trappin' this cat? Just dangle a rock an' he comes runnin'. *Pathetic.* But I figure you don't do shit for *me*, I'll do shit to *him*."

Tyrell gave a nod and the awaiting thugs went to work. Holding DeShawn's head back, they removed the sock and forced open his mouth. As they yanked out his grill with pliers, their laughter was so loud I could hear it above the screams.

I watched helplessly until he passed out and, still chuckling, Tyrell retrieved one plucked molar and held it to the camera. "We got ten fingers after this, Deveroux. Then ten toes. Then we start workin' on the eyes. Your choice how much this bitch gotta go through." He stared right into the lens. "Be on the corner of Woodrow and Tyler. Midnight. Alone. No tricks. We'll send a car up. An' don't forget, Deveroux—we be watchin' your every mothafuckin' move."

The video abruptly ended, leaving me and Bert staring at a dead TV, and for a long while neither of us spoke.

"That Martina's cousin DeShawn?" Bert finally asked. I was too numb to talk, but when I nodded, he told me, "These cats ain't foolin'. What you gonna do?"

"I don't *know*." I admitted. "But I *can't* raise Nario. Ain't *no* way I'm bringin' somethin' like *that* back into the world." My hands shook and I sat down. "You gotta Ouija board 'round this joint?"

"'Course. What you got in mind?"

When I told him, Bert shook his head. "You *is* one crazy bastard. Y'know that?"

"Any better ideas?"

He was quiet until a smile chiselled his massive face. "After all the shit we done faced together, y'know it's ride or die 'tween me and you, Zeke. And wit' *that* plan, we sure as *hell* gonna die *sooner* than later."

I WASN'T ON the appointed corner five minutes when a tinted-window Chrysler 300 rolled up carrying three thugs who frisked me before the silent trip across town. The whole ride the driver eyeballed me in the rear-view like I was gonna disappear if he blinked.

The Wayne County morgue is the last stop on life's train for anyone in Detroit; when we pulled to the rear loading dock, Tyrell and another hoodie-wearin' mutt stood watch near the already-open door, and I wondered how many under-the-table Benjamins it took to gain access at that hour.

"Lazarus Man shows up," Tyrell snickered after his crew guided me up the steps. "Too bad. Woulda been fun givin' DeShawn a bolt cutter manicure, know what I'm sayin'?"

"Where's he at?"

Tyrell smirked. "Chickenhead's safe. We get what we lookin' to get, you get his whack ass back. An' if you thinkin' this gonna go any other way but mine, think again, Deveroux."

He flashed a gat at his waist, and I scowled. "If we here to do it, let's do it. Don't need you runnin' lip the whole time."

"A'ight, then. Have it your way." He gestured to the open door. "Let's go."

They led me through a long corridor and down a series of staircases to a lower level. The cold worsened the deeper we went, and I felt dead eyes on me; at the end of another hall two more thugs guarded a door marked STORAGE ROOM 1A, but they weren't alone—a flickering man in an outdated, high-collared suit and a sad-eyed little girl hovered nearby. I shivered, stopped, and Tyrell looked at me.

"S'your problem?"

I motioned with my cane to the corner. "We bein' watched."

Tyrell peered in the direction of the spirits before prodding me forward with his piece. "I don't see shit. Keep goin'."

The interior of the storage room was lined with drawer coolers; one on the left was already open, the tray slid out and occupied by a sheet-covered corpse with exposed feet peeking to the ceiling. Tyrell marched ahead of me and yanked the upper portion of the shroud down.

"This Nario?" I asked. For all I'd heard, he wasn't nothing special: just a hefty, broad-faced dude topped with cornrows, scar on one lip, a few old, healed-up bullet wounds on his torso mirroring the new ones that'd snuffed him out. Tyrell motioned to the body.

"Go on, Lazarus Man," he taunted. "Do you thing."

I stared at him, then Nario. I closed my eyes and saw Fenkell, heard the screams, smelled the sulphur. I'd sworn that night never to raise spirits again, but now there I was, back to the wall, that demon's voice mocking once more: *Make your choice, ghost-eater. Make your choice.*

A scuffle in the hall broke my thoughts. There was a shout, the sounds of struggling, and when I opened my eyes, Tyrell was looking around me to the doorway. When I turned, the thugs who'd driven me there backpedalled into the room while three unfamiliar mugs brazenly burst in behind them waving Wessons like they was pullin' a bank job.

"*Levonte?*" Tyrell snarled. "The *fuck* you doin' here?"

A brute with bushy hair hidden under a do-rag smiled a callous, thirsty ice grin before boldly stepping forward. "You think we wouldn't know what's goin' down tonight, Tyrell? I *own* these streets, no matter what you think. *Nobody* makes a move wit'out me knowin' it." Levonte studied me next. "So this be The Resurrector? Yeah, I know *all* 'bout *you,* Deveroux. Thought you was dope shit back in the day, huntin' haunters wit' your crew 'til you got one'a your soldiers *and* your lady-boo killed. Way I hear it, though, when you tried bringin' her back you had to put her down again 'cause she came back *wrong.*" He peered at Tyrell. "Bet y'all didn't know *that* fun fact, or you wouldn'ta been so hot to have him do what you wantin' him to do."

The thug beside Levonte bristled; blood seeped through his baggy jeans along one calf, and I knew he'd been the dude I'd stabbed in my apartment.

"Watch that cane. Cat thinks he's Zorro," he warned, but Levonte still took another step ahead.

"Don't worry 'bout it, G-Don. *None* of these fools be leavin' the morgue." His glare stayed on Tyrell. "I'm gonna do them just like I did Nario."

Tyrell swore then, roared past me, and grabbed for Levonte. In a blink a fight broke out between both crews, a storm of fists, spit, and blood. When Levonte sent Tyrell to the tile with a pistol-lash across the face and readied his Wesson for the killing shot I made my move.

I dove for Nario's body, clasped one hand over his eyes, the cold, ancient phrase slithering from my tongue: *"Invoco te, spiritus mortuorum, veni in mundum iterum Pilatus foras . . ."*

I invoke thee, spirit of the dead, come forth again into the world. Instantly that harrowing, frigid static bloomed in my skull and rippled down my arms, so intense it felt like my soul was being torn apart. The room blurred into a shifting ink-smear, and from faraway I heard a scream before the lights wavered, brightened, then blacked out altogether.

"The fuck's *this?*" Levonte shouted in the dark. A breath later, light returned: the brawl had stopped and I was on the floor, but by then nobody was paying attention to me.

Nario sat up, eyes blank and face slack, like a sleepwalker roused from a deep dream. He blinked and scrutinized his own hands with a newborn's curiosity. At the other end of the room all the thugs stood frozen, terrified as Nario scanned each of them until his deathly stare settled on Tyrell and Levonte.

"Where . . . Where am I?" he asked, tone a garbled, groggy mess. Upon hearing the words Levonte pushed away from the others and stumbled back towards the door, his once-concentrated determination suddenly diluted with dread.

"T-This be a trick, homey," he stammered. "I *killed* you, man! I killed you!"

Levonte bolted down the corridor then, repeating his declaration as he retreated. His horrified flight was quickly imitated by the other thugs until only Tyrell remained, nose bloody and gazing with childish awe from the tile. He glanced feverishly from Nario to me, opened his mouth to speak, but instead crawled away like a scared back alley dog. Abandoned in the room, my heart pounded, then doubled its pace when Nario turned his unsteady sight towards me.

"Where am I?" the revived body asked again, clearer this time. And then: "Zee?"

I could barely breathe, but a pained smile caught me anyway at the recognition of the old nickname. "V-Vernell? That you? That really *you* in there?"

What once was Poppa Nario slowly nodded. "I'm cold, Zee." The voice was coarse and didn't sound anything like Vernell's used to, but the tag was something he'd called me years before Fenkell's doom. It was him. "H-How'd the hustle go down?"

My smile widened then as I opened my clenched fist to reveal the small bone hidden in my palm, the *memento mori* Bert kept of his brother.

"Good 'nuff, I think," I propped myself up with the cane. "Let's get the hell outta here."

I called Bert from a phone in the morgue's lower office, and he came in his old Cadillac to pick us up. On the way back to his shop a gloomy dawn snow started in, but none of us said two words.

IT TOOK MOST of the morning for Vernell to warm up, adjust, and be able to speak properly. He and Bert talked for hours after, awkwardly at first, but then just like brothers, laughing and joking and talking 'bout old times. It was weird hearing familiar stories from back in the day slide from the mouth of a stranger, but after a while it didn't matter.

"Where you been all this time?" I asked Vernell when Bert was called out front—even a ghost-speaker like me didn't know for sure where anyone went after the Big Blackout, but Vernell just shook his new head.

"Can't tell y'all, Zee. Some things you gotta see for yourself, know what I'm sayin'?" He looked at me then. "But just so you know, Martina ain't mad at you."

I wanted to ask more, but then Bert returned, seriousness staining his face. "Some cat just told me DeShawn was dumped on the corner of Kelly and Morang this morning. Fool's alive at the hospital, but ain't in a good way. Word is Tyrell and Levonte split outta Detroit like bullets, too."

"They's worried Nario's gunnin' for 'em." I said. "It's what you said 'bout retribution—to them the reaper done rose with their names on his lips. Ain't none of 'em gonna stick 'round now."

Since then the 'hood ain't been the same. Thugs that hung out for years skipped town, frightened of stories a dead man walked among them hungry for revenge, and we decided to feed into the con, rebuilding Poppa's crew and playing like Nario was still Nario, except this time we planned to run shit *right*. Wasn't gonna be like it was before with bodies stacked from ceiling to floor: we had it, everything that'd been his—cash, cars, *everything*—and we were gonna use it to protect people 'stead of kill 'em. Sounds whack, but that's life. A hustle every minute, one to the next.

Early Christmas morning I bought some flowers and went to see Martina. The Evergreen Cemetery on Woodward was blanketed in dirty snow while I limped among the headstones; I hadn't been there in five years, not since Fenkell, not since the choice I made, and I worried 'bout what to say.

A hundred mournful, gawping spirits lined the path as I walked, but none of 'em tried to connect with me to pass on whatever messages they had. It was like they knew I wasn't there for that, and they just watched me go by. At the end of a long row near an oak tree I found what I was looking for. Unlike the others, Martina's ghost wasn't waiting, and I wondered if Vernell had been wrong.

"Sorry this took so long, Boo," I whispered as I set the flowers down. "Sorry 'bout everything."

I hoisted myself up, looked around and didn't see anything, but when I turned to walk away she was there, a smiling, soft outline against the snow. Our eyes met but we didn't speak, and a second later she was gone again. I stood there a bit before leaving. Outside the gates, the streets were awake and mean as always.

Final Flight

Cherry Potts

HOW MANY TIMES have we danced in the thermals, just pretending . . . how many times have we aped the mating flight, practising for when we were grown, for when we might be queen? This time it's real, and wrong, and wonderful, and right, and wicked; and I shriek my delight in her, my worship of her, my intoxication, my need; oh, Light, how can I stand it? The feel of her wings brushing against me, as she courts an updraft, her singing as she dives and turns, laughing as she closes, and flits away again, until finally, she comes to grips and we plummet, in a tangle of limbs and wings. The roar of blood in my ears, the feel of her mouth on my neck, my throat . . . the suck of the wind above the Edge, the sudden ice as we fall into the Shadow, still clasped each to the other, urgent in our loving, neither willing to let go and spread wings once more, each willing to die in the other's embrace . . . almost.

She twists suddenly; shrieks and banks, pulling fiercely away, her wings are Shadow against the gold of the sky. I marvel at her glory, and almost forget to save myself. One wingtip brushes the barren darkness of the valley, and I lift, feeling incredibly heavy, incredibly light, impossibly complete, and yet incomplete. I rise in a tight, urgent, spiral; back to the Light, back to her, my queen.

And she comes to me again, and there is a strange hungry look in her eyes, something quite different from the laughing delight of a moment before. She craves me, would, I think, kill me, but she still knows me, just. And I know this strangeness. It wells in me too. This is completeness, this is life as it should be, this is her right, my right, and it will be our own unique disaster.

A PIECE OF the sky fell today. A shimmering displacement of grey-blue cloud made momentarily solid, spinning out of control. I kept my eyes on it, groping for a hold on the rock, crouching low, my eyes stung by the wind; expecting . . .

Nothing happened. A soft whirring, whining noise; a sudden flash of what could have been fire, but wasn't, gone in an instant.

I had become so used to anticipating a fall from above, and here it was, utterly different from my imagining, terrifying in the explosion of nothingness, the lack of warning, of ritual. But because I had been expecting *something*, for weeks now, I was ready to believe what I saw. So although I would have thought I had imagined it, but for the smell of burning, I knew I hadn't.

I felt the air bounce back from her passing, even up in the wildness of the winds on the Edge, and no matter what I wished, this was not who I had looked for. I turned, and I saw where she fell, her wings fluttering uselessly about her.

I say wings, because that's what I thought they were, despite the wrongness of them. I had no better word.

The Air-borne I had been watching from my safe rock sailed off, never noticing the extraordinary newcomer, and I crawled down from my perch on the Edge, keeping to the still air to leeward of an outcrop.

Her camouflage was good. If I hadn't seen her fall, I wouldn't have known she was there. If I'd taken my eyes from her, I wouldn't have found her again. As with the displaced sky, the rush of air in all that tumult, it was simple chance, or destiny.

I inched down the lee of the Edge, enjoying the stillness of the air there, a good spot, a gentle place; if you were not falling.

That very stillness had trapped her, no uplift for those wings, only the fast descent, and the cruel insistence on reality that is the Edge.

The outcrop petered into more general cliff, and a ledge of sorts, not yet to the base of the valley.

She had gathered herself together, wrapped her wings tight about her like a cocoon. There was a box beside her knee, about the size of her paw, the paw that was frantically beating at that box with a desperate urgency, trying to dislodge its bent lid, its jammed lock.

I cleared my throat.

The paw flew back into the cocoon of wings, and she flinched away from me, whimpering. The fact that she made no attempt to run confirmed that she was hurt. It is a long way from sky to earth, even if you only fall half the height of the Edge.

I stayed put, letting her get used to the idea that I was there; no threat.

She stayed perfectly still, gauging my intent. Decision registered in her frightened face, and she turned back to her box and hit it a swift sharp blow. The lid sprang open, and her shoulders slumped. She flicked something from the box into her ear and dragged herself round to face me. She moved in perceptible jerks.

Fear, not cold; but cold would hit soon, she wasn't dressed for the tooth-sharp wind from the Edge.

"Hello," I said.

A listening expression on her face, her throat muscles worked for a moment, then a disembodied voice came from the little box she clutched awkwardly to her chest.

"Hello," it said.

I lowered my gaze to the box then looked back at her face.

Nice eyes: treacle brown; blood smeared across her lip and chin.

"Do you need help?"

Again, that listening expression.

"No," the box said.

I laughed.

"Are you cold? Hurt?"

She held her paw up, slowing me, waiting for whatever it was the box did with my words.

"Yes, cold, hurt. I can manage."

"Oh yes? How?" I asked.

"My friends will find me," the box said dispassionately. There were tears on her face.

"I will be your friend," I said, pulling the topmost layer of fur from my back. She shrank away, wiping the tears and fresh blood from her face, shaking her head.

I crouched lower, trying not to loom over her fragility and flung the fur about her shoulders. She shuddered at its touch. I watched her face, considering.

Not the weight.

A wry twist of her mouth. She ran her fingers through the thick grey fur.

She raised her head a little, meeting my eyes for the first time.

"Thank you," she said, and I was startled at the sound of her own voice, gravelly, but tight and high with stress.

The use of her own voice made me suddenly want to re-establish the barrier, throwing up formality in the face of her attempt at direct communication, but still, she was injured, and there was only me to help.

"You will permit me to help?"

But what help can I offer, I wondered. *Out here, days from civilisation? A civilisation I am forbidden.* Refusal would be best. If she rejected my offer, I could walk away, get back to my business, and leave her to be rescued by her friends, or die. I eyed the fur about her shoulders. It felt like a promise made.

She was fidgeting with the box. She glanced up, paws curled protectively about the shiny damaged thing.

"My friends will come."

I looked up, half expecting some other glimmer of light to break into a fragile flying body. Instead I saw Shadow.

"Shadow will have fallen here. Your friends will find you first?"

She tried to look up, but her injuries prevented it. She twisted about watching the dipping sun, and the Shadow of the Edge crawling like a tide across the dust.

She did not need to answer.

"Shelter?" she asked at last.

I carried her, scarce the weight of a hatchling. She trembled, pain and fear. Yet there was trust in the way her uninjured limb hugged my neck.

Trust. Hmm.

SO HIGH WE are flying, but I can feel the drag of the earth, even up here. I can scent the presence of others. We are no longer alone; somewhere between the burning delight in each other and our life-affirming dive, we have each become queens, rivals; each other's enemy.

The trail of winged suitors spiral after us: Oh, Shadow, not just suitors. The Queen.

She screams defiance, rage, challenge. She is glory, but hers is the glory of experience and age; and I can *smell* that she is no longer all-dominant. Somewhere in her body chemistry, she has admitted her age, and permitted my, *our,* maturity. I tilt into the wind waiting for her to rise to us. Some quiet part of my mind says: *this is your mother, your life-giver, your protector, your home*; but my entire body-bone-sinew-muscle-blood-feather, screams back at her, *all this is mine.*

But her challenge is not for me. She passes me with scarcely a glance, all her energy focussed upon my sister-lover-rival . . .

MY MEAGRE SHELTER, never designed for two, my lengths of bone and twined rawhide, my furs. She looked at it as though the animals might still be alive, as though the low entrance was a mouth that would swallow her. I could not carry her in. I had to put her down and drag her in behind me, whimpering against the pain I caused in the doing of it. She leant against the rock wall, hugging herself away from the touch of bone. Dark in the shelter, only the tallow lantern to light within, even before Shadow touched here.

I removed more furs, laying them on the ground, making a comfortable sleeping place. I did what I could for her cuts and bruises and her broken bones. I poulticed and I bandaged and I splinted as though I knew what I was doing, but I did not, for she was not of my kind, I did not know how her bones ought to go, beyond the simple logic of straightness and joints. It was a great fortune that she had broken nothing I could not guess at.

Her wings for example: they were a little like a bat's, strong flexible struts of something a little like bone, but not organic—I could tell from the smell—with some woven fabric stretched over, that sprang from the shoulders of her closefitting clothes. I glanced with curiosity at the way the muscles of her back worked, the smoothness. Those false wings could never have done more than glide.

She needed painkillers, but I had none.

I offered meat and milk. She refused by feigning unconsciousness. I let her be. I ate and I drank. I took more layers from my body as the food burned in my stomach, easing cold from my bones. And then I curled up, and I thought how her presence compromised me . . . and I turned to see her watching, her eyes wide in astonishment. Her little box was making clicking noises, her throat working silently. I let her see that I was watching her, and the throat muscles stilled. A form of speech, or of record?

I blackened my digits in tallow and soot, and I wrote upon the wall.

The Shadow is upon us.

My calligraphy was once considered very fine, and even with these limited materials—hard rock, soft tallow, powdery soot, the words were a thing of beauty. I said the words, pointing to each syllable. I tapped her box and said the words again.

She flinched.

I had not expected her to understand the meaning behind the phrase, but perhaps among her own scholars, there was a similar concept.

She spoke.

Her language.

She tilted the box so I could see the grey section, covered in hieroglyphs. She spelt out the syllables, and the box spoke to me, translating.

"I walk through the valley of the shadow of death."

Ah, now I saw we understood one another. I wrote that for her, an elegant phrase, making good use of the concept of the Shadow. It pleased me. She reached and pointed out *Shadow* in each of the phrases.

"Shadow," the box said, then her own voice, "Shadow." She took my paw and traced her own hieroglyph with the remaining sooty tallow on my pads.

"Shadow," I said. She nodded. Tears were dripping unheeded from her eyes. I wiped them away, smearing tallow onto her cheek. She laughed, but her paw, wiping away the smear, trembled still.

I turned away, and crawled out into the creeping darkness, to speak to the voice of Shadow.

I CANNOT SEE, cannot watch, blinded by my own need to fight, raging at the suitors, keeping them away from the battle above, I patrol round and around screaming at them to stay away. Showered by falling feathers, spotted with spilt blood, I keep the spectators away from the combat, queen against Queen, into the slowly deepening sky. When the end comes it is in silence. She does not scream her triumph; she just allows the broken body to fall in a graceless spiral. I do not wait for it to hit; pushing against the air, forcing my already tired wings upward, to make my own challenge.

There is a moment, when I gaze at her bloody face, when I think it is over already, but that otherness is still in her eyes. Breath heaves in her and she roars her ownership of the sky. Oh Light, but she is beautiful, and mine; and craving battle. She means to kill me; it is in that look.

I call her name, over and over again, and for a moment she sees me. She turns and pulls mightily out over the Shadow, screaming as she goes, taking us where they will not follow. A long way we fly, and finally she wheels above me and strikes, and I fear her, but this is not a death strike after all, she pulls up almost playfully, and laughs, breathless with exertion and emotion.

"It is mine," she says. "Mine."

"Yes," I say, for she has taken on the mantle, there is no question but that she controls the hive, the very sky is hers to do with as she will. And so am I; I am not her rival. I do not want what she spreads her wings for. The suitors are not my suitors, I would never want them, could never want them, although she, it seems now, does. And I am no longer her sister, for she can have no sisters. I cannot be a suitor, which leaves me only servitude. And yet, the fire in me, the pride, the need, these are not the feelings of the hive, I am not a supplicant, I am her equal, and she knows it, and . . . I taste the air . . . she fears me.

She shakes her head, and blood flicks out onto my breast. "You have been scented. They know that you are also queen.

They will want you."
"I don't want them."
"It makes no difference."
Her voice is like thunder; I do not know how she does it. She is Queen from wingtip to wingtip.

She approaches almost delicately, renewing her courtship dance of before, and my heart skips and dives in a graceless curtsy, that she must feel. She closes again and grips and holds me, and I want her so badly, but I am so afraid of her. Her face is against mine, her paws holding, talons flexing slightly so that I gasp, and she laughs. And then she is so gentle, carrying us both on her mighty wings, as we turn slowly in the glorious sinking redness of evening. And I shudder under her touch and shudder and shudder again, and she laughs a small secret laugh and lets me loose to spread my wings and shudder quietly to myself some more, before I return to her and give back her gift.

I SAT AT the entrance of my shelter and looked about me, at the clear sky above, all golden with the Light given to the Air-borne, at the sullen darkness of the Shadow flowing out from the Edge to close night about the valley. The valley of the Shadow, where the sun never quite touches the river, where night never quite leaves, where the only way to Light is the long climb up the Edge. The extreme cold of that place made me shudder even through furs, and my furs lay behind me in the dark fug of the shelter.
    With her.

AND WHEN WE are done, we ride the cooling air, wingtip to wingtip, gliding in thoughtful silence. Her eyes slide to mine.
    "When the time comes," she says, "I will come out here for my final flight."
    I look down at the blackness of the Shadow and the seemingly bottomless gorge that is the Shadow beyond the Edge.
    "Here?"
    She blinks slowly, the yellow of her eye eclipsed for a moment, and I shiver . . . the darkness below has almost sucked the Light from the sky; there is a greenish tinge to the cloudless arc above us.

"You know you cannot come back with me."

I suppose I had known, but somehow I allowed myself to forget. I do not respond, absently scanning the darkness below for some small scuttling creature to stave off the hunger that is beginning to creep into my consciousness.

"Wait for me," she says, and I turn my head, not understanding. There are tears rolling down from her amber eyes, tracking through the feathers of her face. She banks away from me suddenly, and up, up. I watch, not comprehending, tired, hungry, my heart full of love, and a peace I did not know was possible. She folds her wings, and dives, talons first.

WHAT COULD I ask of darkness, then? My safety, *our* safety, was compromised by her presence.

I searched the dark presence of the Edge, listening to the wild shrieking of the night bird's prey, gripped in talons, the abrupt silence as the fight was squeezed from it.

I shut my eyes, darkness in greater Shadow, and waited for my answer.

Darkness did not speak to me, and I raised my head, opened my eyes, and looked up.

The golden upper air mocked me, Air-borne whirled above, barely specks in the glow, the occasional glint as a wing caught the low light, and I imagined them laughing, *stay in your darkness earth crawler, learn to love Shadow.* Save that they did not know I was there, crawling in my darkness, waiting for them to fall. They did not know, *yet.*

Shadow entered my heart. Ice took hold of my blood.

I REALISE TOO late and am folded into Shadow with the first strike of her weight against me, falling into silence and bewilderment and pain, from which I fear to wake.

But I wake.

I have never felt so strange, so bereft. An involuntary keening shakes me, mewling like a starving fledgling, crying out for my mother. And she is there, caressing, soothing; those unexpected tears once more on her face.

"What have you done to me?"

But I do not need to ask; not really. A long slow shudder goes through my body, so utterly unlike the shudders she has let loose in me before, that I sob.

"I have made you a shelter, I have caught you some game, enough for many weeks; I have lit a fire."

I lean my head against her and weep, and she cradles me and hushes me.

"You must keep the fire alight, at least until you have healed."

Healed? I will never heal.

"Why?"

She is silent a long time.

"There can be only one, and I cannot kill you."

"You have killed me." She pushes me away a little so that I have to look at her.

"I have given you a choice. You can make of it what you please. You can live and wait for me, or you can die, if that is what you want. But you choose, every moment of every day, you choose."

"You are Queen."

"Now, yes. This is how I resolve the choice we had. One of us could die, and one of us could be Queen. For the hive, you are dead. For me . . ." her voice dies for a moment and she bows her head, "for me, you are Queen." It is scarcely a whisper.

"Me?"

She nods.

"Stronger; more beautiful than any other."

"Me?"

If she had not taken my wings, I would laugh, I would be proud that my Queen thought me better than her. And yet, the only way she can be Queen in her own eyes, is to maim me?

"I don't understand." I want to sleep, to weep, to scream, to . . . Light, I still want her . . . even after this.

She carries me to the shelter she has made; my Queen carries me, to a shelter she has made herself. She lays me down gently, so that my wings, my *lack* of wings, are not in contact with the ground or the furs that she had ripped from the animals she has laid in the coldness of the ready-made larder that is the cave beyond the shelter. There is water within reach.

She lies down beside me, limbs protective, face against mine, until I sleep.

She thinks I do not wake when she goes, but I know the

moment she stirs that she is going, leaving me.

THE SHADOW DRANK its fill of me, the hours I sat there, reminding me that I could not go home, that I had no friends to come find me; and that her friends could not be mine.

I watched the Shadow crawl up the far side of the valley, watched the golden sky turn through red to darkness, watched the distant stars.

At last my bones screamed for warmth louder than the muffling silence of Shadow could hide from me. I staggered as I stood, and limped to the shelter, expecting her to be asleep, but I could not escape her. Rigid, wild eyed, the tallow lamp carefully tended. I watched the tension slip from her, and realised she thought I had left her, alone in the dark, with death stalking the richness of Shadow. I shook my head, gathered up the nearest fur and wrapped it tightly about me. She shifted awkwardly, lying down as close to the wall as she could get, leaving me room to lie beside her. I looked at the space between the wall of the shelter and her well-wrapped body, as though I had a choice. I did not want to lie beside her, but there was nowhere else. I wormed into the space, careful of the lamp. She lifted it out of my way, and I knew it was partly to prevent me extinguishing it. She could not bear the dark. I have had to learn to live with it, she need not. I turned my back to her, but the shadow I cast on the wall disturbed me, unnatural, misshapen, awkward. I turned again and stared at the words smeared onto the wall above her. I willed the shapes to cease being words, to be a landscape, or pattern of tide on estuary sand, or . . .

I slept. I dreamt. I dreamt I was Air-borne again; banking in the sunlight, pelt warm in the balm of Light. The strength of my wings a glory, and I was chasing a small darting bird for the pleasure of it; not that the bird realised, and it shrilled in terror. But then I was the prey, sharp talons rending at my back, feathers whirling about me, hot blood running down my neck and shoulders and breast; and the pressure of air was not wind, not the speed of my flying, but the unmistakable buffeting of falling.

I woke sharply, to the tallow still glowing, and a stranger leaning above me, a questing paw on the great scars where my wings should be.

I think I would have killed her then, were it not for the tears falling on my bared shoulder, precisely where feather gave way to pelt, a sensitive spot, where the splash of her weeping could wake me. She covered her eyes and flinched back out of my immediate line of vision. I sheathed my talons carefully, one by one, and waited for the fear of falling to recede and my heart to stop pumping with the remembered weight and energy of those wings, my wings, spread in Light. A few tears of my own fell before I could look at her again.

SOMETIMES I IMAGINE her life, and wonder how many chicks she has raised, how many suitors mated and killed. Sometimes I regret that I did not challenge her, that her life is not mine . . . sometimes. Once she lets a spent suitor fall, almost at my feet, and I look up to see her gazing down, screaming with triumph, and I wonder, does she see me? And I look at the broken body on the fringe of Shadow, and it stirs. Still alive. I creep towards him, know him . . . a nest mate. I turn his face into the Light, and wonder whether he is live enough to survive, live enough to mate and give me chicks, but it is loneliness talking, it is Shadow eating my heart, and even when he opens his eyes and stares, and speaks my name, I know there is only one thing I can do for him. He tries to purr as I crouch beside him, and I lick the blood from his face. After I have ripped out his throat I lie beside him, with his limbs and wings curved about me, his tail draped across my feet, as we must once have lain as nestlings; and I keen softly for the feel of another's belly fur against my back until his body warmth fades and the weight of him no longer comforts.

SHE STILL HAD her eyes covered. She had not seen my weeping, perhaps had not seen the talons spread to rip the heart from her.

She did not move, waiting for whatever retribution she had earned, and I wanted, sorely wanted, to cast her out into the night to freeze. Instead I picked up her buckled grey box. She flinched a little then. I spoke far more gently than I felt she deserved.

"What did you think I was? Did you think we breed wingless *here*?"

She uncovered her eyes and looked at me.

"I did not know anyone could survive . . . that."

I shrugged.

"I know of no one else who has."

"But you . . ."

I waited, curious to see how much she understood, whether I would have to kill her after all. She shook her head.

"I must tell you something; I must tell you a thing I should not tell."

I frowned. I couldn't help myself.

"Don't give me your secrets."

"I must. I do not know how else to explain that you can trust me."

"I don't want your secrets."

She looked at me cautiously.

"Am I breaking a taboo?"

I laughed.

"By the Light, nestling, you have broken at least ten already, if I was going to be offended and offer your heart to Shadow, I could have done it many times over."

"Then . . . ?"

I sighed. I could not kill her if she offered me trust. Perhaps she had worked that out for herself.

"Tell me then."

"I'm part of a scientific expedition from another planet. We have been observing your culture . . ." she hesitated, ". . . the culture of the flying people up above, that is, for years."

I nodded. "I knew you were there. So do they."

She was shocked. It spoke from every muscle in her body. She really should learn to school her reactions better.

"Do you think we are stupid? All those automated recording devices? They will have had to issue an instruction to the nestlings to leave them alone. Believe me; you have not recorded much about us that we were not prepared to let you see."

She smiled weakly. Perhaps she did not believe me.

"The thing is," she said cautiously, "when we first came, the similarity of behaviours to several lower species on our planet led us to believe that you did not have a true civilisation. We were looking to exploit resources and we cannot do that where there is a civilisation."

"Lower species?"

"Forgive me, I can't translate it any better."

"You mean animals."

She ducked her head apologetically.

"Birds, obviously, but also—some insects."

"*Insects?*"

She bit her lip and had it bleeding again. She mopped at it absentmindedly.

"Bees, wasps, ants . . ."

I shook my head.

"We have these creatures. They are nothing like us."

She kept silent for a moment, thinking how to answer me.

"Culturally, you are more like them than you are like us."

I looked at the wall, the words, behind her.

"Are we?"

She twisted awkwardly and smiled.

"We have an ancient, ancient myth, that creatures such as you once lived amongst us. Or perhaps there was only one—I am not sure—but she was beautiful, and long-lived and incredibly wise and frightening. It did not suit us at first, to believe that you could be of that kind."

"And now . . ."

"We know better now. *I* know better now. We were clearing up, getting ready to leave, since there is nothing for us here, when I saw you; up on the cliff face. And you were different. The others are not interested, now that there is no opportunity here; but I am interested in what there is here. I am interested in you."

"So interested that you lost your thermal."

"Yes."

"So interested, perhaps, that you did not tell anyone where you were going."

"Yes."

"And you think that your friends, who are interested only in what there is not, will come looking for you?"

"Yes."

I tried to divine any uncertainty, but I could find none.

"Why?"

"Because I am . . ." the phrase was untranslatable.

She frowned at the box, still held loosely in my paw. I held it out; the tips of my talons grazed the inside of her wrist as she took it.

"That is one of the ways we are different," she said sadly. "I will try to explain. We are mammals, we suckle our young, we pair bond, although not exclusively. We have no neuter, we are all either male or female, and it easy to tell which we are. I cannot tell whether you are male or female or neuter."

"You have a very weak sense of smell."

"That too."

"I mean that I know you to be female. I can tell that you are a mammal, and that you have lain with a male fairly recently, by how you smell."

I had embarrassed her.

"I am . . ." that phrase again.

"Pair bonded?" I offer her. She shrugged, shook her head, nodded. I scorned her uncertainty. I *knew* what I was.

"I should have been a queen." Why did I say it?

She looked at me not believing, but then her eyes slid to where my wings should be.

"Your people kill your queen once a new queen emerges."

"Yes. And if two queens vie for the same right, they also fight. And one of them must lose. I lost."

Too many words, sticky words with a weight of memory and hurt clinging to them, hard to shake off, but I must do my best to ride the thermal I had chosen.

"You survived. That would not happen among the . . . on our planet."

"It shouldn't happen here." I pulled the furs tightly about my shoulders, watching her adjusting to the fact of my femaleness, my potential, my failure, my . . . mystery. I let amusement flood through me. Silly chick, her scientists would really struggle if they were to find out about me. And the amusement died. They must not find out.

"You are certain your people will come?"

"Yes."

"Can they travel the Shadow?"

"We travel space, this is nothing to us."

I let my scorn show. She lowered her proud head and smiled uneasily.

"We have [untranslatable], and coverings that allow it. I am like a . . . new hatched chick without it."

Nicely done, appealing to my maternal instinct, of which I had none, reaching out across species, offering me a metaphor that I could grapple with. Clever little chick.

"Will they find you before Shadow retreats?"

"Probably."

"I cannot be here when they find you."

"I do not want you to go."

"What choice, little helpless chick? You would freeze in a matter of minutes. You can think up an explanation for how there came to be a shelter here. I will watch for them and come back when you have gone . . . you will need to wipe whatever you were recording, if it will not fit your story."

"I can't."

"Then you must destroy the box."

"They won't find me without it. I said nothing that could harm you."

I found my talons flexing. *And if they find you dead? What will they do?* I wondered. But we were beyond that, she and I.

"So you must leave your box here. I must listen and watch for these friends of yours. How will they come? And how soon?"

"We will hear them first. A noise like . . ." she hesitated, " . . . like wind across a cave mouth." She imitated the *whup* of a shallow cave, with a wide mouth, in a wind of some strength. I inclined my head. I would recognise the out-of-place-ness of that sound, and my hearing was excellent.

"I cannot leave the box here. They will ask for it. We are going, there is nothing we can do that would bring harm to you."

She didn't understand.

"Soon?" I asked.

She nodded.

THIS TIME I wrapped myself carefully; her "soon" might be hours yet. I checked she had her taper and enough tallow to keep her in the Light. I crawled out into the darkness, and the bitter cold, to wait for whatever came.

I had grown used to waiting.

I SEE HER, out here, testing the thermals, finding the dead spots, the cold that never goes, the sucking of Shadow. She hunts out from the Edge, and she mates above the valley, I see how she drops prey and suitors with equal indifference, and watches the way the bodies fall, testing the air. I imagine her coasting the darkness too, flying through Shadow like an owl, I can almost believe she has a plan.

I CROUCHED IN the Shadow once more, but I did not speak to it this time, I listened to it crackling with darkness, I listened to my own breathing, to the wind wuthering up the Edge and blustering amongst the stacks. It was a long wait. Two hours, perhaps three, before I heard that noise, a wild wind across a cave mouth, where there was no cave. They were far away still, at the end of the canyon, and moving slowly. Whatever night vision her species possessed was not equal to Shadow at its depth.

I crawled back into the shelter.

"They're coming."

She tilted her head, listening, but her hearing was not as sharp as mine, and the sound was a subtle one, amongst the many voices of the wind.

"I can't leave the box," she said again, "but there is this."

She pulled a bundle out from beneath the furs of her bedding. Her wings. She pushed them towards me, spread them. She had mended the broken struts. She looked at me, silently, until I touched the fragility of the mesh with outstretched talon.

"They should carry you. Perhaps only once, but they will camouflage you, you've seen that." So she did understand, after all, something at least.

As I gathered the wings to me, my shoulder brushed the symbols we had drawn onto the rock, smearing the meaning. I reached out and wiped the surface more forcibly, blanking out our shared understanding of Shadow. We had also a shared knowledge of Light. She smiled, and raised her head suddenly. She had heard that noise for herself.

I was out and climbing the sheer rock-face above the shelter before she could think of more to say. Reaching up in springs and leaps, towards the first glimmer of light in the sky beyond the Edge. I heard the craft change its tone to a soft panting as it found a safe place to land, I heard her voice, gravelly, young and high, like water in a stream bed, speaking words I couldn't understand, and another voice answering, followed by a sob, and a murmur that needed no translation. The panting changed to the wind across the cave mouth, then to a fierce mosquito whine, dwindling gradually. I looked up and caught a flash as the first rays of Light caught some reflective surface, a brighter gold in the golden pool of dawn.

I stayed where I was, crouched against the wall of rock, and carefully unfolded the wings. Guide cords led from the tip of each rib, and she had done her best to adapt the fixings to my frame. I tugged the cord, it seemed strong enough. I shrugged the contraption onto my back and experimented with how the control cords fitted and what did what. The jacket was too tight, I had to rip it part way across the back to get the front edges to meet.

Would it hold me?

Long enough perhaps.

With care, I could fold the wings to me so that I could climb unimpeded. And I climbed, up to the Light, to the very lip of the Edge.

I crouched above the Shadow, with the first warmth of Light on my back for . . . since . . . I closed my eyes and curled my toes and arched my back in ecstasy. I had forgotten what the real Light was like, what it *was*.

A purr rumbled through me, and I blinked slow delight at the first touch of dawn.

No time now. I fumbled the cords awkwardly into place, tugged anxiously at the jacket. *Will it hold me*? I spread the wings, all but invisible, even to me, and felt the wind tug at once, lifting me. I gasped. Was this *fear* shuddering through me as my feet lost their grip on the earth?

I had forgotten. In all my dreams of flying, I had forgotten what it is, truly, to fly. To feel the power of my wings carry me . . . and this was not flying, there was no power, these were not my wings, nor were they *hers*, arched above us both. I let the wind pass, and sank back to earth.

MY LAST SIGHT of her is as she flies into the dawn, weariness in every wing stroke, my bloody torn wings clutched to her. She does not know that I see, she does not know that I hear the wild keening as she goes.

It is that weeping that keeps me alive, more than anything else she did to ensure my survival.

SO THE EDGE, and something to carry me over; to soar, or to plummet. When was it I grew weary of waiting? Was it when I lay curled in the embrace of the dead nest-mate with his blood drying on my talons, or only last Shadow, when a stranger wept for my torn body?

I turned and looked once to a horizon from the past, the fertile plateau rich in rivers and game, bright with sunlight, and noisy with insects and bird call. And something more: the urgent uneven beat of headlong flight, a shriek of defiance. I scanned the air swiftly ... *where?*

AND NOW, I see her, flying for her life above me, some fresh young upstart determined to break her, as she once broke me.

And I watch and I wait, as I promised; but I am still making that choice; hour-by-hour, moment-by-moment.

Will I live, or will I choose to die?

Will she live, or will I choose to let her die?

I UNFURL THE wings and spring away from the Edge, into the Light.

The Ravens, Before Returning

Ellen Huang

And who says we should go back
to the one who cursed us this way?
Who says we should like our black feathers,
iridescent in the dark, clipped away
to weak, bare arms that dropped
human objects just the same?

Oh dear sister, you did us no wrong
in seeking to know us more
But if you had waited, you would see
we never once called you to harm
a finger, to sever a single digit
of your brave and beautiful form.

We only called you to seek out the truth
and spare a wise pause for the birds
and deliver to them a kindness,
as if any of them could be your brother.

Their Disappearing Edges

Giselle Leeb

I OWE EVERYTHING to my adoptive mother, except, say, the stars.

My earliest memory of my real mother is of flying with her among the soft blurs of bats, looking down at the garden of the house where I was to live until I was eleven. I was very little then and for a long time I thought it must have been a dream.

Most children hope at one time or another that they have been adopted. And we did too. We'd sit on the bench at junior school, the twins and I, and discuss the possibilities. Nothing was out of bounds. Nothing was real, really.

So imagine our surprise when the man and the woman came to our house. They knocked on the front door when Mum was in the back garden hanging out the washing. We were not supposed to answer the door to strangers, but I knew right away that they were not average folk. They were beautiful, with delicate features and dark floaty hair, their clothes flashing silver from shadow, like the trout in the stream at the bottom of our garden.

"Could you call your mother?" said the woman, her voice a soft bell.

I invited them in, the two tall, thin people. They look a bit like me, I thought, comparing them to Mum's solid body as she came through, wiping her hands on her apron.

I'd never seen Mum so pale. I could tell that she knew them as they looked past her to where the three of us stood, curious, lined up behind her chair. Their expressions were politely interested, as if they were assessing our features.

There was a long silence.

"We've come," said the man at last.

"Oh," said Mum. "Are you sure?"

The woman nodded as tears ran down Mum's face.

I stared at Mum's back, and I brushed against soft shadows flying with me and my real mother in the night. *I will never drop you.* They *were* like me. It was their eyes—piercing and light—that made me recognize them.

Mum did not turn and look at us. "Pack your things," she said in a choked voice.

I left my mum's house with a few changes of clothes and the Polaroid camera that I was given for my eleventh birthday, the day before the visit. The film was so expensive that I had only taken one photo so far. I'd persuaded Mum to pose at our front door, looking out at the garden. It was summer and the awning was covered in clouds of climbing roses. Her smile was half-hearted—as if she had guessed what might be about to happen, I thought later. I put the photo in my pocket.

And so, at eleven o'clock on a sunny morning, we left our front door with scarcely a thought about the woman who I'd believed up until then to be our real mum. I waved goodbye, far too excited to be sad, dazzled as I was by our new parents.

What did we expect? We'd thought our parents would live in a grand palace of some sort. They left us inside a ring of trees with a couple of wooden stools to sit on, which we had to take turns in sharing. We sat together and talked about what our new life would be like. Our real parents were probably preparing the palace, we decided.

The odd thing was, although we had only gone as far as the bottom of our garden, we felt as if we had travelled a fair distance. I stood up and stared towards Mum's house. It looked slightly faded, like an old photograph. *Photographs!* I got out my camera and carefully positioned our front door in the centre of the frame to take the picture. *Before it disappears altogether.*

I bagsied one of the stools that summer morning and peered at the photo as it brightened into life, while the twins knelt beside me looking over my shoulder. This is what we saw:

OUR HOUSE, SOLID, real. I am standing at the front door, barely walking, hanging onto the doorframe. Mum is standing behind me. She is looking down at me with a puzzled expression, as if she can't quite work out how I came to be there. I am staring with desperation towards the faerie ring. I toddle towards it. She scoops me up and turns away.

I RECOGNIZED MYSELF from the elephant pyjamas Mum kept in a chest in her bedroom. Tears burnt my eyes; they splashed down onto the picture until it smudged into dark. For the first time, I missed my mum, and I missed my real mother too.

At lunchtime, our new parents appeared from behind a tree with a bowl of red berries. Faeries never lie, but they avoid explaining things directly. I found out how long we were to stay in the faerie ring by eavesdropping as we scoffed the berries: one hour for each year we'd spent in the human world and then our lives as faeries would begin. What this life would be like, I could not imagine.

The berries tasted sour, but also sweet. After lunch, we scarcely had time to cover ourselves in leaves and huddle together in a dip in the ground, before we fell into a dreamy sleep. I flew among soft shadows and I felt comforted, but when I woke, the sky was dark, as if it was holding onto something. I rubbed my eyes and gazed at our front door. It was further away and less distinct.

While we slept, the faeries had left us a verse—written on a leaf—and a small, round cake. The cake looked golden and delicious, but somehow I did not want to eat it. I gave it to the twins and they gobbled it down. Besides, I had found a crust of bread that Mum must have stuffed in my jacket pocket before I left and I nibbled on it slowly to make it last. Bored, I sang the verse over and over, while the twins laughed and danced around the ring.

A THOUSAND SHADOWS of a thousand trees,

A thousand shadows of a thousand shadows.

MY BROTHER AND sister did not tire of the game. They threaded in and out of the trees, weaving the light with their golden hair, while I grew listless and hungry.

Perhaps I'm not like my new parents after all. I sat glumly on my stool and stared at the mound in the middle of the circle. Could it be that the faeries lived there, although they were as tall as human beings? I walked closer and took a picture.

MUM AND I lean from the window of my little room at the top of the house. We are looking at the mound covered in stars in the garden. But the stars are twinkles of frosty light threaded into the earth. Bats dip past in silent black motion, hardly perceivable except as a shudder. I want to fly with them, but my mum is clutching my hand, as if to keep me there.

WHEN I WAS little, I'd thought that the sky had fallen down. After I saw the photo, I knew that the mound was shining from the inside out, my real parents two stars hidden away from us inside it.

The twins danced over to look at the picture, then flitted away. "A thousand shadows of a thousand shadows," they chanted.

Where are my mothers?

At teatime, our parents returned. And though I had longed to see her, my new mother seemed distant as she sat opposite me, saying nothing. *When she flew with me, the warmth was all my own.* I couldn't help sneaking another picture of my old front door.

I STAND WITH the twins in the garden, staring towards the faerie ring. We are strangely pale; we are almost shining. Mum comes out of the house with a man carrying a suitcase. He is arguing with her, pointing to us and then to himself, but he looks frightened. Mum shakes her head before he turns away and disappears up the brick corridor between our house and next door.

I RECOGNIZED HIM from the photo I once found hidden behind

the bathroom mirror. I knew who he was: he was the man I had supposed was Dad.

The afternoon light slanted into my eyes. I averted my face and aimed the camera straight into its rays. Never look directly at the sun, Mum always said.

MUM RUNS THROUGH the corridor towards the garden. Her face is contorted, a fierce sun, orange fire streaming down her cheeks. She wipes the flames from her eyes, but the threads of fire remain attached and her fingers burn the bricks; they become light as scraps of paper, the house vanishing behind her. She stops outside the ring. The twins and I sit inside it, laughing among glimmers of silver. Mum looks hungry, desperate, like she will agree to anything. Even eleven years.

I GLARED AT my cold faerie mother. I would escape from this woman who had given me away. I would escape back to Mum. *But she stole me first.*

My real mother returned my look without a smile, and then she simply faded away.

The twins were quiet after that. They sat reading the second verse that our mother had left for us.

I SAW A woman running, through the forest, through the trees,
   Her look turned back, I saw her, she sank me to my knees.

SHE HAD ALSO left a dish of tea. I sipped just enough to wet my lips and passed it to the twins. I ate my last bit of bread as they drank with relish. Twilight fell, half sun, half moon. *I am so hungry.*

I did not know where to aim the camera. I pressed the button and the photo slid out as white as when it went in. The twins did not even look up when I waved it at them. It gleamed like a ghost in the half-dark.

After night fell, the only warmth seemed to come from the stars above us. I pointed the camera at them.

PINPRICKS OF LIGHT burn into black, before we appear—my brother and sister, and I. We sit in the heavens and we eat mouthfuls of stars. But the more we eat, the thinner we become, and their number does not seem to go down. We eat more and more. But our bellies glow, quite empty.

I STARED AT the photo, and then at my hands holding it: they shone a little in the dark. I could hardly see the twins, except for their newly burning eyes. *I scarcely know them.* I could not hide my surprise at our distance, but they seemed not to care or notice.

I shivered when a fresh breeze blew from the direction of our old house. I peered into the dark for hours, trying to make out our front door, but the house had disappeared. I sank my head in my hands. *I am so hungry.*

The whirr of bat wings made me look up. I smelled something. Rich meat and gravy. Pastry. *Mum.*

I zoomed in on where I guessed the kitchen window might be. The camera flashed bright in the dark night.

STEAM RISES FROM a freshly baked pie as it cools on the windowsill of my house.

A PIE! MUM had left a pie for us on the windowsill. *On purpose?*

The twins did not look at me as I cut a lock from each of their golden heads; they stared longingly at the faerie mound as if it was already home. I wove their hair into a fine thread and tied it to my brother's arm, before I started towards the windowsill.

For a long time, there was only silence in the pitch dark as I inched across the lawn, clutching onto the thread. But the smell of the pie grew stronger and my stomach rumbled as my old house emerged from the blackness, its outlines indistinct except for the windowsill and the pie. These were in colour, as if light shone on them from inside the house, but no matter how hard I looked I could not see beyond the sill. When I eventually reached it, I felt behind for a gap, but my hand touched solid brick.

I could barely stand from hunger. I stumbled back to the ring, guided by the thread, the pie heavy under my arm. I divided it into three equal wedges, but the twins shook their heads. I was as thin as them by now, but, whereas they looked healthy and glowing, like our real parents, I was sickly. I felt at that moment that I was hardly the oldest anymore.

Do they even remember Mum? I could not meet their burning eyes. I sat with my back to them, my tears flowing freely, and shoved the wedges into my mouth one by one. As I ate, the kitchen window came into view behind the sill. I yearned for a glimpse of Mum. And she did appear briefly. I willed her to look at me, but she only stared down at where the pie had been, her hair grey in the yellow light, and I thought that she had been planning to eat it herself after all.

But I felt that pie going down, solid inside me, and I knew that I was at least part human. I looked again and my front door had reappeared.

The twins gazed at me with their faraway eyes, and I could no longer find words that they would understand.

I showed them the photos. "Mum's house. Our mum's house," I said.

Pale and glimmering, they stared at it without recognition, and I understood that she was not theirs anymore, and scarcely mine.

I steadied the camera to make sure that I got the last photo of my brother and sister exactly right. In the faerie ring they are almost invisible, twinkling silver outlines shining against black.

As I held onto the golden thread and made my way alone across the grass, my mum, who I had scarcely noticed in my previous life, grew dear to me: her cheeks cherry-red, her eyes dark brown—unlike mine—and her voice soft with sorrow. She was not dainty, my mum; she was strong and capable, what people call "alive".

I suppose it makes sense that the last photo is of my real mother, as much as you can ever see of a faerie. It was years before I could forgive her. When I finally took the pictures from the drawer where I'd hidden them, I saw that she had not forgotten me. A verse appeared on the very last photo I had taken, blinded by tears, before I travelled home.

I SAW A woman running, through the forest, through the trees,
    Her look turned back, I saw her, she sank me to my knees,
    She saw me, I saw her, how strangely we were pleased.

I REALIZED THAT my real mother is not as cold as I had supposed; she was not unaffected by losing me for a second time. It is just that, for faeries, each of their years is many of ours.

When I got back to the house, there was an old woman sitting in Mum's chair, looking out of the kitchen window towards the faerie mound.

I recognized her from her brown eyes. "Mum," I said.

"My angel," she said. "How tall you've grown."

I held her hand, and we smiled at each other for the rest of that afternoon and on into the night.

Mum and I had agreed that she'd put me down as her grandchild in her will and nobody asked any questions after her funeral.

I bake a cake with two candles for my brother and sister on their birthday. Although they will outlive me, young and thin and golden, I feel sad that there will be no one to do it for them when I am gone. I leave it in the faerie ring, but I make sure that each time I do, I cut the golden thread that seems to grow of its own accord up from the ring of trees to my windowsill.

I don't do much else at the moment. I like to sit in Mum's chair and watch the bats take flight at dusk. Something will happen soon and I will leave home.

My skin has grown coarse and my hair has darkened to brown. I am no longer so slender. In fact, people say that I look very much like my own dear grandmother. But they also say that they do not know where the light in my eyes comes from. They always remark on this. I have never tried to explain and I have never tried to extinguish it.

Swanmaid

Bronwynn Erskine

HAPPILY EVER AFTER is a prince to break your curse and carry you off on his white charger to a castle and a crown. It's a dress of embroidered feathers and a hundred roasted swans for the feast. It's an endless stream of troubadours who sing to you of the years you spent bound beneath your curse's weight as if you do not dream every night of swansdown.

You watch the horizon from the battlements, torn between hope and fear, until one morning the spring thaws yield up a crooked V of long-necked shapes against the rising sun. Though you've told no one, the guards have all seen you watching. It's not hard to guess what for.

The prince is full of swagger and boast that night. (When is he not?) He calls for a hunting trip. Invites his gentlemen with a laugh and what he must think is a sly glance in your direction.

He's still laughing later, when he invites himself to your bed.

He always thinks himself the height of humour when he's drunk, but it's all too raw tonight. Too real and too cold and too much harsh truth. He stomps off when you start crying, muttering darkly that he'll trade you for a better swan.

That's all you are in his mind. In all their minds. The swan who turned into a woman. You're a story, a miracle. A prize to grasp and a treasure to covet. You lie awake for hours while the thought runs 'round and 'round in your mind, chasing after the truth you've kept from yourself all along. Your cloak of feathers fell away when the prince spoke your name, but you'll always be the swanmaid.

In the morning you ask your most trusted handmaiden to fetch you swan feathers. Her eyes are wide and solemn, but she only bows her head and does as you ask.

All through the summer you sew in secret, in the quiet hours when your ladies are gone about their own tasks. White silk thread pierces the shaft of each tiny feather, and the cloak begins to take shape.

The prince goes hunting. He returns with dead swans to heap the feasting tables and laughs ever more raucously with his gentlemen. For each swan he brings you, broken-necked and gutted, you sew more fervently.

Through the summer your stitches grow more certain. As fall draws down upon the castle, you notice how much faster the progress goes. But still you fret. Will it be done in time? The leaves turn to gold and flame, and you feel the weight of time dragging at you whenever you must lay aside the needle to attend to the duties of the prince's court.

The first snowfall spurs you with panic. You sew all night by the light of guttering candles. Time is drawing short now. You feel it in the weight of your bones, in the darkness of your hair when you catch sight of your reflection. In the savour of meat upon your tongue.

In the thin grey hours of morning, gritty-eyed, you stitch the last feather into place. Your handmaiden's eyes are wide and dark as she fastens the hundred pearl buttons up the back of your feather-embroidered dress, but there is the shadow of a smile as she lifts your feather cloak onto your shoulders.

The guards stare and whisper as they catch sight of you in the corridors and on the stairs up to the battlements.

The sun is just cresting the eastern hills, and the long-necked shapes have waited for you. They rise from their resting places as you reach the castle wall, close enough that you can hear their wings drumming the clear, cold air. The sight of them steals your breath away with fear and hope.

It's easier than you expected to step to the top of the parapet.

You hear the guards cry out behind you, but the swans cry out more sweetly. You spread the wings of your feathered cloak wide and step forward.

You fall, or else you fly.

Happily ever after is the chains of your curse broken. It's wings that can break a strong man's arm and carry you far from any cage. It's sisters around you, sheltering you in their wake when you're not strong enough to keep going on your own. It's freedom, and the wind sifting through your feathers as you head south to a gentler winter.

The Whippoorwill

Kevin Cockle

THE FOKKER DR. I Triplane with its distinctive yellow cowling
made Josh think of a butterfly or a bat, so sudden and unlikely
were its evasive manoeuvres. "This is Werner Voss' last
combat," the sylph said as she created the mirage to illustrate.

It was fifty below zero with the windchill, but "Sylph" and
Josh sat in balmy comfort on a bench overlooking the Bow
River, Sylph maintaining the temperature around the bench
while dissipating the resulting condensation-fog. Josh wore a
light jacket more for the benefit of any unlikely onlookers than
out of necessity. Inside the mini-dome of warmth, it smelled like
a tropical island beach. It smelled like summer.

How she loved her fighter pilots. At least in that brief
window between WW1 and the jet age with its fly-by-wire
controls. "Used to be you had to strain against the wind-
resistance on your control surfaces," she would say. "The pilots
could feel me, and I them. Like the sailors before them, but with
resolution orders of magnitude finer. Like orchestral music,
Josh, in your terms. Like hearing a moving aria in the Paris
Opera House, sitting with someone you love. I can't really
reduce the dimensionality into your frame of reference exactly,
but that's what comes to mind. Nowadays, I can't feel anything.

Most planes don't even have pilots. Shame."

Voss—outnumbered eight to one at this point—executed one of his weird flat-spin horizontal turns and put a few holes into McCudden's S.E.5a, scattering the British pursuers once again. Sylph created the mirage out of ice crystals in the air, refracting light to get the colours; playing with shadows to create the appearance of depth and density. She had explained her lensing mechanisms to him at length, but as always, he marvelled at the imagery as though it were magic. The dark evergreen backdrop of the Edworthy cliffs across the river made the planes stand out so vividly, Josh felt as though he were flying pursuit himself. More than once he flinched and ducked at the incoming spray of Spandau machine gun bullets.

Yesterday, it had been all about Hans-Joachim Marseille, the young German ace of aces in North Africa. A *Rotte* of Bf109s had roared up and down the Bow River valley as Marseille pulled off deflection shots out of steep, banking turns Messerschmitt engineers had claimed would be impossible. "Of course," Sylph had chuckled, "the math hadn't accounted for the air being sentient. I couldn't resist helping out now and again. My darling Joachim."

Voss dipped and rolled, turning into his attackers when he could have escaped. "You know these were the bad guys, right?" Josh smiled. It wasn't all Germans all the time—she loved her Yeager and Bader and Bishop too, but she did seem to have a special affinity for the other side of the hill.

"Yes," Sylph sighed. "But they were so exquisitely doomed." She turned her face to look at him with playful, crystalline eyes. "Who can resist such poignancy?"

He blushed, shook his head. "Don't start," he said.

Up close, you could see right through Sylph to the skeleton-boughs of the frozen aspen trees that lined the river. From a distance she seemed solid enough, but sitting beside her, Josh could see the limitations of water vapor and light tricks. She had, for whatever reason, given herself shoulder-length hair with a grey polished-steel sheen, and a handsome, high-browed face that favoured severity over traditional norms of feminine beauty—at least as Josh understood them. She wore a royal blue skirt suit and jacket that presented like the garb of a headmistress at some prestigious private finishing school.

When he'd asked her about her choices, she'd just shrugged and said it would be too hard to explain. It hadn't even occurred to him to question that.

Her voice, and all the other sound effects she created, were sort of "auto-tuned" out of ambient noise in the background. The sound of cars or trains or shouts or sirens in the distance would be transformed, repurposed by Sylph manipulating air density, changing frequency and wavelength by changing the medium. These compression techniques Josh had understood at least, in the context of his own music-industry background. Such as it had been. He had heard techs talk about "Fourier analysis" even if he couldn't do it himself.

"Why me?" he asked under his breath, as though he weren't certain he wanted her to hear him. Machine guns rattled; low-power piston engines strained under combat duress.

"You know why," she said. That auto-tuned trill. " 'As Above, So Below.'"

"But I don't understand that though. Not really. I'm not . . . I'm nobody special. I'm not smart—most of the things you say go right over my head. I just don't get this. You. Us."

Sylph watched as Werner Voss—twenty years old, and dead from a single bullet through his heart—crashed into Belgian farmland. The scene changed: a galleon floated in mid-air; the Flying Dutchman. "You know how you get calls from telemarketers?" she asked. "Like, way more calls than you remember ever receiving in the past?"

"Sure?"

"It's because you still use a landline. That information gets shared, and pretty soon, calls start converging on your location. The more you pick up, the more you get."

"Because I don't have a smartphone."

"Those fucking smartphones! And smart fridges and toasters." Sylph clenched her fists in mock rage. Josh grinned in spite of himself. "It's your goddamned internet. Like a beehive; all I hear is a constant buzzing. Truly. It reminds me of the time before humans. You may as well all be plants and bacteria again. The cosmos is changing, Josh. Contracting. I'm being focused more and more on people such as yourself."

"Like fly-by-wire? Only, I guess it's everybody, not just pilots?"

Sylph turned her head and smiled. "It's exactly like fly-by-wire. That's it exactly. And you say you aren't smart!"

That made him chuckle, but then he winced, his breath catching as a sharp pain shot up from his hips through to his lower back.

Sylph's face was suddenly impassive, her polar-blue eyes watching Josh closely.

"I'm sorry, Sylph," Josh said. "Have to lie down for a bit. Been sitting too long."

Sylph stood as Josh gripped his cane, steeled himself, then lurched to his feet. Pain lanced from his right knee, cascading up and down his spine, and he grit his teeth in response. Slowly, gingerly, he made his way back the way they had come, following a path cleared and dried by Sylph's micro-targeted scalding air blasts. Wouldn't have been possible otherwise, the streets rutted with ice, the sidewalks hopelessly uneven with uncleared snow. With so many abandoned townhouses in the complex, few folks fit enough to shovel the walks were left.

"You should have that checked," Sylph chided as she walked beside him at his halting pace.

"Should have a lot of things checked," Josh grimaced. He knew he was in trouble, with a knee that needed replacing, and undiagnosed degenerating neuropathy on his right side that had prevented him from building guitars and playing them. He needed help, but public healthcare—along with so much else—hadn't survived the disintegration of confederation. He could afford one of those back-alley "chop shop" jobs ("No wait-times!"), but he just wasn't there yet, emotionally, intellectually. Apparently the cosmos wasn't just changing for air elementals.

Not for the first time he reflected upon his sheer ability to endure as both a blessing and a curse. When other people would have acted for better or worse, Josh just hunkered down, covered up, took more hits. It was the story of his life.

"Do 'Cheatin' Heart'," Sylph asked, penetrating his mounting gloom.

"No, Sylph . . ."

"Come on. You know who you sound like? To me?"

"Sylph . . ."

"Townes."

"No. Stop it."

"Townes Van Zandt. You do. I hear an echo of him in you."

"Townes Van Zandt was a genius. I'm a never-was hack."

"'Your cheatin' haaaart . . .'"

Josh smiled as he heard Hank's backing band start up in the air all around him. Sylph loved the whining twang and yodelling transitions of Hank Williams and could reproduce them perfectly. She said Hank packed enormous musical information into almost every word of his phrasing. Josh took her word for it.

Eventually he joined in. How could he not? Her enthusiasm was infectious.

IN THE BEGINNING he had been terrified.

He'd started seeing her in dreams before the first cold snap in September and had been unnerved by the persistence, night after night, of the imagery. But when she had appeared on the street dressed only in her headmistress get-up against the sub-zero cold, staring into his kitchen like something out of the Overlook Hotel, the sight had nearly broken him. He wet himself, hobbled into the bathroom, locked the door.

The terror of seeing some sort of ghost was quickly displaced by the more fundamental horror that he was losing his mind. He spent a week in that condition, wondering if he had become psychotic in his isolation. Not knowing who to call. Not having anyone to call. Worst week of his life by a long shot, and that was counting all the times he'd lived in his car, or had to force himself to stop drinking.

Ultimately it was Sylph herself (Her? Itself? Josh had settled on "her" as the path of least resistance) who had calmed his fears on that score, taking him outside in weather that should have killed him. "See?" she'd said. "You're wearing a golf shirt. How much more proof do you need? Crazy doesn't protect you against frostbite. I do."

And so the winter progressed. Calgary didn't get Chinooks anymore, so when winter hit, it was no joke. Josh would have had a world-class case of cabin fever if it hadn't been for the outings with Sylph down to the river. Once the fear subsided, he was always and only fascinated by the weird miracle of her. *You can get used to anything*, Josh reflected, and not for the first time.

On the first of October, the condo manager cancelled the group cable contract, leaving Josh without television. Most people streamed, but Josh didn't know how, and though he knew he could learn, he was happy enough just reading. Didn't have digital radio, but had a record player and a basement full of vinyl albums. Story of his life: when change came, he just hunkered down, rode it out, let it wash over him. Adaptation had always struck him as over-rated, somehow. Not to mention stressful.

He'd come back to Calgary years ago to look after his brother when cancer had got its hooks in. Two years of DIY medical misery, compounded by the hyperinflation that had attended Alberta's separation, and the near-collapse of the public sector in general. Carl had had the money to get treatment, but it would have meant selling the condo and using every last dime to buy what? A few more years in a place that had become no country for old men? "Fuck that," Carl had said every time Josh brought it up. "I got a better plan."

Carl's better plan had involved transferring title of the condo to Josh. Then he'd invested in a basket of US equities and taught Josh how to write out-of-the-money puts and covered calls on them. He could do it online, generating a steady trickle of US dollar income, which was the only non-crypto of any use in Alberta. Wasn't conceptually difficult, but it did take rigorous record-keeping and an organized mindset. Carl had had just enough time to hammer those skills into Josh before the end. The little brother acting like the father, as he always had, much to Josh's everlasting gratitude and guilt.

For a while, things had stayed stable. Manageable. Carl's clockwork solution had proven remarkably robust, all things considered.

When Sylph had first appeared to him however, tremors had begun to shake Josh's house of cards. The income-drip was sufficient for his bare-bones needs, but it was getting hard to make payments in cash, or even with his old-style credit card. The last cab company had gone out of business just in time for lethal winter, and busses hadn't run in Calgary for years. And Carl's old Mac was slowing, crashing more often. These were Big Things to Josh; existential threats. The smartphone he had thought he could get to the finish line without, was starting to seem more and more inevitable. It was getting harder and harder to hunker down in this networked environment. An environment that seemed to be actively seeking him out, purposefully becoming aggressive and hostile towards him.

He had to wonder if these stresses had played a part in getting Sylph to materialize. Her referencing "landlines" didn't seem coincidental, the more he thought about it. *Maybe it was now or never for her,* he wondered.

Maybe we don't get Chinooks because she can't do them anymore.

Maybe "As Above So Below" implied "As Below So Above".

He wasn't even sure what that last thought meant exactly, but it bothered him all the same.

ON DECEMBER 7TH—Joshua Abel Neumann's sixty-second birthday—three things happened to and around him. Big Things: cosmic dominoes.

First, he awoke to another email from Cecille:

Dear Josh:

Did you think I would forget? Happy birthday. You better still be alive, bastard. Return this email, or call me. I know you have my number.

Not to nag you or anything, but let me just remind you that your room is ready here. Penticton is warm (ish); our farm is turning a profit; you know you love it here, and Don's looking forward to seeing you again. I'm serious—you need to get the frick out of Dodge. I know that's scary for you—you don't have a passport, you don't want to be a stateless refugee, you don't drive anymore, yadda-yadda-yadda. Suck it up and get here.

I'm not doing all the work: you call me. Today. Let me know you're okay.

Love,

C.

He read the note over and over; thought of a bunch of things he could say, and didn't. Had he really not responded to her last email? A quick check of his sent-mails confirmed it was so. He resolved to call her later on that day. Maybe after breakfast, if he could work up the charm.

He was halfway through a packet of instant oatmeal when he heard the sirens. Ruled out the fire department because it didn't exist; ambulance seemed expensive, cops unlikely, unless the board had decided to bid for service. That *did* happen occasionally, with squatters taking over the odd abandoned unit, and gunplay being a little beyond the purview of the average board member. Josh put his chips on "cops", tuned into the community newsletter for updates.

In a few hours, the story was told. Edna Halston, 82, of Unit 3999, had been found on the bench out front of the little copse of trees on 37th street, dressed only in her slippers and nightgown. She'd been there all night, frozen solid in an upright, seated position. Comments speculated wildly, eventually landing on a consensus that she'd gone looking for her little dog (dead for over a year now) in a demented haze, and settled on the bench where people would have seen her a thousand times over the years. Seemed plausible enough.

A lovely, pastoral spot as Josh recalled. He passed it every time he went down to the river, to sit at his own favourite bench. Not wearing a nightgown perhaps, but not much more, given the conditions. The only thing between him and Edna's fate, was Sylph.

The thought settled in his chest like a physical weight. He stared at the newsfeed for the next couple of hours, hitting "update" like a rat seeking a dopamine-bump, praying for more information.

That night, like an incantation of sorts—bell, book, and candle—the third thing happened.

In the cold, clear darkness outside, he could hear Hank's voice:

Hear that lonesome Whippoorwill,
He sounds too blue to fly . . .

He thought about getting his parka and boots, his toque and gloves, but then he thought he was being silly. Instead he composed himself, got his cane, and headed out into the night with just his usual windbreaker and running shoes.

IT WAS ALL so overwhelmingly beautiful, Josh felt tears on his cheeks for the first time in half a century.

"Happy birthday, Joshua," Sylph said, casting a glance at him as they sat together overlooking the frozen riverbed.

She had created the electric hues of an Aurora Borealis, then simulated the illusion of flight through the undulating light. In the dark, under frigid, indifferent stars, the feeling of motion was uncanny. As the Aurora slid past, a warm breeze caressed Josh's face, moved the last wisps of hair surrounding his balding pate. He had never experienced anything like this. Perhaps no human being ever had.

But then he thought of the open-cockpit pilots of WW1 flying through clouds made incandescent by moonlight. Maybe that would have been close.

After several attempts to speak, Josh croaked: "I haven't said thank you as often as I should have, Sylph. This is . . . this is astonishing."

"My pleasure, Josh." He could feel her smiling in the dark.

"For everything. I know you've been making sure my furnace doesn't crap out. My windows don't ice-up inside. You make it possible for me to get exercise; give me an excuse to get it. Thank you for all of it."

"Thank you, Josh. It's more of a two-way street than you realize."

"About that," Josh swallowed, mouth suddenly dry. "Did you know Edna? I mean, was that . . . you know . . . you?"

Sylph seemed to consider her words carefully before answering. "I know what you're asking," she said, "but your pronouns don't really do me justice. I'm a distributed being—a collection of vector fields and gradients. When I localize to interact with you, I'm this, I'm "me", the Sylph you know. But when I localize for someone else, the odds of me being exactly the same thing are . . . well. They're not zero, but they're not great."

"Okay. But you know what I'm saying, right? I don't know how to get the logic right, but did you—did some version of you—kill Edna?"

"Yes, Josh, I did."

"Okay."

"Because she asked me to."

Josh didn't know what to say. Aurora light played upon his frowning face in shades of green and mauve and violet. Sylph

103

filled the silence with measured tranquillity. "She had been a teacher, and the government had stopped paying her pension. She'd run out of money. I'd been heating her house these last few weeks. Think she was down to her last can of creamed corn. Yes, she was increasingly confused and disoriented, but she was very lucid when she made her request. She had wanted to take advantage of the clarity.

"We went to her favourite spot and talked at length about the life she'd led. It had been years, she said, since she'd been outside at night. Even just that was a wonder for her. I promise you it was nice for her. Peaceful. And never final: had she changed her mind at any point, I would have taken her home, and continued to care for her as best I could.

"She felt no pain. When she was ready, I called down a jet of air from the stratosphere, and gave her instantaneous mercy. And that was the end of her."

Josh nodded.

"Are you okay?" Sylph asked.

"Yeah. I'm just . . . she was what? Ten doors down from me? I never made any effort at all to know her. Feels like I could have . . . I don't know."

"Don't feel bad. There's nothing you or anyone else could have done."

Josh accepted the verdict in silence. First, because the moment seemed to call for silent reflection. For Edna, and for himself.

And second, because Josh knew that every word he uttered contained an infinite number of sin waves of different frequencies in superposition, most of which no human could hear, but all of which Sylph would detect. She could hear intention he didn't even know he had. And though he loved what she had done for Edna, and appreciated what she did for him, he knew in that moment one certain thing he wasn't sure he wanted to share.

He was certain he didn't want to be one of Sylph's doomed fighter pilots, no matter how pleasant she made the flight.

THE NEWLY-PURCHASED smartphone was undeniably sleek and black and opaque. It sat on the table next to the cappuccino Josh had bought, both objects so alien in aspect as to appear to be works of art to his way of thinking.

The kids at the kiosk had been nice, once they'd gotten over the shock of meeting a grown adult who didn't have—had never had—one of their indispensable machines. They'd done some set-up formatting for him, downloaded the banking and payables and ride-sharing apps he needed. He'd bought the coffee to test out his newfangled purchasing power, and to get off his feet for a few moments. The phone wasn't complicated. Exploring it for fifteen minutes was enough to convince him that he could get himself home in good shape.

Cappo finished, he pushed himself upright by the food court tabletop, secured his phone, gripped his cane, then headed in the direction of what he hoped would be Safeway. He vaguely remembered the mall layout, but it had been awhile, and the place had been entirely redesigned as a kind of museum or amusement park. You could still shop here, but it was ridiculously expensive. What you were paying for was the experience. And the heavily armed private security, aided by their state-of-the-art surveillance AIs.

Store fronts affected a retro 1960's design motif, encouraging patrons to think of themselves as members of an apocryphal suburban middle class. Just plain folks. The canned music was similarly vintage, playing all the old Christmas standards: "Rudolph"; "Frosty the Snowman"; "Baby, It's Cold Outside". Mall employees dressed in period costume: part retail help, part living displays. It struck Josh as an updated version of Heritage Park, the old faux-pioneer town that had been a big attraction when he was a kid. *Come see what life had been like in the Good Old Days. Remember?*

Eventually, he found his way to the grocery store and headed directly for the main exit. He was sweating, nearly exhausted: he wasn't used to bearing the full weight of his winter panoply. Grocery stores all had good places for cars to pull over, so he'd always used them as transportation nodes. He'd had to pay a neighbour one hundred US dollars for the trip up the hill; getting home would apparently cost a fraction of that.

He stepped through the automatic doors and immediately felt his face tighten in the arctic air. A knifing breeze reminded him of Sylph's penetrating gaze; the uniform metallic-grey sky brought to mind her hair. A silver-coloured smear in the cloud cover told him where the sun should be, but he couldn't feel it. Not even a little bit. That too, reminded him of her.

"It's all been swell, Miss Carousel," Josh murmured. A line from his favourite Townes Van Zandt song—one of Townes' melancholy, ambiguous "goodbye" tunes, even though the moment seemed to resonate more strongly with the implicit betrayal of "Pancho and Lefty". He hoped Sylph could still hear him, even if she could no longer appear to him. But deep down, he knew it didn't work that way.

He sent a text for a driverless car that promised to arrive in 2.35 minutes.

He pulled his hood around closer to his aching cheeks; turned his back to the wind.

He was afraid. He had traded a doomed, comfortable universe for an uncertain and dangerous one. He had done that intentionally. It was all on him. He had made the one move that meant he could never again stop making moves.

He could almost feel the mysterious whole of his self being reformatted as activated pixels. Could almost hear the telltale cosmic, white-noise buzz.

"As above, so below" indeed. He finally understood.

Nephele, On Friday

Elizabeth R. McClellan

It's harder to find her than it once was.
You've got to know what bars
allow her to smoke inside. Outside
it doesn't want to gather into a wreath

for her face. She wears as little
as possible for the weather, all drapes
and scarves without substance.
In the neon glow and low light,

she looks solid, and drinks beer.
"For the bubbles," she says, cigarette
flaring. "They taste good." She doesn't
fade away to mist, and she doesn't age.

She melts her features to fit her latest ID.
She showed me once, a slow shift
that left my stomach on the ground.
"He left me that. I suppose so I wouldn't

wear Hera's face forever. That gets
messy later. Not that he ever cleaned up
loose ends, but she was smarter than him.
I was not made for him and that kept me safe."

She drains the froth and catches the bartender's
eye. "For a given value of safety. Clouds are
used to passing over, and even being passed
through. Bodies are different. All salty

and rigid and held down to ground, like
trees that can walk. All compact, with
insides and outsides that aren't supposed
to change places. But you don't say no

to the thunderbolt. Dressed as a queen,
but not for long—I had the modesty
of raindrops, after all, and my instructions
were to lead Ixion into a trap. So I did."

A shadow falls over the corner of the bar,
the pungent smoke going blue to grey.
"I did. And I was rewarded. Eventually.

After my first and forgotten son, all
testosterone and cloud-shifting, who knew
that horses are wind made body too,
and had my clever grandchildren, men

fleet as horses but thinkers. Rewarded
with a king, a son of virtue and quick wit,
my Athemas, son of Aeoleus, a bit of
a nymph himself, who did not mind

my shifting moods or morphing face,
who delighted in Phrixus and Helle,
who asked, for the first time, how it was
to have a body, and shuddered

when I told him it was a horror, a curse

to be flesh and not vapor. 'When the children
are older,' he said, and meant it,
watched me finally sublimate. The sky

was an old friend in with a new crowd,
but the birds do not forget a queen.
The birds told me the moon's sister had
burnt all the seeds before they went to ground,

bribed the Oracle, to open a way
for her fine sons. I remembered being solid,
stole the gold from a sunbeam, made
a flying ram. I remembered rams as fierce

and clever. Perhaps I should have
entreated with my grandsons, who so
loved a rampage." The ashtray is filling.
The glass goes bottom up. For a while

she does not speak, and her face shines
when she does. "My Helle. Never harmed
a soul. But clouds know about water. Rivers
draw us down. More nymph than daughter.

And remembered, at least, by sailors,
who always watch the clouds. Phrixus
made it. Escaped the moon sister for
the sun's boy. Sent my ram to Zeus,

who started all this. No loose ends. Just
water changing state, sea to sky." Her pack
is empty, her glass is too. "Why do you
come down then? For beer? Cigarettes?"

"To be solid," she said. "One thing a cloud
can't be. It's awful, having a body. But
I don't want to forget how. It's all I have left,
the memory of how to be meat."

Elizabeth R. McClellan

Outside she bums a last smoke, waits
until we're alone, starts to fade, grows
amorphous. I gather the cool damp fabrics.
They'll be clean for next week, when

Friday morning a little gale will gather them
off my back porch, so I know to hit
the bars that night when the wind whines
and one cloud stubbornly covers the moon.

Golden Goose

Chadwick Ginther

BLINKING LIGHTS AT the end of the Cessna's wings flashed like tiny lightning in the night sky. The dick in front of Ted Callan had called shotgun, which left Ted's knees crammed into his chin. Despite the dragon-scale invulnerability his tattoos provided him, his legs were numb. Former football players weren't meant for small planes.

The dick in question was Loki. God of mischief, Loki. He'd dressed like a glam rock star today, sporting bright purple hair, oversized sunglasses that made him look like a bug and a significant number of tattoos. He'd said he wanted them to match, to help Ted "blend." Ted was covered head to toe in tattoos, but Loki's disco ball shirt and leather pants didn't really match Ted's jeans and black t-shirt. At least Loki hadn't said "trust me." Those two magic words always meant Ted's life was about to go to shit.

"Trust me," Loki said. "This is a much safer way to travel."

Unsaid, was Loki's original reasoning he didn't bother to share with the pilot. "They'll be expecting us on the highway."

Today was the first time Ted had flown in an airplane since he'd been tattooed by a trio of Norse dwarves in a grotty motel room in Winnipeg. Those dwarves had wanted to use him to

111

bring back the good old days of myth and magic. They'd given him nine gifts—and made Ted a lightning rod for trouble.

An inky storm cloud tattoo, like his dragon scales, a gift from the dwarves, moved just under the skin of Ted's chest, matching the clouds outside the plane. That tattoo responded to the weather. The weather responded to his mood. Which meant a lot of unexpected thunderstorms. Truth was, the tattoo may be recent, but the storm had always been in Ted's chest. It was only the damage that got flashier with the dwarves' handiwork.

It was almost two years to the day since Ted had received his nine legendary gifts—and since Loki had introduced himself. He'd lost a few gifts, and traded a sun for the sword along the way. But he still had the storm. The hammer. The sword. The horn. The horseshoes.

Ted had expected something to pop up to mark the anniversary, but not that someone would steal his car. Granted, Loki had stolen the car for him, but Ted still wanted his ride back.

He'd spent the last two years fighting monsters. Protecting people from the rising tide of mythological bullshit. One thing he'd learned: if you let a monster take something from you, you have to fight to take it back. If you didn't, they'd keep taking. It was just a car. But it was Ted's. It'd been a gift. And he'd get it back.

He took a deep breath. Flying had been enough of a pain in the ass, between the cramped accommodations and increasingly Orwellian security theatre. A death by inches. Ted hadn't been looking forward to the flight even before Loki had booked the smallest plane he could find with a pilot trading an opportunity to build hours for gas money.

Ted grunted, shifting toward the window again.

"Want to switch seats?" the trickster asked.

"Yes."

"Lots of room on the wing, buddy." Loki pointed a cocked finger at Ted, and mock-fired with a wink.

Ted snorted a laugh. Loki hadn't said switch seats with *him*.

He still wasn't sure the flight was a good idea. Takeoff went okay. Now they just needed to land safely. Except like Ted, trouble followed the trickster like the running of the bulls.

He wished he could smoke. The growing twitch of nicotine

withdrawal did nothing good for his bad mood.

Ted pinched the bridge of his nose.

"Nervous flyer?" the pilot, a young woman named Amy, asked him. She'd turned to face him and her headset looked like Princess Leia buns on the side of her head.

"No, ma'am, I'm not," Ted said. He tried to smile. "Just need a smoke."

"We should be landing in a couple hours."

"Ted has many gifts," Loki said. "But patience isn't one of them."

Amy didn't get the pun. "Why are you two heading to Flin Flon?"

Ted had no idea what to tell the pilot. He sure as shit couldn't tell her the truth. Loki saved him. In a manner of speaking.

"Kind of an anniversary for us."

"Congratulations!" the pilot chimed, her smile as bright as Loki's sequined shirt.

THE DRONE OF the engine was lulling, coupled with Loki chatting up the pilot, but out there, something in the air was following them. He could feel it.

And it held a grudge.

Which could be goddamned anybody.

Rain pattered the windscreen. The clouds could be hiding anything. Wind tossed the small plane, cracking Ted's head into the window.

"Whoa. You okay?" Amy asked.

"All good." Ted smiled as he rubbed his head to sell it.

Loki gave Ted a long look as the pilot turned back to her instruments, muttering at the storm and scanning the sky. Ted couldn't do anything but worry. Which made the weather worse. More rain. More wind. And that made the flight bumpier, and Ted more worried. And the storm grew.

"Relax," Loki said, as if forgetting that few things riled Ted up faster than being told to relax.

"I'm. Trying."

Loki mimicked Ted's clipped tone. "Try. Harder."

The stars went out and the sky lit up with lightning. They were surrounded by thunderheads. Rain blew past the plane too fast for Ted to see.

Amy whistled, "Nothing like this in the forecast."

"Crazy, right?" Loki said. "Weather's as unpredictable as a redhead."

He knew what Loki was getting at. He also *knew* there was something out there, but he couldn't see it. And it had nothing to do with his red hair. He tapped his boots on the floor of the plane and drummed his fingers to a Zeppelin song no one else could hear, trying to calm down.

Ted would've felt better with his feet on the ground. Something about having his toes in the dirt and calling to the sky felt entirely different. Hippy dippy bullshit. But it was one thing to bring the lightning to him, and an entirely different one to be up among it. In the sky, trapped in a fragile winged tube, the storm felt vaster somehow.

He nudged the thunderheads. He didn't know what effect bold action would have on their plane. Even his "gentle" attempts seemed problematic. The pilot's grimace intensified, and she twitched with every flash of lightning; but she kept them in the air.

IT WASN'T SOMETHING following the plane, but many somethings. Ted caught silhouettes in the lightning flashes. A flying "V" on either side, and one behind them; their honking cries audible over the engine and rain. It wasn't the dragon Ted had been looking for, but it might be worse.

Geese.

So. Many. Fucking. Geese.

Even with a brisk tailwind a goose shouldn't be able to catch a plane, but no one had told these geese that. Ted had seen a Canada goose drive off an angry bull. Geese didn't give a shit. They were the Canadian honey badger. Maybe they could fly over two hundred klicks an hour just out of spite.

"I'm diverting around this storm. We're gonna land in Dauphin and ride this out on the ground." Amy sounded to Ted like she was trying to hide her nervousness, but wasn't quite there.

Once they were on the ground, he'd bet bourbon to beer he could take whatever came at them. But they had to get there first. He felt the storm's motion, the roiling clouds, the flashing lightning, the buffeting winds, and his tattoo moving to match. Ted felt like he was drowning. Being so close to the storm, so far from earth, Ted swam against that storm. It wanted to lash out as fiercely as possible. It wanted to destroy.

He wanted to destroy.

But he couldn't.

He wouldn't.

If he gave in to the flash of the lightning and the peal of the thunder, Amy would definitely die. Ted would be fine; the horseshoes tattooed on the soles of his feet allowed him to walk on the air. Loki would be fine. Loki would always be fine, no matter what Ted did.

He caught flashes in the lightning and the rain. In every flash of light, the flying wedge grew closer, and larger. And their honking cries louder. It filled the sky as much as the storm. They surrounded the plane, pacing it. Their tightening proximity nudged them directly toward the centre of the storm.

Ted did better with threats he could hit. The hammer tattooed on Ted's right forearm gave him the strength to go toe-to-toe with monsters. It also drew giants to Ted like flies to shit.

It wasn't fucking fair. Those geese probably weren't even geese. Loki was a shape-changer. Lots of giants were. And since the dwarves had given Ted the power of Thor's hammer, Mjölnir, along with his storm, the giants had carried over their grudge from the god to Ted.

He looked out the window. The geese were closer.

Motherfucker.

One goose turned its head and stared. Right. At. Ted.

"Can't you outrun them?" Loki asked.

"You'd think so." Amy didn't seem happy that it hadn't already happened. "But apparently not. They can climb higher than our service ceiling. If they want to catch us, they will."

Ted took off his boots. "I guess I better fight them."

Amy turned, shocked. "You better *what?*"

Wind buffeted the plane side to side, up and down. They hit an air pocket and dropped like a rock. The greasy burger Ted had eaten before getting on the plane wanted out. He choked it down. The geese were back on them in a moment.

Lightning traced across the sky and Ted bent a bolt toward the furthest goose he could see. Missed. Another bolt was building. He could feel it.

Trying to nail a single goose an indeterminate distance away was different than hitting a giant. The more bolts he called, the bigger the storm got, the more likely the plane would get hit by stray lightning. Ted couldn't direct them all. He hit one. He was sure he hit one.

"Stop it!" Amy yelled. "Whatever you're doing, stop! You're going to get us killed!"

"Point of order," Loki said. "He's gonna get you killed. We'll probably be fine."

"*Not* better."

Amy banked the plane away from a wedge of geese, but one broke from the formation and landed on the wing with a thud, forcing it back to true. Its neck craned toward the window, black eyes glittering, white chin straps electric in the storm. It was huge. Fucking ostrich huge. It slammed its beak into Ted's window, spittle streaking across the cracking glass until it was lost in the rain.

Amy asked, "What do they want?"

"To kill Ted," Loki answered. "Maybe me too?"

"Oh, that's all? I should let them have you."

"Maybe they want you?" Loki jumped as a second goose slammed into his door. "It's hard to tell who's pissed off who sometimes. Hit any geese with your plane lately?"

Amy stared gawp-mouthed at the trickster but said nothing.

A thud above, a second goose on the wing. They banked sharply, Ted cracked into the window. Amy rocked the plane trying to shake the geese. A third goose landed on the nose and the plane dropped into a dive. The pilot side door tore off and a goose darted in hissing and honking. Ted punched it in its stupid goose face and knocked it off the plane. But there were more. Lots more. And they were driving the plane into the ground.

Ted released his seat belt buckle and put his hand on the pilot's shoulder. "Time to bail."

Loki nodded and turned into a harpy eagle. He screamed at the goose trying to bite him. Amy screamed at Loki.

Ted didn't have time to answer or reassure her. He tore her seatbelt free from the air frame and jumped out of the plane taking Amy—still in her seat—with him. Loki followed Ted out the gaping pilot's side of the plane.

The geese swarmed the trickster as Ted and Amy tumbled, ass over tea kettle. Loki disappeared in the clouds. The spinning was getting disorienting. Ted held Amy tight to him and let her seat fall. He unclenched his curled toes, his bare feet touched the air with intent, and they stopped dead.

They stood, suspended in the air. Amy checked to see if he wore a parachute. Double checked the sky for the telltale silk, and a reason why their plummet had stopped.

A wedge of geese dove at Ted, and he changed direction, the horseshoe tattoos allowed him to pivot as if he were a running back on a football field instead of in the clouds.

"Hang on," Ted said.

A skein of geese, moving together like starlings, chased another flying shape backlit against the flashing clouds. More came after Ted. Loki would be fine. After all Loki had survived, including the end of the world, he wouldn't be taken out by some fucking geese. Ted needed to keep Amy alive. She hadn't asked for any of this shit.

Her hair stood on end as he gathered the storm. No plane to worry about anymore, but he still had to be careful. A lightning strike wouldn't hurt him, but Amy would take the full brunt of any stray bolts. Lightning flashed from cloud to cloud. The lightning followed the same path across the storm tattooed on his chest, in time, arcing from there to his tattoo of Mjölnir.

In the brightness of a flash, he bent the lightning to the geese.

They were too close. The thunderclap that followed was loud enough to scare shit from a wolverine. Lightning bisected several of the geese like they were meat on a spit. Their afterimage burned on Ted's retinas through closed eyelids and in the moment it took for his vision to clear, more geese were on them.

They hovered as they flapped, snapping at him and Amy. Ted dropped. The geese collided in a thunder of honks and meaty thuds. As Ted fell, he spotted a goose he'd struck with lightning, gliding roughly towards the earth, still smoking, but alive.

"Tough fuckers," he muttered, but he was long past believing these geese were local.

Ted kept the geese away. Drop. Dodge. Light 'em up. A

simple plan, but effective, and eventually the geese flew off.

TED AND AMY landed amid some jack pines and rocks. There was no sign of Loki.

Ted and Loki had come a long way since the first time they'd met and Ted had wanted to beat the shit-eating grin off the god's face. Now Loki was more like a brother. And sister. And sometimes a weird aunt who kept trying to help him get laid. In a way, the god of mischief was the only family Ted had left.

Amy slapped Ted's hand away. "So remind me why you needed a plane?"

"I can't fly."

The pilot looked at the sky, still flashing, and blinked away a fat drop of rain. "Coulda fooled me."

Ted waited for Loki to spring out from the bushes. When the trickster didn't appear, Ted asked Amy, "You okay?"

"I'm not hurt." She paused and shuddered at the distant honking of geese. "But I'm pretty far from okay. And you owe me a plane."

Ted didn't want to antagonize her by pointing out—as Loki surely would had he been here—that *technically* they owed her uncle a plane. Or diminish her statement by saying she'd get used to it. He didn't know that. Maybe she would, maybe she wouldn't. Getting used to magic was a fucking lie anyway. He'd been balls deep in magic for years now, and there was always something that came up to make him shake his head, and go "why? Why the fuck would anyone . . . Just. Fucking. Why?"

"Smoke?" Ted offered Amy the first unbroken cigarette he'd tapped out of his pack.

"No thanks. I don't smoke."

"Mind if I do?"

"Knock yourself out."

Ted lit the cigarette, savouring the butane, the crackle of the paper catching, and the peace of the first drag. He inhaled deeply, exhaling the stream of smoke away from Amy. "I should probably quit." He snorted a bitter laugh. "Loki says it would be the end of the world if I tried. Again."

"This usual for you?"

Ted nodded. "Usual in the unusual. Giant geese problems are new."

Amy asked, as if afraid of the answer, "What . . . what are you?"

"I'm Ted." He didn't have a clever answer for what the dwarves had done. Ófriður, they'd named him. Weapon. Troublemaker. Un-peace. "I'm just a guy."

"Just a guy," Amy threw his words back at him. "Never seen another guy do what you just did outside of a movie."

Ted braced himself for the "but they were better looking" dig that Loki might've provided, but it never came. "Loki is, well, Loki. He's a god. Small 'g.' Mythological motherfucker of mischief."

"Wait. Loki is *Loki*-Loki?"

"Last time I checked."

Her eyes narrowed. "Wait, if he's Loki, does that make you—?"

Ted cut her off with a laugh. It would piss off Big Red and Dead to no end to hear that. "Nope. Similar portfolio. I fight monsters."

"What monsters are there in Flin Flon?"

"The kind that stole my car."

"I'm in this mess, because of *your car*?"

"It's a magic car."

Amy groaned. "I wish I'd never met you."

Ted heard that a lot. His dad always said wish in one hand and shit in the other and see which one fills up first. He didn't repeat that to Amy. The advice hadn't helped him growing up, wouldn't help Amy now.

SOMETHING RUSTLED IN the bushes and deeper in the trees. Ted's first thought was Loki had found them. But that didn't seem right. Ted and Amy weren't in the middle of anything embarrassing, so there was no need for Loki to show up now, of all times. And Loki didn't give warning to his arrival.

Ted hopped to his feet and got in a boxing stance. Lightning crackled from his storm cloud tattoo up his right arm to Mjölnir.

Amy called out, "Who's there?"

Ted put a finger to his lips and mouthed, "They've found us."

"Who?" she mouthed back.

"Geese."

The air seemed to go out of the clearing as the honking and screaming began.

It wasn't geese that came tearing out of the woods first. It was campers dressed in filthy jeans, flannel, and down jackets that seemed a bit heavy for early September. They were drenched. From rain, from sweat, Ted wasn't sure.

"Run!" the lead camper yelled. "They're right behind us!"

Geese burst out after them, hissing and honking. They flapped their wings as they ran, a few took to the air in great leaps, landing between the campers, separating them.

"Get behind me!" Ted called. He dug his toes into the sodden earth and felt for the storm. "Get out of here! *Git!*"

The geese didn't listen. Instead, they advanced in a semi-circle.

Amy yelled a warning. "The campers—!"

Ted spun to see the campers grinning at him with far too many—and too sharp—teeth. Their eyes had gone all black. Two of them had pulled a sleeping bag over Amy's head and two others scrambled to get the drawstring at the bottom tight as she kicked them.

"Oh, fuck me."

Ted didn't see where the first bolt of lightning hit. Two campers he'd turned his back on threw a sleeping bag over his head too.

Ted fought to break out of the bag. But the fabric wouldn't budge. It stretched with his every punch and kick. He stepped into the air. Something hit him from behind. Several somethings. A baseball-bat-heavy goose kick. He shook off the strikes until one caught him behind the knees. He tipped backward, and the geese piled on him.

The air inside the bag reeked of stale farts and wet marsh. Their rasping bills sawed at his pant legs as they clasped his ankles and tried to stuff him fully inside. He kicked and hit something solid. It squawked as the beatings continued. Dragon-scale invulnerability was great and all, but he still felt things that couldn't kill him. And the rocking and rolling from all the goose onslaught left him dizzy. He couldn't focus on where to call the storm. Rainwater seeped into the sleeping bag. Distant thunder rolled. He could still feel the storm, but he couldn't use it.

The sword. It'd stopped the biggest, baddest giant Ted had ever fought. It would cut through a fucking sleeping bag. The sword formed in Ted's left hand. It was too long to swing in the tight confines of the sleeping bag, it was damn near Ted's size, but the brilliant white-blue blade slid tip first through the sack. Ted could see.

He spun the Bright Sword in a wide arc. The geese danced away. Avoiding the light, or the sword's edge, Ted wasn't sure. But now he could see where Amy was, and that the geese surrounding her were running at him, bellowing in anger.

"Goddamnit." He hated this part. But it wouldn't be the first time he'd called a bolt from the sky right on top of himself. He paired his storm tattoo with the sky. Small lightning danced over his body, bright as his sword. Instinctively, Ted reached for the sky with his hammer hand and brought the lightning home to Mjölnir.

The stink of ozone filled his nose, then fire. Feathers burst aflame. The water drenching his body boiled away. All in an instant. Then, honking cries of pain were drowned by a thunderclap. Ted had a feeling of weightlessness as he was blown off his feet. He hit the ground before he could set his feet under him.

He hurled the rags of the sleeping bag off his body. A ring of geese lay on the ground. Stunned or dead, Ted couldn't say. He took a moment to confirm. Their chests pumped like a slow bellows. The geese were alive. Bully for them. A couple of down jackets were left in a smoking pile, their owners disappearing into the woods.

Ted recalled the sword into his arm and braced his hands on his knees, catching his breath as Amy wriggled out of her sleeping bag. He stood and cracked his back, digging a fingernail into his ear. It did little to stop the ringing.

Where the hell was Loki?

Ted helped Amy to her feet as the stunned geese stood. Ted groaned and readied for round three. It didn't come. The geese took flight, honking with laughter.

Honking, at least. But it sure as shit felt like they were laughing at him.

TED COULDN'T HELP but feel they'd been travelling in circles. He'd hoped to salvage some supplies from the wreckage, maybe even his fucking boots, but no luck.

Whatever the goose things were, they reminded him of a story he'd heard about swan maidens. Shape-changers who could take a swan form thanks to a feathered cloak. He'd seen Freyja's falcon cloak in action before. This type of magic wasn't new to him. Although why the hell anyone would want to turn into a fucking goose, he had no clue.

Of course, swan maiden cloaks were a *gift*. Goose cloaks seemed like a curse.

There was an old joke about Canadian geese being where Canadians deposited their hate and ill-tempers. Ted didn't know about that—he'd seen plenty of shit that couldn't be blamed on geese. Maybe whatever was affecting these campers had made that saying literal. Ted didn't know how it may or may not spread.

TED LOST TRACK of how long they'd slogged through the muck. His watch was toast. In the distance, where the trees started to thin, he saw something. A wall, maybe? They crept closer. It wasn't a wall. It was a nest. An island-sized nest. Impossibly big. See-it-from-fucking-space big. Instead of being woven from grass, entire trees were crammed together and glued in place with mud, stacked to the clouds.

"I do *not* want to meet the goose that lives there," Amy said.

"You and me both."

A handful of geese landed, almost disappearing against the nest. They preened their chests and Ted thought he heard a zipper sound. A human stepped out of one big goose, then the next, until all the flock appeared human. They shook their coats of feathers, turned them inside out, and put them back on. They were quite the crew, wearing matching red down parkas.

They carried sacks, presumably offerings, or prisoners. None seemed large enough to hold Loki, but Loki being Loki, any, or none of them could be the trickster's prison.

The nest shuddered, shaking as if by a tornado-wind. A dragon-sized neck snaked up and over the nest's edge. The humans climbed up the black bill and scrambled up the neck. Ted held his breath waiting for the titanic goose to spot and devour them. It didn't. When all of its campers were aboard, it lifted its head and brought them into its nest and out of sight.

"Welp," he said to Amy. "I'm going in."

"You're *what*?"

"Loki's got to be in there. I'm getting him out."

"In. There."

"He'd do the same for me."

"Really?"

"He'd probably be the reason I needed rescuing, but he'd show."

Amy considered that. "Okay. Let's save him."

"'Let's?'"

"You two owe me a plane. I'm not letting you out of my sight until I get it back."

Ted held out his hand. "Okay, partner."

This time she didn't slap it away and nodded. "Let's go."

"Put this on."

Ted handed Amy one of the trashed parkas from the ambush. He'd put the fire out before they'd been completely consumed. Both still had feathers sticking out of it and were more rips and tears than coat.

Amy wrinkled her nose at the parka. "I don't want to turn into one of them."

"You won't." She didn't look convinced. Ted sighed.

He put his coat on first, and walked out of the trees and toward the nest. When he didn't change, Amy followed. She still looked dubious. Beyond dubious. Incredulous. Shit sakes. Ted had turned into Loki. He hadn't said "Trust me" but he may as well have.

"You didn't ask for this. You weren't meant to get caught up in this. And I'm sorry. I'm doing my best."

"Your best."

"I'll try to keep you safe."

"Try. No promises?"

"This is the real world, and magic is just as real. Shit happens. I've learned not to make promises I can't keep."

"Thanks for being honest. I guess." Amy took another long look at the nest. "What do I do if one of them comes at me?"

"Grab it behind the head and snap its neck."

"Won't that kill whoever is inside?"

"The people inside seem to be entirely in the body of the goose."

"How does that even work?"

Ted shrugged. "Fucking magic."

He joked, but he needed to remember, there *were* people in those goose bodies. Maybe they were innocent. Maybe not. He'd been lucky not to kill any of them with his lightning. Once he'd dealt with the big fucker, they'd see what happened. But Ted didn't kill people. Didn't even like killing monsters if he could avoid it.

Big Goose lowered its head for them, honked loud enough to shatter the windows of a truck, and spread its bill wide. Its tongue warbling from the cry, thorny spines pointing back towards its throat. Each of those spines was big enough to impale a person. Shit. They were bigger than most people. If it got Ted in its mouth, he'd have to fight his way out through the stuffing chute.

Its heartbeat was audible as it regarded them, eyes black as slough water at night. It closed its bill. Ted waited a moment before clambering on. Stinking, marshy exhales wafted over him from the goose's nares. Ted climbed between the eyes to the neck. He checked over his shoulder. Amy was still following him. So far, so good.

Big Goose lowered them into the nest. At its centre seemed to be a clutch of eggs. The goose things carried their prizes toward it. Ted and Amy followed. If Big Goose had captured Loki, that's where he'd be. After ten minutes of walking, they didn't seem any closer. It was kind of like trying to walk across the High Level Bridge in Edmonton while drunk, though there was more goose shit to dodge here.

"Nothing good about goose shit," Ted grumbled.

Ted really wished he'd been able to find his boots. His feet would never feel clean again. Another ten minutes walking and Ted wanted to burn what remained of his jeans. When they finally reached the "eggs" Ted saw they weren't eggs at all. They were camper trailers.

"The fuck?"

"Greetings, Ófriður."

The voice was loud. Loud as the thunderclap when Ted had dropped lightning on himself. He spun around and Big Goose's head was *right there* behind him. Grinning. It knew who Ted was. Knew the name the dwarves had given him. It had to know one more thing.

"Where's Loki?"

"My golden goose?" The big black and tan prick honked a laugh. "If you can find him, you can keep him."

The goose things flipped their parkas, and changed.

"Ted . . ."

"Amy, get in one of those trailers. Now. Lock the door."

She nodded and ran. Something about this fight didn't smell right, and it wasn't the goose shit. Ted couldn't put his finger on it. It smelled . . . cold. Like the time he'd been too impatient to defrost his old freezer and took a screwdriver to the ice, puncturing the Freon canister. He didn't have any time to consider it further. The geese were on him.

Ted grabbed one by the neck with each hand and spun, swinging them to clear a path for Amy to get to the nearest trailer. The geese didn't make as good a weapon as Ted had hoped. He snapped one's neck like he was flicking someone with a wet towel. The goose went limp in his grasp and he hurled it at the growing crowd. He did the same with the second goose. It barely delayed them. The geese were back on him in no time, slamming him with their bony wings, and knocking him into the slimy ground.

Ted heard the click of the trailer door closing behind him. These geese could probably tear through its walls like they were paper, but Amy was as safe as he could make her. Time to cut loose.

He pointed at Big Goose. "Give my friend back, fucker."

"Friend?" the goose howled with laughter. "*Loki* is your *friend*? Loki has no friends. The only thing he has of value is his name."

The sky rumbled as Ted cocked a finger at Big Goose. "Guess again."

Big Goose laughed as the first bolt hit home. And kept laughing as Ted peppered it with lightning. The goose was bigger than anything Ted had ever fought. Too big. None of Ted's bolts had any effect. Ted gave up on the lightning and ran up into the air and out of the goose shit. Big Goose's neck moved too fast for Ted to grab, and it flattened him into the mud with its bill. But he caught a foot as the enormous goose took to the air, tipping the camper trailers in the downdraft.

The goose felt real. Hit like it was real. But it couldn't be. If there was anything out there this big, Ted would've heard noise. Ted called lightning. *All* the lightning. Enough to strike any and every bit of the giant goose's body. He knew why he'd recognized the cold smell. Illusion. None of this was real.

Big Goose rippled under the lightning strikes. And disappeared. A second, smaller goose appeared, leg still clutched in Ted's hand. Smaller, but still pretty fucking big. Over twenty feet tall. Ted knew this shape was real.

Big Goose slapped at Ted with its heavy wings, buffeting him into the—now much closer—edge of the nest. It turned its head to the sky and honked as it took a giant greasy green dump on one of the trailers. It noticed Amy peering out of the roof of one of the overturned trailers and ran, wings spread, toward her.

Sweet musical Christ.

Ted jerked Big Goose's hind leg until he heard something pop. He dug in his heels and hauled against the bird's immense weight. There was no traction in the muck, and the goose dragged him along. Ted stepped up into the air, and his horseshoe tattoos bit in. Big Goose stopped dragging him, and Ted hauled it back.

It honked its displeasure and whipped its head around, slamming into Ted. Its rasping teeth shredded what remained of the already damaged down jacket. Ted released the goose's foot and grabbed it by the neck, suplexing it onto its back. Mud and shit splashed, coating the trailers. Ted scrambled on its belly and punched. He kept the goose's neck vise-locked in his left hand while he punched with his hammer hand. Every time Big Goose got too bitey, Ted punched it in its stupid goose face instead.

He punched until it stopped honking. And he kept punching, punctuating every hit with curse. "Fucking . . . goddamned . . . geese . . . where . . . the . . . fuck . . . is . . . Loki?"

"Ted! Stop!" Amy called.

He stood, sweating and panting on top of its unconscious breast. He really needed to quit smoking. The feathered cloak shrouding Big Goose had torn, and Ted recognized the face he'd been hitting. It was Loki's giant form. The trickster's face was mangled and bloody, but he was alive. He might not've been if Amy hadn't stopped him.

Ted cradled Loki's head. "I'm so sorry."

A booming laugh filled the nest, but this time, there was no nasally honking. Ted looked up, way up. Standing by the cluster of trailers was a giant, better dressed than most. Looked like he'd actually had a suit tailored to his hundred-foot size, and kept his beard groomed with something other than mud and blood. "Pity. Would've been lovely for him to die at the hands of his adopted family. Again."

"Giants," Ted muttered. "Why is it always fucking giants?"

"What, you don't know me?" Ted didn't recognize the giant, but he knew the look. He had the glow of a man who'd just taken a twenty-minute shit on company time.

"Should I?"

The giant smirked. "Útgarða-Loki. You *will* learn it, Ófriður."

Útgarða-Loki. Ted didn't need to learn it. He knew it. Loki of the Outyards. The giant who'd tricked Loki (no mean feat) and Thor (a considerably easier feat) for shits and giggles back in the days before Ragnarök.

"Motherfucker, I'm ready for you right now."

"No, thank you. But we'll meet again. Soon."

The giant smirked and everything was gone. The nest. The giant himself. Everything but the vehicular "treasures" and the goose shit. They were standing in a campground littered with giant green turds, cars and trailers, a crumpled Cessna, and some very confused campers standing in piles of rotting feathers. A gleaming metal cube rested in a fire pit. Ted's magic car.

Ted had no doubt Útgarða-Loki would turn up again. He wasn't looking forward to it. He was fucking exhausted with fighting old grudges from another world. But he'd keep at it. There was no other choice.

"What happened to you?" Loki said looking up. He rubbed his jaw and groaned. "What happened to me?"

"Long story."

"That wannabe's always wanted my name for his own. Made me think you were him. Thought I finally had him down. Until you started hitting me for real." Loki's form shifted to the one he'd worn on the flight, hiding his injuries. "Did we win?"

"We're alive." Ted said, bouncing the cube on his palm. "I got my car back. I'd call it a win."

"A win?" Amy said. "What am I gonna tell my uncle?"

"The truth?" Loki said.

"The truth?"

"You hit a bird. A big one."

She groaned.

"Or," the trickster said with a smile. "You landed to get out of the storm. And you let me fix it."

"How?"

"Trust me."

"It'll buy you some time for us to fix this."

"Fix it?" Amy gestured at the wreckage. "You're a certified aircraft mechanic? How can you fix this?"

"That Outyard wannabe isn't the only one who can play with illusion." The trees swallowed the wreckage. "I'm not a mechanic, but I know someone who is."

"They won't want to help," Ted said.

"I'm charming as hell, and if that doesn't work . . ." Loki rubbed his jaw. "Ted can be *very* convincing."

The House with a Pond with a Girl in It

Christa Hogan

"IT LOOKS LIKE something out of a horror movie." Matt squinted up at the dilapidated, two-story house that would be his new home.

"The inside's better," his mom said. She exhaled a final cloud of white smoke and crushed her cigarette butt in the gravel. "It has good bones."

"Do they belong to the previous tenants?"

"Very funny." She slung a trash bag over her shoulder. "Grab something from the car, will you?"

Matt retraced his steps. The car's door groaned as he wrestled it open. He surveyed the cardboard boxes and trash bags crammed in the back seat. He selected the box decorated with *Thrasher* stickers and his skateboard first.

Not that it mattered. The new house was in the middle of the sticks. He wouldn't skate until they moved again. But then that probably wasn't so long to wait.

They'd moved six times in as many years for twice as many reasons. Matt had a name for every place they'd rented. There was The One that Smelled Like Reefer, and The Place Over the Drummer's, and The One Where We Only Lasted a Week.

He'd liked the last place they rented though—The Apartment On the Blue Line. It was in a rough neighbourhood, but at least he could take the blue-line bus to the skate park every day.

Mom was already heading out of the house for another load when he climbed the front porch steps. As he passed, she peered into his box, which was full of used trucks, wheels, and old grip tape.

She frowned. "Not just your own stuff either."

"Yeah, yeah." He let the screen door slap shut behind him.

The inside of the house was even more depressing than the outside. And what was that smell? Like something rotten. And old people. A chill went through him. Wait, did old people *die* in here? That would explain how his mom could afford to rent an entire house.

The last house they'd lived in was The One Built Next to a Landfill. They couldn't drink the water or use it for showering, dishes, or laundry. But at least he'd had his own bedroom and didn't have to sleep on a couch or, worse, in with his mom.

Matt took the stairs to the second floor two at a time, eager to claim his new room. The upstairs hall was ten degrees hotter than the downstairs and lit by a single bulb. Matt pushed open the doors lining the hall one at a time, heart sinking farther with each empty room. She hadn't mentioned that the house wasn't furnished or air conditioned.

The last room had a mattress and a cheap, plastic-looking dresser. Matt dropped his box on the mattress, sending up a cloud of dust motes. He coughed and went to open the only window, but it was stuck. Great. He used the edge of his t-shirt to wipe grime from the glass and peered out.

The view wasn't anything special either. The backyard was little more than sand and weeds surrounded by pine trees. The evenly spaced rows of trees looked purposeful, like the tobacco plants in the fields they passed on the way there. Or bars on a window.

"Matt, I'm serious!" Mom called from downstairs. "I need your help."

He groaned. "I'm coming. Jesus, Mom!"

"Language, kid!"

Like she was some kind of saint.

Matt started to turn away from the window when something caught his eye—deep in the pines, a shimmer of light across water. Huh. Well, that was new at least. He'd never lived in a house with a pond before.

"SORRY ABOUT THE pizza," Mom said for the tenth time.

They'd opened the takeout box to find the cheese stuck to the lid, the crust and sauce already cold. Matt chewed his slice mechanically and said nothing. He was too hungry to complain and too annoyed with her need for his approval. He could have told her that no-name pizza from a backroad gas station wouldn't exactly be gourmet. There was a reason it only cost five dollars.

She was quiet for a while, but not still. She was never still for two seconds when she was trying to quit. She fidgeted in her chair, with her hair, with the congealed cheese on her slice of pizza. She was already itching for a cigarette, and she'd only officially decided to quit (again) an hour ago.

"Sorry about the electricity too," she added. "And the water. Tomorrow I'll go into town and get it all turned on."

Matt grunted. He wasn't just mad about the power or not getting a hot shower or the cold pizza. He was fed up with moving. Fed up with having to rely on her for everything. Fed up with her promises that this time would be different.

He was sixteen, too old to believe in her fairy tales anymore. There was no fancy job or rich boyfriend or winning lottery ticket in their future. Just fast food, soul-sucking work, schools where he didn't fit in, and overdue bills until he was old enough to move out on his own.

"I'm not hungry." He pushed his plate away, nearly knocking over the red tapered candle between them. The flame spluttered and smoked.

"Careful." Mom slid the candle farther away, leaving a trail of red dots on the table's scarred surface.

He pushed back his chair.

"Hey, where are you going?"

"My room."

"First, eat your—Oh, fine."

He grabbed the heaviest flashlight from a box by the fridge.

If he was going to spend a dark night in The Murder Mansion, he needed something that could double as a weapon.

He made his way to his room and searched every dusty corner for serial killers and poisonous spiders. When he was satisfied, he locked the door and sat cross-legged in the middle of the floor. He shone the flashlight against the side of a bright white box for lighting.

Then he took out his cell phone. His battery was dead. Perfect.

The full, dismal reality of his life sank in. Sometimes he felt like he was surviving one endless moving day. He couldn't remember going to both the first and last day of the same school, and he'd never stayed anywhere long enough to have a real girlfriend. How sad was that?

Sweat dripped from his forehead. Damn but it was hot in this house.

Matt stripped off his shirt then got up and went to the window. A square of yellow light from his room shone on the weeds in the backyard. As he tugged at the window with both hands, his shadow hovered and jerked inside the yellow square. Like a moth caught inside a streetlamp.

He banged the heel of his palm repeatedly against the window jam until the glass rattled and shivered. Finally the window budged, an inch.

Matt exhaled with frustration. Why was nothing in his life ever easy?

At school, he had to work twice as hard as other kids just to keep up. He was so far behind that he'd end up in remedial classes, again, which was sure to put a serious dent in his girlfriend prospects. New school; same old bull shit.

Maybe he should just drop out, like his mom did when she had him. Get a job. Save some money. Buy a car and drive to California, to a city with actual skate parks. He'd get discovered. Get a sponsor. Go on tour and compete in the X Games. He'd have no trouble finding a girlfriend then.

Air trickled in through the opening, lukewarm, moist, and— Matt sniffed, frowned. Directly below his window, a tiny orange light burned bright for a moment then dimmed. A puff of white smoke drifted across the yard. He heard a familiar sigh of relief.

Matt dug his fingernails into the soft wood of the peeling

windowsill. Who was he kidding? She would never quit smoking—she hadn't even made it through the night—and they would never quit moving. He would never get a girlfriend. Nothing in his life was going to change for the better.

"SURE YOU DON'T want to get out of the house? See town?"

Mom pushed her cheap, white plastic sunglasses up into her beige hair. When she squinted into the sun like that, she looked about sixty. It was like seeing into his own future.

"I'll stay here." He stepped back into the house. The outer door slapped shut between them, its screen blurring her face. She looked younger again as she shifted the thin strap of her vinyl purse higher on her shoulder.

"Suit yourself. I'm stopping at the grocery story after the power company. Any requests?"

"Food."

"You got it." She made a gun with her forefinger and thumb and clicked her tongue against the roof of her mouth. "Call me if you need anything."

"Phone's dead," he reminded her. "No power."

"Right." She stared down the long drive. "Well, if it's an emergency, walk up to the road and see if you can flag someone down."

"If it's an emergency, I'll bleed to death before I get there."

"Maybe you should just come with me."

"Buh-bye, Mom." He started to close the inner door too.

"Unpack some of the boxes in the garage, okay?" she called just before the door closed.

Matt twisted the bolt and watched through the wavy glass as she drove away. Clouds of dust marked her progress. Hadn't taken much convincing for her to leave. Maybe she was sick of him too.

He turned and faced the dark, empty foyer at the bottom of the stairs. Now what? Normally he liked being home alone. He'd watch whatever he wanted on TV—none of those relationship talk shows Mom liked. And he'd raid the fridge, make a huge triple-decker sandwich with nothing but sweet pickles and American cheese.

But no power meant no TV and no refrigerator and no air conditioning. They'd managed to open a few windows, but it didn't help much. He'd slept in a pool of his own sweat all night and woke to find his bare arms and chest covered in mosquito bites. His entire body was on fire, and the house already felt like an oven.

So, fine. He'd go outside. Work on unpacking a few boxes, like she asked. It was cooler outside any way, and that would keep her off his case for a while. Besides, most of the food was out there.

Matt went out to the garage and rolled up the door to let in some light. Then he rifled through the boxes marked "kitchen" until he found a bag of corn chips. He broke open the bag and ate them while he checked things out.

The old tenants had left all their stuff in the garage. Probably got evicted too. A red kayak perched in the rafters and a pair of fishing poles hung on the wall beside a shovel and a rake. He finished off the chips, tossed the crumpled bag back into the box, and wiped his hands on his jeans. The fishing rod was hunter orange and longer than him but weighed next to nothing. A lure like a flattened silver spoon with yellow feathers was tied onto the line. He touched a finger to one of the hooks buried beneath the feathers and drew blood. He sucked on his finger, impressed.

Fishing wasn't really his thing. Outdoors wasn't really his thing, unless you counted skating, which he didn't. There was something about the way the rod fit in the curve of his hand that he liked though. And any way he was bored.

When he stepped out of the shade of the garage again, the fishing pole rested in the hollow of his right shoulder. He would check out that pond. See if anything lived in there.

Matt crossed the yard and followed the line of trees toward where he'd noticed the water shimmering the day before. Nothing but weeds grew beneath the pine trees. Amber-coloured sap oozed from the trees' bark, which was thick as armour but crispy like scabs.

The pond was farther from the house than he'd thought. By the time he reached it, a line of sweat dotted his upper lip and the armpits of his t-shirt were damp.

The pond was almost a bigger disappointment than the house, which was saying something. It wasn't much bigger than a swimming pool. The water was oily black and smelled rotten.

Slimy green plants matted the surface. Matt certainly wouldn't be eating anything he caught from it or swimming in it, but . . .

He studied the rod and reel until he figured out how to release the line. Then he did his best imitation of casting, something he saw in a survival show once. On his first try, the lure snagged in some branches behind him. It took him a quarter of an hour to untangle it.

The second cast went wide and landed in the green slime along the edge. He cast another half dozen times before the lure zinged through the air and plopped neatly into the centre of the pond. He was a natural.

He let the lure drag the line down toward the bottom of the pond. It ran so long that he started counting. When he reached twelve he stopped. How deep was it?

He rewound the line until the lure clanged against the tiny metal loop at the top of the pole. To his own surprise, he cast again. And then again.

Sometimes his casts went wide or came up short. With every cast, he improved, though he didn't get a single nibble. Probably nothing lived in there. Or maybe the fish were hiding. Did fish do that?

Stubborn tightness settled in his chest, like sometimes happened when he was trying to land a trick. Well, he had all day.

He cast again, then went to sit in the anaemic shade of a pine tree. He held the rod in one hand and scratched at his mosquito bites with the other. The sun was intense now. His eyes watered, then grew heavy. Bugs buzzed so loudly in the heat that it felt like the sound was inside his head. He closed his eyes.

The sound of a car's engine woke him. He winced as he tried to sit up. *How long had he slept?* His arms and legs were now covered in mosquito bites *and* bright red with sunburn. *Ouch.*

He heard a car door slam, then the front porch's screen door slap shut. Mom must be home—with food. Maybe the power was on too.

He got to his feet and stumbled back toward the house, only belatedly remembering the fishing pole. He retraced his steps to the edge of the pond and turned in a slow circle, searching.

He'd fallen asleep with the pole in his hands—he was sure of it—but there was no sign of the pole anywhere. Rod, reel, line, and lure were all gone.

"YOU WON'T BELIEVE the story about this place," Mom said when he walked into the kitchen.

She was putting away groceries. Plastic bags covered every surface and when she opened the refrigerator door, the light came on inside. Sweet baby Jesus—they had power! Matt grabbed a cup from an open box and poured a cold glass of water from the fridge's tap. He drained it down in one gulp.

"Oh yeah?" he said, only half paying attention to what she was saying as he tore open a bag of Oreos and stuffed two in his mouth.

Mom chewed her lower lip. "Maybe I shouldn't tell you about it. You're already having nightmares."

He stared at her, mouth full of chocolate wafer and cream filling. "M-m-what?"

"Oh, come on. You can't hide it from me. You were yelling in your sleep last night."

He tried to protest, but she'd bought the store version cookies again and the white cream-paste had glued his tongue to the roof of his mouth.

"It's not like you're having night terrors again or anything though," she continued. "Not like you—"

He choked down the cookie. "I haven't wet the bed since I was twelve!"

"I know, I know." She threw up her hands in surrender, a can of peaches in each. "Would you please stop shouting at me?"

"I'm not—" He pinched the bridge of his nose. Took a deep breath. "Just tell the story."

Apparently, when she gave their address to the lady at the power company, she got an earful. Everyone in town knew the house's history. Which was guaranteed to make school fun for him.

"The lady said that the house dated back to before the Civil War," Mom said. "The original owners, the Walters, had two kids. A daughter and a son. But something was wrong with the girl."

Matt frowned. "Wrong how?"

Mom traced a circle around her temple with one finger and whistled two shrill notes. *Cuckoo.* "The family kept things pretty quiet. No one ever knew the details. They took her to doctors all over the country, but she always ended up back home."

Matt exhaled, secretly relieved. A crazy daughter. That wasn't so scary.

But Mom wasn't done yet. "The younger brother grew up, left, and never came back. Until what happened to the parents."

"Wait." He tensed and swallowed down the residual chocolate slime from the cookies. "What happened to the parents?"

Mom bit her lip. He could tell she was torn between sharing a really juicy story and having to listen to him talking in his sleep. "Well," she said finally, "after the war, they lost all their workers."

"You mean slaves."

She flushed. "Yes, I mean slaves. So the Walters sold off some of their land and rented more to sharecroppers. Then they planted what was left with timber."

That explained the even rows of pine trees. Nothing natural grows that neat and tidy.

"No one in town saw them much after that. Eventually, the Walters stopped coming into town at all. When a preacher from their church rode out to check on them, he found the daughter floating face down in the pond, naked. The parents had been dead for ages."

A chill ran up his arms. "You mean, forty whacks, like Lizzy Borden style?" He made a hacking motion.

Mom blanched. "God, Matthew. Maybe we should forget about cable for a while. No, they just got old. The daughter wandered around until she fell into the pond."

They died of old age *at the same time*? He shivered. Something didn't add up there. And why was the girl naked? Or was that just a grisly detail added by the locals?

"The parents weren't dead *inside* the house?" he asked finally, remembering the smell when he'd first walked in.

"No!" Mom said a little too quickly. "This was like a hundred years ago, Matt, and it's just a story. Probably not even true. I'm already sorry I told you."

That made two of them. The house was creepy enough without dead old people and crazy naked ladies lurking in the back of his mind.

"Did you get any of the boxes in the garage unpacked?"

"Uhhh." He blinked, caught off guard. She could change subjects so fast it gave him whiplash.

"And would it kill you to help me put away the groceries?" Mom sighed and shoved boxed mac and cheese onto the same shelf as a new jar of pickles. No one would ever accuse her of being organized.

"I need help, Matt." She turned to face him, arms crossed. She looked suddenly tired again, old. "I can't do all of this by myself. I know you don't like it here. I know you're mad at me for making us move again. But we needed a fresh start. Things are going to be different this time. I promise."

A dry laugh escaped him. "Yeah, right. Different. How's quitting smoking going for you, Mom?"

Her mouth snapped opened then closed.

He was already walking away.

"Matthew!"

He needed to slam something, but none of the doors inside the house closed properly. He stormed onto the porch instead. He threw the front door shut so hard that the watery glass panes shivered. The sound reverberated, like a gunshot, through the pines.

He stood, chest heaving. Sometimes he hated her so much he could taste it on the back of his tongue—like pineapple left too long in the opened can. Acid and sweet and metallic.

He clenched and unclenched his fists as he waited for her to come after him, to beg him to forgive her for moving again, to make more empty promises she wouldn't keep.

But she didn't. That was a first. Maybe she was finally giving him space. Or maybe she didn't want to deal with him anymore.

The rage slowly leaked out of him, leaving him shaky and nauseated. That's when he noticed the damp footprints on the porch and the fishing pole leaning against the wall. The lure gone. The loose line spooling over the peeling floorboards.

THE NEXT DAY, Mom registered him for school. He'd start the following week.

By Wednesday, she had a job as a cashier at the drug store. She had a second, part-time job lined up doing drive-thru at a McDonald's in the next town.

"I think it's time you got a job too," she said, not looking at him. "We could use the money."

He said he would think about it.

She started at the drug store on Thursday. And on Friday, the girl showed up on the front porch for the first time.

Matt hadn't noticed the porch swing until he heard it creaking back and forth. So when he followed the sound outside, it took a second for his brain to register that there even was a swing, much less a girl using it.

She sat with one foot tucked underneath her and used the tiptoes of her other foot to keep the swing in motion. Water dripped from her dark hair and ran over her bare shoulders to wet her white cotton dress. More water dripped from beneath the swing and soaked into the floorboards.

Matt glanced at the empty driveway and then back to her. "Can I help you?"

She had a full mouth with lips a deep red that was almost purple. Her eyes were black, or at least a really dark brown. When she blinked he could see she had bluish, almost translucent eyelids.

"We're the same age," she said. Her voice was young, much younger than she claimed.

"Oka-a-y."

It was a mile to the closest road, much less another house. She wasn't even wearing any shoes. Where did she come from?

"Do you live around here?"

She didn't answer, just kept staring and swinging. She was starting to give him the creeps.

He tried again. "What's your name?"

Nothing.

"I'm Matt."

"Matt," she repeated, and for some reason he shivered.

Maybe her parents were the previous tenants. Maybe they sent her to get their crap back. He remembered the fishing pole then.

"Hey, did you take the fishing pole the other day and then put it back? Was that you?"

Mischief glinted in her eyes as she pushed up from the swing. Her dress fell just above her knees, her skin impossibly smooth and pale.

139

"I want to show you something, Matt." She went down the stairs, leaving damp footprints behind. When he didn't follow, she turned back. "Are you coming?"

He shook his head. "I'm good."

She was pretty, but definitely off. Following her anywhere, even in broad daylight, was the equivalent of going into the basement alone, without a flashlight, when a known axe murderer was on the loose. He'd seen the movie; he was not going to be *that* guy.

She tilted her head to one side. The sun caught on a strand of her hair and turned it a deep blue-violet. He tried not to stare.

"You don't have to be afraid of me, Matt."

"I'm not—" he squeaked, then cleared his throat. "I've got stuff to do. Sorry. Some other time."

She lifted her thin shoulders and let them fall again. Then she walked away. He watched her go.

Once she rounded the house, he raced inside to the back door. Through the window, he saw her cross the yard and pass between the armoured trunks of the pines. He eased open the door with a low squeak and stepped out. She didn't turn.

He trailed after her, keeping his distance, watching to see where she'd go. He followed her all the way to the pond and kept watching as her head and shoulders sank beneath the water's surface.

"How was your day?"

"Fine. I think." Matt pushed around wrinkled, reheated peas on his plate.

"Did you . . . go somewhere?" Mom's voice was weird.

"I don't think so." He couldn't remember much after she left for work. He must have slept all day.

Mom set down her fork with a short sigh. "Are you going to tell me what happened, or do we have to play twenty questions?"

He dragged his eyes up. Her mouth was set in a thin, tight line. "What do you mean?"

"You know we don't have money to replace your shoes every time you decide to go wading in the mud."

"What shoes?"

"Those Vans I bought you. They're ruined. Do you know how

long I had to save for those? How did they get so wet?"

Matt didn't know what to say.

Her fingers curled into fists on the tabletop. "I don't get my first paycheque for a month. It took all my savings to pay the deposit on this place."

He stared back at her, mute. He knew he should say something, feel something, but she was already saying and feeling too much for the both of them.

She leaned closer and squinted at him. "Your pupils are tiny. Are you stoned?"

He struggled to understand the question. "Am I—"

"*Stoned*, Matthew! Did you take something? Whatever it was, tell me right now, or I'm taking you to the ER and having them pump your stomach."

She was on the verge of tears. Something clicked inside of him then. "Mom, I didn't take anything. I'm just tired."

He *was* tired too, groggy, like when he slept in too late. He felt like he'd been asleep all day, dreaming about a girl and a house just like this one.

"I don't need new shoes," he heard himself say. "I'll clean them up. I'm sorry, Mom. Don't cry. I'll do better this time. Things will be different here. I promise."

HE STARTED SCHOOL on Monday. The kids blurred together in his mind. Teachers and remedial classes too. Days and weeks. Everything was blurring, bleeding together. The only thing that seemed clear was Naya. That was the name of the girl who had shown up on his porch, the girl he'd followed into the pines, the girl who lived in the pond.

At night, he'd sneak out the back door, where she would be waiting for him. They'd make love, in the house at the bottom of the pond, in her bed at the top of the stairs. Then they'd lay together, arms and legs tangled like weeds. Afterwards, they'd sit on her porch swing holding hands, watching the rows of pines sway in the blue-green light.

It was a strange kind of house, but the closest he'd ever come to having a home. Naya said that was because he belonged there like the rest of them. He could stay forever if he wanted to. No one ever had to leave once they chose to stay.

She never talked about any of the other people who lived in

the house at the bottom of the pond. They were all beautiful as Naya and just as unreadable. Men, women, kids of all ages and colours. He couldn't tell how any of them were related. He decided not to ask too many questions. If this was a dream, he wanted it to last forever.

He told Naya he'd think about it, but he knew Mom wouldn't understand. So each morning, he walked back home, collecting his Vans from the edge of the pond. He kept them there so they didn't get muddy. He didn't want her to worry.

MATT SAT UP in bed. His room was dark. His cell phone said it was 4:56 am. Voices thrummed outside his window—a man's and a woman's. Or was he dreaming again?

"You belong with us."

"I can't."

Matt got out of bed and went to the window. Mom stood in the backyard in a tank top and her underwear. The sight of her pale thighs filled him with revulsion and protectiveness at the same time. Who was she talking to?

He pressed his face closer to the glass. A man stood just below his window. He wore loose pants and a white cotton shirt. His wavy hair curled around his neck and glistened in the moonlight.

The man glanced up then, straight at Matt's window. A jolt of recognition went through Matt. He was one of the people who lived at Naya's.

A second later, he wondered why he'd ever thought about a house in a pond or a girl who lived there. That couldn't be real. Yet here was a man from Naya's house, talking to his mom.

"Come with me," the man said again. "You belong with us."

Mom took a step back. "He needs me."

"He's leaving you," the man said, and Mom stopped. "He's been leaving you since the day he was born. Soon, he'll be gone. You'll be alone again."

Her shoulders drooped, but she said, "That's what it means to be a mother."

"Your son doesn't appreciate you. And you resent him."

Matt's stomach lurched.

"I don't. I don't resent him," Mom said, but her voice shook.

"He deserves better. You both do." The man put out a broad,

pale hand. "Let him go, and come with me. I can make you happy. You'll never worry again, and your son will finally be free. It's time to come home."

Mom hesitated a long moment, but then she took his hand.

"Mom?" Matt banged the heel of his hand against the glass. "Mom!"

She didn't look up.

He raced from the room and down the stairs. He threw open the back door just as his mom disappeared beneath the pines.

"Mom!"

Matt stumbled down the back steps and across the yard to the treeline. Roots and rocks bit at his bare feet. Branches clawed at his face and arms. He ran until he saw the pond—a blue square, like a window lit by the moonlight. Mom was already waist deep and wading farther out.

"Mom!"

Matt splashed in after her. Cold mud sucked at his feet and ankles. Thick, viscous water that smelled of ancient, dead things soaked into his shorts, his shirt. The water rose up to his throat. Soon he wouldn't be able to touch the bottom.

Mom's hair fanned out over the water's surface. She was floating, and then she started to sink.

Matt lunged forward. Foul pond water flooded his nose and burned down his throat. He gasped, trying to breathe even as he reached for her.

"Don't go!"

Something pale hovered in the water ahead, just below the surface. A bloated face with opaque staring eyes and a hungry mouth. Matt choked down revulsion and reached one last time for something—anything. His fingers brushed against soft fabric. Mom's shirt.

He closed his fingers and pulled with all his strength. Water rippled out around them, splashing against the shore with a thick, slurping sound.

She was heavy. Why was she so heavy?

"Let her go!" he spluttered, tugging harder, grabbing hold of one of her arms now. "She belongs with me!"

He fought and kicked back towards shore. Mud squished between his toes, liquid first, then gradually more solid. He held tight to her arm and a fistful of her shirt and dragged her into the shallows and through the reeds. They collapsed on hard, dry soil.

Matt twisted around then, clenched hands full of rocks and loose dirt and sand and pine needles. He expected to see the man's bloated face. Instead, he saw Naya.

She stood in waist-deep water, moonlight glistening on her bare breasts. Water ran from her dark hair and into the shadows where her eyes should be.

"Naya." His fists unclenched. Pebbles and sand trickled down his bare legs and bounced off the hard earth. "I—" He took a step forward, pond water lapping at his ankles, desire stirring higher up.

She said nothing, only lifted a slender, pale hand toward him. Water cascaded from the tips of her fingers, sending tiny concentric circles splashing against her perfect navel.

He wanted her. He wanted to be with her, to stay with her.

Mom stirred behind him. She coughed, a wet, gurgling sound. "M-matthew?"

Naya's perfect, serene features shifted. Her lips parted, and he saw the glint of sharp, white teeth.

A sob of horror escaped him, followed by a roar. He clawed up fistfuls of earth and stone and flung them at the pond, screaming obscenities.

The stones struck blank air and plinked into the pond. He stood, feet planted wide, chest heaving, waiting for the man to return, daring Naya to show her beautiful face again.

The pond's surface rippled once, dissatisfied, then fell still with a sigh.

MATT BENT OVER his mom and helped her to sit up. Her eyes were like black pools as she blinked at him.

"I need a cigarette," she said, at the same time as he said, "We need to move."

Then Matt sank down beside her. They stayed there a long time, not talking, watching the pond. Nothing moved. The sky turned pale. Still nothing. The sun rose. It all seemed like a dream now.

Eventually they got to their feet. Mom looked embarrassed and crossed her arms over her chest. Matt cleared his throat and looked away.

When they got back to the house, Mom took down her purse from the kitchen door. She pulled out a crumpled pack of Marlboro's and started to shake a smoke from the pack. Then she frowned, as if realizing what she was doing. She tossed the pack in the trash and got out her keys instead.

Matt went to his room to collect his phone and box of skateboard stuff. He stopped off at the kitchen before leaving. He threw in some crackers and peanut butter and a knife from the drawer. They would get hungry soon.

Mom was already in the car when he stepped out onto the porch. "Remember the place by the railroad tracks in Richmond?" she asked, as he got in.

He said he did.

"I wonder if it's available again?" She put the car in reverse and did a k-turn.

"I liked that place," Matt said. There was a park close by with handrails and ledges to grind on.

"I can probably get my old job back." Mom looked hopeful.

Matt nodded. "Sure."

As they drove away, the house grew smaller and smaller in the rear-view mirror. Through the trees, sun glinted on the pond's surface. Matt thought he saw something, someone standing in the tree line. Then the car turned a corner, and they left it all—the boxes of stuff they wouldn't miss, the house, the pond, the girl who lived in it—behind.

Research Log ~~33

Rowena McGowan

Research Log 04.55.~~33

Well, here I am in my new digs, with my new diploma in black magic clutched in my clever, clever hands! I know a lot of the other students are into all that modern stuff now—bungalows, bamboo walls, even room sharing—but I'm a traditionalist. I've settled in a nice stone tower overlooking a lush parkland surrounded by a dark and foreboding forest. Well, I mean, it's not *that* dark—they're only poplars—but I think they have a nice threatening appearance to them. And I'm pretty sure you can still call something a tower even if it only has three stories, as long as it's round. Which my tower is. Because it's a tower.

But enough about my living quarters. I've finally decided what I'm going to do with my magic. I've decided to go into swan maidenning. Swan maidenwork? Anyway, I want a flock of swan maidens. You just can't beat the classics, and I think it looks really impressive.

I've made a slight alteration to the spell, though. I've read a lot of black magical history and the thing about maidens, especially princesses, is, they always find a prince. Always. Or at least some clever third son who will eventually earn riches and glory though his origins be humble. And then the maiden and the boy will fall in love, and then best-case scenario you've lost your swan maiden but more likely you're getting thrown off your tower or stabbed with a silver knife or something.

It just gets messy.

So I've created a slight refinement of the swan maiden spell. Instead of returning to human form every night, *my* swan maidens will just stay swans. I know it's not quite as romantic, but I think it'll be safer and I won't have to find housing for them. They can live on the pond, just as soon as I finish digging it. Or start digging it.

Anyway, I think this will be one for the history books. Birds are so much easier to deal with than girls.

RESEARCH LOG 04.58.~~33

Well, I have my swan maiden! I wish I was a better artist so I could draw the scene. I had it all planned out, did some research and everything. I picked a nice sunny day, conjured a rain cloud and deposited myself right in the courtyard of the nearest castle (note to self: bring a change of underwear when you travel by raincloud). There was my princess, picking flowers or walking around or whatever it is that princesses do. I don't know, I wasn't really paying attention. I probably should next time, it might make princess-catching easier.

"Princess Belladora!" I boomed. "I have come to punish you for your sins!"

I don't actually know what she did wrong, but I'm sure she did something. Princesses be sinning. It's a fact of life. Anyway, I sort of swirled my cloak around her (it kind of got caught on her shoulder buttons but I don't think she noticed) and swept her away. I screwed up the wind angle so we got back to the tower later than I meant to, but by the time we got there the spell had taken firm hold and I had a swan in my cloak. Incidentally, feathers everywhere. I dumped her in the pond and went to get changed.

Huzzah! Mission accomplished.

RESEARCH LOG 04.59.~~33

Today was ~~a total disaster~~ not a success. Apologies to future me if my writing is a little difficult to read. I think my arm is broken.

It started out pretty well. When I woke up I was still riding the high from yesterday. I went to check on my captive. She was floating on the surface of her pond, her head tucked into her wing, looking exactly like any other swan. She looked up as I walked towards her and I think she was glaring at me, but I might be projecting. Bird faces aren't exactly expressive. I mean, it wouldn't surprise me if she was glaring. I mean, I know her transformation was her just punishment for, y'know, stuff, but I bet she thought I was being wicked for wickedness' sake. Whatever. The ways of spellfiends are not for the common folk to know.

Anyway, I'd brought out some food for her, a nice big bucket of birdseed. I shook it at her and called to her and she just stayed on the lake looking at me with what was probably supposed to be either anger or disdain or some combination of the two. I yelled at her again and told her that she'd better come eat because birdseed was all she was getting. Slowly, she started paddling up to me and waddled carefully onto shore. I had this moment of being really proud of myself. And then she reared up and spread her wings.

I didn't really notice when I was doing all my hocus pocus, but swans are ~~terrifyingly huge~~ really big. And then she charged me. One second I was standing straight up, backing away slowly, the next I was on the ground with two white feathery masses smashing down on me.

Every time I tried to cast a spell or even get up, she hit me again.

I ended up curled up in a ball on the ground with my arms over my head. I'm not sure how long the beating went on. Long enough that there isn't a single part of my body that isn't bruised, that's for sure. Eventually I guess she got bored. By the time I'd decided the coast was clear and begun to haul myself off the ground, she had flown off.

I could go after her but honestly, by now I'm not sure there's much of a point. She's probably already found true love—princes are everywhere these days—or at least some friendly white witch who's good at reversing curses. Seems like a waste of energy trying to find her.

~~Also, I don't want her back.~~

RESEARCH LOG 04.60.~~33
Owwwwwwwww.

RESEARCH LOG 05.18.~~33
Bought a naturalist's textbook. Turns out swans are highly aggressive.
I may have to rethink my strategy.

RESEARCH LOG 05.19.~~33
After careful contemplation, I have decided to abandon swans as a transformation subject. I know that swan maidens are traditional but, like, what a cliché and also, so hard to feed. And you have to dig out a big pond for them and then you have to make sure it doesn't get too grungy and it's really way too much work. And honestly, all that white is soooo last season. I need something brighter, something glamorous.

That's why I have decided to switch to peacocks.

Peacock maiden. It just rolls off the tongue.

RESEARCH LOG 05.33.~~33
Minor setback. Turns out peacocks are incredibly beautiful, jewel-like birds. Peahens, on the other hand, aka maiden peacocks, kind of look like chickens.

I mean, really fancy chickens. If these actually were chickens, they would be really impressive chickens. They've got these lovely head crests and their necks are sort of greenish. They're nice. They're just not as impressive as the bird I thought I was getting.

Anyway, that's a minor setback. I have a peacock (peahen? Sounds boring) maiden now! I couldn't find quite as impressive a princess on short notice. In fact, I suppose technically she's not a princess at all. But I feel like the second eldest daughter of a lord with a lot of land is basically a princess. Also, I'm sure she would have ended up marrying a prince, which makes her technically a princess-in-waiting, ergo a princess.

It counts.

She seems to be settling in okay. Thank goodness! I had to do some quick renovations, since peacocks don't live on ponds.

Filling that whole thing in was *not* easy. And I guess I needn't have bothered, since she totally ignored the little shelter I laid out for her and climbed up a tree.

RESEARCH LOG 05.34.~~33

Sorry again to future me for bad writing. I didn't get much sleep yesterday.

I was curled up in my bed, dreaming of a magical future wherein I owned a whole flock of peacock maidens, when I heard the most awful noise outside my window. I thought it was a person shrieking at first. I jerked up in bed positive that someone was being murdered. But there was something sort of . . . caw-y about it? I threw open my curtains and came face to face with my peacock maiden. She was sitting in the branches of the tree outside my window. As we stared at each other, she opened her beak and made that noise again.

I guess peacocks scream?

I closed the curtains and went back to bed but I didn't get much sleep. It's fine. How long can one bird scream, really? And I'm sure I'll get used to it.

RESEARCH LOG 05.38.~~33

She won't stop screaming. *Why won't she stop screaming?* I just want to sleep.

RESERCH LOG 05.45.~~33

She's still screaming. Why is she still screaming? Don't birds ever get tired????????

RERCH LO 55

Still scream. Why screa? So Tird.

RESEARCH LOG 06.02.~~33

After careful consideration, I have decided to release the peacock maiden. I do not have facilities that are adequately equipped to deal with such an exotic specimen. It's better for both of us if I release her back into the wild. Well, into the village. Whatever.

She was dreary looking anyway. Maybe I should start kidnapping princes instead.

RESEARCH LOG 06.25.~~33

I have done some intensive thinking and I've concluded that my issue might be that I keep using wild bird species. Domestication is a long process whereby a wild animal is selectively bred for traits that make it easier for humans to use it. And one of those traits is a good temperament. That's why you can sleep with a dog on your bed, but if you try to pet a wolf, you're just begging to have your hand ripped off. So logically, if I use a domesticated bird species, it'll be way easier to deal with.

Therefore, I've decided that my next maiden will be a goose maiden. I know it's not quite as romantic sounding as a swan maiden, but it'll be easier to deal with and anyway, geese have a long history in folklore. I mean, most of them lay golden eggs or are herded by goosegirls that are secretly princesses but hey, tradition is tradition.

Anyway, it'll look like a swan from a distance, and that's all that most people will see anyway. Sometimes my genius amazes even me.

RESEARCH LOG 06.27.~~33

I couldn't find another princess on short notice, but I snagged a merchant's daughter, and I feel like that's pretty close. Performed the spell and the goose maiden is now safely stored in the shed. I'm ~~a little embarrassed~~ not quite sure about the whole domesticated bird thing

I'm giving her a night to settle in and then I'll go check on her tomorrow. I envision a long and fruitful working relationship.

RESEARCH LOG 06.28.~~33

Geese are basically just swans but meaner.

Note to self: visit apothecary for more bruise cream.

RESEARCH LOG 07.21.~~33

You know what are the worst? Big birds. I mean, the feeding costs alone might bankrupt me. I'm a one-person operation. I can't take care of a bunch of large birds on my own. That's crazy. Plus they're dumb-looking. They're all round and weird. I have a tower. I have an *aesthetic* going and it doesn't include a bunch of boring, sloppy waterfowl. I need something sleek, something classy, something that just screams "magic" and "arcana".

So I've decided to get into crow maidens. I mean, crows are super magical, right? They're all black, they've got long, threatening beaks, I'm pretty sure they live in towers anyway.

It was meant to be.

I really feel this is a fun, bold new direction that will really blow people away.

Also, I bought a cage. You know, just as a precautionary measure.

RESEARCH LOG 07.40.~~33

I have my crow maiden. I'm so sick of scouting out princesses and ladies and stuff so honestly, I just grabbed the first pretty girl I saw. Whatever, she was running around carrying a bunch of jewellery. That probably means she's at least rich, right? I don't know why it matters anyway.

Just to be safe (I mean, she's not that big a bird, I bet she couldn't beat me up the way a swan can), I got her shoved into the cage before she had time to recover from her shock. Hurray! I even put a padlock on it, just to be extra safe. She can just stay in there until I'm sure she can behave. I'll still bring her food regularly and I gave her a water dish, but I've learned my lessons. Birds stay in cages around here. Try to attack me now, birdbrain!

RESEARCH LOG 07.41.~~33

SHE PICKED THE LOCK ON THE CAGE.
SHE WENT RIGHT FOR MY EYES.

RESEARCH LOG 08/09.~~33

Now that I have sufficiently recovered, I have done some research. I was always taught that nonmagical beings only have the intelligence of the shape they have been transformed into. So I had figured "hey, it's just a bird, no worries, right?"

I consulted my naturalist's handbook. Turns out crows can use tools.

Sod this. I quit. Maybe I'll go into potion making. There are some awfully pretty mushrooms out in the woods. They've gotta be safer than birds.

Eiyri

Laura VanArendonk Baugh

I CRESTED THE ridge and saw the little homesite. A line in the earth had been dug out in the footprint of the house that would be. At each corner, a spray of small stones was scattered to the southwest, as if an angry child had slapped a stack of building blocks.

Well, that was why small piles of stones were built before a house was.

"You'll never be able to build there, Harri Davies," I muttered aloud.

I walked into the centre of the outlined house and looked from southwest to northeast. Yes, two clear peaks stood opposite, the house exactly between them. Harri Davies had been optimistic to hope it would be clear. But a normal fairy path should have merely disrupted the stones, not scattered them like a giant's tantrum. The two peaks were tall— Snowdonia has the highest peaks in Wales—but that in itself wouldn't indicate anything more unusual about the Fae who used this fairy path.

I tucked my hands under my arms to shield them from the mountain winds and walked on, enjoying the misty views.

I bore a Welsh name, courtesy of the father who had

inconveniently died before my birth (so said my mother, anyway, and it wouldn't do to question), and perhaps that had been an element in my assignment to the Manod project. I certainly wasn't foremost among the National Gallery staff, lowly even in the Scientific Department which had only barely begun before the war. But I was available, and my Welsh name might have been thought to be useful, and so here I was.

But that name had only created a curious distance among my new neighbours, who expected me to speak their tongue, know their ways, and be different than my English employers. I couldn't even manage *Eryri*, for this Snowdonia—my best attempt of *air-rare-y* marked me indubitably as an outsider and a pretender. I felt lonelier than I had in London, and so I had taken to tramping the mountains as I waited for our precious deliveries.

"Hullo, Miss Thomas!"

My body knew the call and turned before I could consciously make a decision. Owen Lewis was a local farmer and one of the reasons I walked here. I knew, of course I knew, it was desperate loneliness which made him attractive, but that did not make the feelings less real.

"Hello, Mr. Lewis."

"Owen, please. I think we're good enough friends now that you may call me by my Christian name."

I wanted to call him by name, of course, but that meant inviting him to call me by mine. While I had gone by Carol in London, the chief curator Martin Davies had introduced me here as Canaid Thomas, trapping me in my Welsh heritage and expectations. So as always, I demurred against my will. "Oh, Mr. Lewis, I do count you an excellent friend, but we mustn't scandalize my poor grandmother."

"I hope to meet your poor old grandmother one day and scandalize her properly." Owen grinned, showing his single crooked tooth in a line of better-behaved specimens.

That was unlikely, as I'd never met my poor old grandmother either, but I only chuckled.

"Have you been up Yr Wyddfa yet?"

Owen had asked this at least once a week, and each time I had to disappoint him. "Not yet. But I will."

"You don't know what you're missing."

"I will climb it, I promise." I gave him a smile. "I just have so much to do to prepare for the cases."

He waved his hand dismissively. "Not so much that you cannot take time to walk over the ridges and see Harri Davies' new homesite."

"It won't be much of a homesite," I answered. "Did you see those stones?"

"I have not."

"They're scattered all down like a locomotive passed through them at speed. Not one stone left upon the other, thrown out for yards, and at all four corners. He'll never be able to keep a house there."

Owen tipped his head. "Interesting, indeed. That's an angry fairy, to be sure. But also, I wonder how a London girl knows about fairy paths?"

I shrugged. "I must have read it somewhere, maybe as a child. It sounded familiar enough when he said he was testing, though I couldn't remember where I'd first heard it."

"Read it," he repeated, with a note of doubt but a charming smile to belie it.

"Or don't you think a London girl might read?" I asked. "It isn't all nightclubs and soirees, you know."

"Oh, no, I believe she might read," he assured me. "Especially a clever girl who works with famous pictures. It's only I find it hard to believe she might read up on Welsh tales and old wives' talk, there in all the bright lights and busy traffic."

"I probably read it while researching one of those pictures," I said, though I couldn't offhand think of one. The National Gallery had rather more portraits than fairy tale illustrations. "Anyway, I don't know what poor Mr. Davies is going to do about his house."

"He'll have to move the whole thing, if it's as you say," Owen agreed. "It's bad enough losing a few cattle if you block a fairy path, but if he's set to block something that will knock down four corners of stones, he's risking more than cattle. And I wouldn't for good gold live in the path of such a thing."

A little chill ran through me, as if the mountain breeze had gotten suddenly through my wool. "I should be getting back. We have a big shipment coming in tomorrow."

"I have more than a share of work as well. Have a good morning, Miss Thomas, and I may see you again this evening if you stop by the pub."

I HAD TAKEN a room with a family in the village of Blaenau Ffestiniog, but my work was in the mountains themselves, at a disused quarry. The first plan to evacuate Great Britain's art treasures and historic artefacts had been to send them to Canada, safely away from the London Blitz, but the U-boat danger made that too risky. So an old slate quarry, safe within the heart of a hollowed out mountain, had been found and repurposed. Already our precious stock had begun to arrive.

A Cadbury truck had laboured up the mountain road today, full of smaller pieces to unload, catalogue, and store. No one questioned Post Office vans, candy trucks, or other innocuous vehicles.

I spent the day helping to save Botticelli, Raphael, Vermeer, and Monet from the Axis powers. Each picture was loaded onto a narrow railway, safely carried into the heart of the mountain, and delivered to one of the small brick huts built to shelter them from the damp quarry air. Some of the staff in the new Scientific Department were hopeful that the dark and cool would be better for conservation than the National Gallery's own building and that much restoration might be accomplished while the pictures were in storage. I thought of my unknown colleagues in France, frantically pushing art from abbey to chateau before the advancing lines, and breathed a prayer of thanks that we had seen the need in time.

Our haven was hundreds of feet below ground, armoured within the very heart of a mountain. No German bomber would reach our treasures.

When I had finished cataloguing and packing, I went home to my cup of tea and novel. I thought of going to the King's Head for a drink and a glimpse of Owen, but I had my poor old grandmother to think of.

I woke to the sound of horns and shouts. My first thoughts, conditioned from London, were of an air raid—but of course that was foolishness in Blaenau Ffestiniog. I rushed to the window, but the narrow old road was empty.

I threw on a dressing gown and ran down to the door,

slowing as I noticed that no one else in the house seemed to be awake. There were no other disturbed sleepers stumbling out of rooms, no one else calling for answers. Had I dreamt the sound? But no, I could still hear it—not loud, but distinct, outdoors. I went to the door and unbolted it.

There was enough moon to see a bit, and now that I could look both up and down the road, it was even more plainly empty. I pulled my gown close and chewed my lip in confusion. But I could still *hear* them—something like a horn, and voices, and the baying calls of hounds. And the calls did not come from up the road, but from the hills, and I turned toward the moon.

The light came through and around them, but they also bore their own light, glistening and sparkling like dewdrops or diamonds on their clothing. Men on horses—such horses!— raced along the crest of the hill, in costumes like Waterhouse or von Holst might have imagined in paint, with a pack of white hounds coursing along with them. And as I stared, chilled with the night air and the sight, I saw that none of them quite touched the ground.

The Hunt, someone said in my mind. *It is the Hunt.*

It did not feel as if the thought was my own, but it must have been, for without wondering for even a heartbeat I knew the Hunt—knew its leaders, wild and dark and wholly Fae, whirling through the sky like a terrible wind, as unfeeling and as dangerous; knew its followers, huntsmen eager for blood sport and death, seeking just quarry of evil men; knew even its hounds, spectral white and red beasts who would run their exhausted prey to the ground and then return to their own otherworldly home.

I did not have time to wonder at how I knew this, for I was wondering instead at why my feet were carrying me off the road and toward the hill.

I stopped abruptly, my heart racing, terrified. Had I been called in some arcane way? Was I about to be stolen away by fairy folk? Was I hallucinating or sleepwalking, dreaming some hideous dream to endanger myself? Was I mad? Was it some late effect of a dangerous gas in the old quarry?

It was too late to wonder. The Hunt had spied me, and the horses swung in a wide angle toward me, each fluid and kinetic movement its own work of art as grand as any of the masters I'd studied.

I could run, but not fast enough. I could see at a glance that the horses were not at their utmost speed, and I could never reach the road, much less go inside and bar the door, if their riders did not wish. And the hounds would never give up my trail if I had become their quarry. No, I had to face this as I had faced down irate superiors or handsy sailors. I straightened my spine, lifted my chin, and folded my arms across my robe as if it were a Worth gown and I Empress Eugénie, about to royally receive a supplicant I planned to refuse.

The hounds reached me first, as the horses began to slow. They poured around me, circled, and came back. I like dogs well enough, but the size and significance of these gave me pause. They were white, with patches of red across their ears and muzzles. The red on their ears was their own colouring; the red on their muzzles was not. They sniffed me, and then they began to wag their tails and lick at my fingers.

"What have you done to my dogs?" demanded a voice.

I looked up at the man approaching on a great black horse. Its neck was arched proudly, its heavy mane flowing like a dark waterfall, and its great feathered hooves made no sound on the earth it did not tramp. The tall man on his back emanated a brooding dark energy, and he was glaring down at me as if I had offended him.

Fortunately my dressing gown concealed my shaking knees. "I have done nothing to your dogs," I answered sharply. "I simply came outside to see what all the noise was. I thought you were an air raid at least. Now that I see you are only some inconsiderate hunters making noise to wake the dead, I shall go home and go to bed."

He cocked his head as the other riders surrounded us. "No, this night we do not wake the dead," he said. "But nor should you have heard us."

"Clearly I have," I said. "And I don't see why that should be so unusual. Don't you often ride as a portent? There is a war, you know."

He scowled. "There is a sort of war, yes, but far to the east and to the south. Your bickering has little to do with me. I do not ride and call for such things. But when I call to my huntsmen and followers, you should not hear." He tipped his head the other way to regard me further, like a raptor eyeing a puzzle. "Who are you?"

"Oh, no. Even I know not to give my name to the Fair Folk. There are too many tales of you taking humans away."

One corner of his mouth turned up. "Dear lady, if you have heard my call to my huntsmen, you are no human."

Shock raced through me like I had touched an exposed electrical wire, and I could not answer. Not human? Ridiculous. But if I believed I was speaking with one of the Fae, then I must believe also that he could not lie to me. Either I was not having this conversation, or I was not human.

"Or not entirely," he allowed. "You have some Fae blood, else you would be sleeping like all the others in this village. Who was your father?"

I was not going to open that box for this wild stranger. "Why not ask who my mother was?"

He bowed his head in acknowledgment.

One of the huntsmen, silent until now, nudged another dark horse beside the leader's and spoke. "Imagine her with her hair piled high and in waves. Would she not look very like the lady called Helen?"

I caught my breath. Helen was my mother's name, and I had often been told I resembled her.

The dark stranger went still in his saddle, and his horse tossed its head. He pressed it forward and leaned to look nearer at me. I kept my chin up and my lip firm, holding his terrifying gaze.

"Granddaughter," he said, "is that you?"

I gaped at him, unable to form any response, and for a long moment we stared at each other in a shared disbelief.

At last he straightened in his saddle. "If you are blood of my blood," he concluded, "you will do more than hear my call to the hunt. You will call us yourself. If you do not call, then you are not blood, and I will owe you no paternity."

Thus for the moment absolved of whatever familial obligations lay upon him, he turned his horse and barked a command. The huntsmen wheeled and flowed in a dark torrent over the land, the white hounds like froth at the horses' hooves.

I stared after them until they disappeared into the hills, faded into the landscape and moonlight like the dream I wished they had been.

I DID NOT sleep that night. I did not tell Owen of my absurd dream. I did not write to my mother to ask if she had made me with a son of the Fae. I catalogued paintings.

Inconspicuous Post Office vans brought us load after load of fine art, safely removed from London's fires. I felt vaguely guilty that my work had brought me to this safe countryside, far from the Blitz. But Germany's bombers ventured beyond London, and we heard reports of bombings in Cardiff, Liverpool, Wrexham. There was little air defence in the north, and we felt vulnerable in our protective obscurity.

"We'll be getting the big boys soon," said my fellow curator Mr. Peters as we finished with today's Caravaggios. "That will be a day's work, and no mistake."

"I'll be glad to have them in," I answered. "And glad of your help to move them." Some of the larger paintings measured twelve feet across even before their protective cases were taken into account. Transporting them into the heart of the mountain would be, as Mr. Peters said, a day's work.

He laughed. "Were I as strong as that, I'd be in the RAF as I wanted, not sitting here moving pictures in the dark."

He never lost an opportunity to remind us that he'd tried to volunteer; I think it was to ease his own guilt as much as for the rest of us. But the RAF hadn't wanted a man with an irregular heartbeat, and so he was still with the National Gallery, preserving culture instead of dogfighting. I thought it just as fine, in its way, but he had not asked me.

I went home to my tea and my novel. It had been a long time since I had been to the King's Head. I feared what a beer might do to my careful resolution to think about nothing at all but my work.

HARRI DAVIES HAD believed his first test flawed; surely some village boy had pranked him by knocking over too many stones to pretend at a fairy path. He had tried again, with the same result. This time he had moved the site of his new house, where work proceeded uninterrupted.

I knew now what could travel a fairy path and strike down all four corners of a homesite, but I did not offer this information.

No one asked.

I did not tramp in the mountains during my free hours. Instead I learned to knit and helped the Women's Voluntary Service to make hats and mittens and mufflers for refugees.

It was a bright and sunny Monday morning when we took the phone call that the first of our largest paintings would be arriving that day. It was a touchier delivery than usual, as of course they could not fit in a forgettable Post Office or Cadbury van and would be on a specialized truck. "It will take them some time to work that through the mountain road," Mr. Peters predicted. "We will have much of the day to ourselves, I think!"

That lasted until early afternoon, when a breathless boy on a breathless pony arrived to tell us that the truck was stuck on the road.

Mr. Peters and I went out in a car. We found the truck on the one-track road which led to the quarry, on firm ground but trapped behind a railroad bridge. The elephant case which protected the precious cargo extended too high to fit beneath the bridge.

"Oh dear," Mr. Peters observed drily. "Let's see what can be done."

The driver met us in a state of consternation, unwilling to be blamed for a bridge he hadn't been informed of. I left the two men to bicker and went to the truck to check the parking brake. This part of the road was a snaky double curve toward the bridge, and there would be no catching the truck if its distracted driver forgot to put on the brake.

I then looked over the bed of the truck and the elephant case. It might be possible to unload the enormous case and carry it by hand beneath the bridge, but that would take more able hands than we had between us, and certainly more again to reload the case on the other side. I sighed and leaned against the dusty truck. The men seemed to have reached an agreement that neither was angry with the other personally, so it was time to start working on solutions.

An aircraft engine caught my ear, and I glanced to the sky. I shaded my eyes and squinted against the sunlight. Then I called up the road, "Mr. Peters? Can you see what that is?"

Mr. Peters turned from the driver and squinted after the plane. I watched his posture go stiff, saw him hesitate to be sure. "That's a Heinkel He 111," he said finally.

I didn't know planes, but I knew enough. "Luftwaffe?"

He nodded. "A bomber." Then he looked at me, coming to join them. "Probably off-course from a Liverpool or Wrexham run. It's only sixty miles or so."

Neither of us said what was foremost in our minds. *Did they know? Did they know about the art?*

Destroying Britain's treasures would be a tremendous blow to morale, a brutal victory for the Fuhrer who had ordered that what could not be stolen should be destroyed. If they had learned—

Mr. Peters shook his head. "See how he's banking? He's probably lost, or has been lost. He might have followed the wrong road or river. It's not so hard to lose one's way over an unfamiliar landscape."

The driver volunteered, "He doesn't look like he's sure of where to go next."

"He's probably trying to calculate how he'll get home again. He needs to find the way, and he'll—" Mr. Peters stopped. "He'll need to drop weight to make it back."

My heart clenched in my chest. "Bombs. He'll drop his bombs. Here." *Here in Blaenau Ffestiniog.*

"A getaway raid," Mr. Peters said slowly. "It might be the town. Or he might look for any sort of infrastructural damage he can do, to disrupt as best he can. Roads, or a factory, or . . ."

"Or a railroad," I finished, my voice hoarse. "Or a railroad bridge." *Or a railroad bridge over a road with a distinctly industrial truck on it.*

Mr. Peters whirled on the driver. "Move the truck! Move it now!"

But I was already running toward the truck, rushing to the bed where the elephant case was strapped, as if I could pull it free and save it by my own strength. I checked the wild notion and yanked open the driver's door instead, ignoring the shouts behind me. I had learned to drive in London; I mashed the clutch and turned the key, urging the engine to catch.

"Stop!" cried the driver, swinging up beside me. "What do you think you're doing?"

"We have to get it out of here," I gasped, stomping the accelerator pedal so that the engine roared to life. "We have to back it down away from the bridge."

"You can't!" He pointed behind the truck. "It's all blind. Why do you think I was stuck here?"

I looked in the centre mirror and saw it wholly blocked by the elephant case on the truck's bed. I looked at the side mirrors and saw the edge of the road, dropping off into the mountainside. An experienced and careful driver might be able to inch down and backward around the mountain curves, but not fast enough to evade the circling He 111.

"Get over," snapped the driver, and he got into the driver's seat as I scooted across to the passenger side. He slid the truck into reverse and eased it backward, his eyes jumping from mirror to mirror as he crept along the edge of the mountain track. It was better than nothing, but it wasn't enough.

The bomber banked at the far side of its circle and came toward us, engines growing louder. I stared at its approach through the truck window, my eyes fixed on the glassed cockpit, like a greenhouse bearing a pilot of death. A bomb separated from the plane, continued forward and down as the plane pulled up, detonated against the stone face of the mountain beneath us.

The explosion was deafening and the truck trembled around me. I might have cried out, I don't know. Everything seemed muted in the seconds after, as I scrambled out the passenger door and dropped coughing to the road.

The road was intact; the bomb had struck too low. Great clouds of dust were roiling up the mountainside, obscuring us for the moment but marking clearly our location at a distance. The pilot could circle at his leisure, an easy return with a more accurate estimate of where to release the next bomb to destroy the road and bridge and truck together.

I stood on the mountain road and screamed, not in terror but in raw frustration. I wanted to move the truck, I wanted to raise the bridge to allow the truck to pass, I wanted to rip the plane out of the sky. My hands worked as if I could reach the He 111.

You will be able to call us.

If I had the time to sit down and think rationally, I would not have listened to the mad voice in my head. But desperation gave me no time to consider, and I could only think of great black horses striding through the air.

165

I dashed up the road to Mr. Peters and the bridge. "Give me a leg up!" I called ahead. "Onto the bridge!"

Mr. Peters looked baffled but, bless him, did not question me as he made a stirrup of his hands and boosted me onto the railway bridge trestle. I climbed, listening for the telltale change in the bomber's engine as it turned.

The railway bridge was not intended for human feet, but I dashed down it as heedlessly if it were a park path. Across the valley I could see the plane banking. It would not need long to align for a second deployment.

I stopped on the bridge and closed my eyes, as if that could help me to call. *I need you. Grandfather, I need your help. I call on the bond of blood and the defence of this our land.*

I thought the words, but not merely thinking. I sent them through the earth, across the stone, down the water, to the people of the air.

Fair Family, I call you to me. Please come and help me.

I felt the response, a physical sensation akin to seeing someone turn in response to a call. But I could not discern an answer. Would they come? Would they recognize me as kin? Was I kin? Was I mad?

I looked up at the oncoming plane, at the glassy cage which held the German pilot, and I could see him distinctly against the sky. I held my place. Huntsmen or no, I was mad.

The truck jerked to a stop dangerously near the edge of the road, and gears ground as the driver frantically tried to pull forward again away from the drop. Mr. Peters stared transfixed at the oncoming plane, but there was nothing for him to do.

The plane's bomb bay doors were open. It was a hundred yards away.

Grandfather!

They came over the mountain behind me, flowing down upon the bridge and around me and then out into the valley air. The white dogs reached the plane first, leaping onto the greenhouse cockpit with savage snarls I could hear even over the engines. Then the black horses and dark riders swept along the nose, and a dozen hunting spears lanced the greenhouse into pieces as the plane shuddered and jerked. The singing dogs poured through the broken glass, filling the cockpit, and the plane twisted from its path.

The horses galloped away and upward, and the leader of the hunt blew his horn. The sound cut through me. White and red hounds streamed from the broken plane as it pitched downward and turned sharply. One wing caught a tree on the mountainside and the plane jerked around, smashing nose-first into rock and falling, impact after tumbling impact, to the valley floor.

The Hunt banked as the plane had and came directly for the bridge. They alighted from the sky and galloped on, coming directly for me, and I saw the black horses snort and toss froth and I squeezed my eyes shut.

They caught me up in a breathless snatch and wind howled around me. I could not breathe, could not see when I opened my eyes, could not even scream in my abrupt terror. After a moment I could discern a more rhythmic movement than the initial jolting tumble, and I could feel someone in front of me. I blinked and gradually recognized that I was seated behind one of the riders on one of the great black horses, and we were in the sky.

I squeezed my eyes shut and held on to the lean, hard form before me.

The horse's pounding strides slowed, and I opened my streaming eyes as we came to rest on a mountain top. My wind-whipped hair stood out in tangles as I slid to the ground, legs weak. Around me, the riders dismounted.

The leader of the Hunt stepped forward. "You called," he said simply. "We came for the defence of this land, which is more imminently imperilled than we had believed."

I swallowed and licked my wind-dried teeth. "Thank you for coming. You saved more than me."

"It seems you are the daughter of my son," he said, and it was impossible to tell how he felt about that. Perhaps he did not know himself. "Our blood is too precious to waste."

I was not sure how I felt about that, either. I managed a safe, "Thank you."

His brows lowered, and I remembered faintly that it was rude to thank the Fae.

"You will need a mount of your own," he said. "And you must learn to hunt."

To hunt? To hunt evil men? To hunt German bombers? What

was he saying?

And then my heart rose in fresh pounding and the wind deafened my ears and I imagined soaring through the wine-dark sky, lancing a Messerschmitt, the sensation of the metal giving way to my spear and the shriek of a dying machine and its pilot—

I shook myself clear, alarmed equally by his suggestion and my reaction to it.

But he had seen it, and for the first time the hint of a smile appeared on his face. "Yes," he said, "I will see that you are taught. Good day, granddaughter Canaid."

I had not told him my name. This final seal on my newfound heritage knelled like the burst of a bomb.

As they lifted into the sky and galloped away, calling to the dogs, I sat roughly down on the mountaintop.

FROM THE PEAK of Snowdon to the quarried mountain of Manod is about five miles as the fairy steed gallops through the air. By land, however, it is nearer twenty at best.

The shop a little below the summit was closed—strictly speaking, the summit was for government personnel now during the war, but I doubted the prohibition could extend to the Fae—and so after a suitable period of physical and mental recovery, I began walking down the path paralleling the narrow gauge tourist railway, which I knew led to a town. It was the wrong direction from Manod Mawr, but it would lead to roads and I hoped telephones.

I had gone a few miles when a familiar form appeared on the slope below me. "Miss Thomas," Owen called, faintly winded. "Are you all right?" He shook his head. "That's not the right question, but I can't work out the right one."

I stood and opened my hands to gesture about me. "I have been to the top of Snowdon."

He folded his face into a smile, but carefully, as if it might crack. "But you still haven't climbed it."

He led me down the mountain and to a Llanberis road, where a battered farm truck awaited our return. We spoke little on the descent and less in the vehicle. Neither of us knew how to address what had happened.

"How did you know where to find me?" I asked finally. It

seemed a safe route around the Hunt, and I was curious to know.

Owen took a long breath, and then he took longer to release it. "Yr Wyddfa was the first place to look," he said. "Arthur defeated a giant here. Arthur died here. Excalibur is hidden here. When a woman is carried off by the Wild Hunt, it is the first place to look." He gave me a quick glance. "And it is a peak on Harri Davies' fairy path."

I smiled.

"I hoped you would follow the railway down, rather than one of the other paths. You're a good tramper, but you don't know the land here."

I nodded.

Owen squeezed his hands on the steering wheel. "You called them, didn't you?"

I looked sharply over at him, but he kept his eyes forward.

"Mr. Peters said—when he was making any sense at all, he said you ran out onto the railway bridge and opened your arms to the sky. He said it looked as if you were summoning the plane. He thought you were taunting it to you, away from the truck." Owen shook his head. "But it wasn't the plane you summoned."

I pressed my lips together. "What did Mr. Peters say he saw after?"

"Oh, the Hunt is visible enough when they're in pursuit. He said he saw black riders and white hounds take down the plane as if it were a red deer." Owen's mouth lifted slightly. "He's not happy to say he saw it, and he says he might be mistaken in all the dust and the shock of the first bomb, but he did admit to seeing it."

A thought came to me. "Do you mean you can see them when they aren't visible to all?"

Owen's chin moved, one quick nod.

"Oh, Owen. I wish—I wish I'd known. I wish I'd had someone . . ."

He turned. "Does that mean I can call you Canaid, then?"

I had not even noticed my slip. And suddenly *Carol* seemed so wrong for these windswept mountains and tracks. "I suppose it does."

LABOURERS WERE DIGGING out the road beneath the bridge, to

make more clearance for the next elephant cases, on the day that the men from London came. They found me in my tiny office, adding to our new catalogue. "Miss Thomas?"

I looked up and noted immediately by their suits that they were not men of the town. One wore aviator sunglasses despite the ubiquitous grey mist. "Oh! I'm sorry, please come in. I—"

"We'd like to speak with you about the day of the getaway raid."

My breath caught. "We did our best—we didn't have the exact dimensions of the elephant case in advance, you see, and so we never guessed the railway bridge would be an obstacle to—"

"We are not concerned about the truck, Miss Thomas," continued the man without glasses. "That is not our ministry's interest."

I hesitated. "What ministry are you from, then?"

He looked to the other man, as if passing off the conversation, and the second man reached to lower his glasses. He had hazel eyes with glints of orange, and the pupils were curiously narrow. "We are putting together a team of specially-chosen individuals," he said. "We feel you could be of great benefit to your country, Miss Thomas."

I did not know who he was. I did not know what I was looking at when he showed me his eyes. But I knew he was someone like me, someone who knew more than I did about what we were. "I should like to hear more about this," I said cautiously.

There was a knock at the partially-ajar door, and he shoved his glasses hastily into place as Owen leaned inside. "Oh, sorry to disturb you, I didn't realize," Owen said. "I just wanted to let Miss Thomas know there was a new horse on my farm this morning. Great black fellow, all mane and feathering, eyes like shiny coal. He had a note elf-locked into his mane, and it said he's yours."

Raven Girl

Alyson Faye

Around the grange's grounds she wanders,
nightgown clad,
barefoot, dewy soled,
no longer caring to conceal her true self,
safe under night's cloak.

She rubs the laurel leaves against her cheek,
absorbing the dusky poison to feed and ignite her soul.

The willows near the waters
warble lullabies of drowned maidens;
whose hair the otters steal to line the nests of the death birds:
the ravens, crows, and jays
who flock to the banks
in their black-feathered hordes.

She throws back her neck calling to her clan.
A fluttering,
a rustling,
a chirruping,
a nestling;

branches laden with shadows,
creak under their burden.
She looks up, *the Raven Girl,*
they called her in the village before the doctors trapped her,
with straps and iron contraptions.
Glossy haired, with ebony eyes,
each empty of an iris,
a tiny flame burns deep
mesmerising,
so the men in frock coats
never meet her eye.

Instead they strapped her to a bed,
reading their Bibles, chanting over
her swaddled form;
in slurred, blurred voices,
melting with their hate.

Come Corvids, come! Gather round me,
weave me a cloak, to carry me away.

The ravens drop purple-hued feathers; rooks rally,
jays entwine stolen silver threads to sew the seams and the
crows,
they bring the wind from beneath their wings to float the
garment.

Willow-woven ties hold it to her tortured body. Behind her the
mansion bursts
with lights and frenzied voices.
She's gone! Bring the traps, Seek her out
Raven Girl laughs to the dark skies,
lifts up her feathered arms,
sucks in a lungful of stars and
rises, shrouded by the multitude of birds.
She is one with them.

Beneath her angry fires flame,
burning her bare soles,
but the fingers of fire do not singe her wings.

Raven Girl

Instead, hectic voices scald the air.

First one crow swoops to peck and claw,
followed by a second, a third rook joins the melee and next
the magpies,
glimpsing treasure
in the pocket watches and gold rings
bombard the men with eager clutching claws.

Raven Girl soars upwards,
breathing in the sky,
sipping the clouds' froth.
As one,
she and her flock, turn, point south and take flight for warmer
kinder shores.

Time to Fold

Mara Malins

I'M PROBABLY THE most famous inmate on the Confederacy jail planet, Yizae. They keep me in an isolated cell apart from the other prisoners, but that doesn't stop me from hearing the catcalls, whistles, and coarse yells of support hollered down the long, soulless corridors. I think of these people as scum of the universe; crime lords, thieves, and unrepentant murderers. And yet to them, I'm worse . . . so much so that I deserve their respect.

At first, I'd been dazzled by my unwanted fame, then uncomfortable, then a deep sense of shame set in. I was being admired for accidentally killing billions of people. The Confederacy has tried to stop their hollering. They don't want a "murdering lowlife" like me being raised to some sort of symbol of rebellion. Their words, not mine.

I came here about five cycles ago. The Confederacy found me, still unconscious, a few days after the battle between the Dragon and Giant and brought me straight here. No trial. No justice. Barely even any hospital time. Just straight into my cell. I didn't care. In fact, I'm probably the only person in the galaxy happy to be incarcerated. After what I did? I deserve to be here.

Even if it was just a card game gone wrong.

It all started with the Night of the Dragon Cards almost seven cycles ago. I combined two of the galaxy's strongest playing cards in the creature arena to create a fire dragon so strong that it broke free and went on a destructive rampage, burning up entire planets and leaving no one alive. Then, to try and make up for my terrible mistake, I played the game again, this time creating a giant to take on the fiery beast I'd created. It worked . . . in a way. Both the dragon and the giant were killed. The death of the giant even revitalised a once devastated and unliveable planet.

There was just one little problem. The life force that the dying giant fed into the planet didn't stop there; it seeped out into the galaxy and all sorts of strange things started to happen. Including bringing the remaining playing cards to life. There wasn't just one dangerous beast now; there were thousands. I'd heard a *Raiju* was holding the farming planet Greta captive with unstoppable thunderstorms, and one of the guards had told me that a group of Valkyries were travelling from planet to planet, killing every man and boychild they found.

That was the other reason why I was happy to be here, locked up in my cell in a heavily guarded jail on a Confederacy controlled planet that housed the universe's worst criminals. It was reinforced, protected, and armed up to the gills to prevent break outs . . . and break ins.

I was currently lying on my hard bed, leafing listlessly through this week's book allocation—*The Laws of a Successful Confederacy Society*—when a loud rapping rang out through my cell. I lifted my head, already knowing what I would see; the morning guard, Teda, staring at me through the small ten-inch by ten-inch gap in the cell door. Teda was a bitch. A bald-headed, feral, buck-toothed, broad-shouldered bitch. She was as ugly on the outside as she was on the inside, and she took great pleasure in provoking the prisoners. My only consolation was that she couldn't touch me; I was a protected inmate and it drove her fucking crazy.

"Enjoying ya book, hoss?" she called to me, snapping her gum between her teeth. It was salamander berry flavoured and stained her teeth red. The sight of it reminded me of my old friend, Poole. He used to love chewing those berries.

"It's thrilling," I lied. I closed the book and rested it on my chest. "Have you read it? Wait, what am I thinking? Of course, you haven't. You can't read, can you?"

Her bug eyes narrowed a little. "Book smart ain't clever in here, girl. You need to be wits-smart. You'd know that if you ever mixed with the real crowd."

"Good thing I have my own little space then, isn't it? I can read to my heart's content."

She pulled herself further through the cell door gap. "If you're enjoying that book so much, I'll bring you the second volume next week."

"Looking forward to it," I replied, forcing a smile.

Teda wasn't fooled. "Is that right? Well, it belongs to a set of thirty-six, each one bigger than the last. I reckon it should last you at least three cycles. Then we can move onto the history of Confederacy if you want. A riveting read."

"Looking forward to it," I repeated, not letting my expression fade. "What do you want, Teda?"

"You have a visitor."

I sat up, the book tumbling to the cold stone floor. "What do you mean a visitor? Who is it?" The only friend I had left was Poole, and he'd deserted me during the battle between the giant and the dragon. I hadn't seen him since.

"How would I know? I'm just here to escort you. You know the procedure, Samus."

I did know the procedure. I followed it every three days—the only time I left my cell—when they escorted me to the freezing cold, dribbling showers. I got up off the bed, wincing as my knees cracked, and faced the wall. I rested my hands on the concrete and waited for Teda to clasp the manacles around my ankles and wrists. Then she bound the chains to a locked steel harness around her own body. In short: I wasn't going anywhere unless I took her with me. Not that escape had *ever* crossed my mind.

Teda walked me down the mostly-silent corridor. It was painted a clinical white and the only light came from the swinging fluorescent strips overhead. At the end of the corridor we reached a little room. Teda opened the door and I walked in, surprised to see an elderly man sitting at a table reading some papers.

He looked up when I entered, letting his eyes wander over

me like I was a fat slug on a piece of lettuce he was about to eat. There was a coldness in his gaze that I immediately disliked. "Sit down," he commanded in a strong voice that didn't suit his frail frame. When I hesitated, he said, "I won't ask twice."

I took a seat, feeling like a school child about to be reprimanded, but didn't say anything. This was his meeting—whoever he was—and I had nothing to lose in listening. But I hadn't spoken about that horrible night between the dragon and the giant to anyone—no matter how much they'd threatened me—and I wasn't about to start now.

"I'm Vutti O'Brien," he said, but he didn't hold out his hand. He looked at me expectantly, as if I should know that name. When I didn't react, he added, "The Leader-General of the Confederacy."

It was an effort to keep my face impassive. Yes, I knew this guy. Or at least I knew his rank. Hell, everyone did. He was the guy rebels frightened their children with. This man had taken the Confederacy from a strong government to a brutal-fucking-superpower in less than a few cycles. It was under his leadership that the rebels had been hunted down and killed like dogs.

"You're Samus? The great player of cards?" Vutti enquired, looking me over again. When I nodded, he sighed. "For some reason I'd expected a man."

I shrugged. "Men always do."

He ignored that. "I've read your file, Samus, and I've gone through every report about both incidents you were involved in." He lifted the paper in front of him and read a line, his brow furrowing. "What the rebels like to call 'The Night of the Dragon Cards' and 'The Clash of the Elements.'" He looked up. "They do like their little legends, don't they?"

I felt a surprising flare of rage at his amused tone. Little Legend? Billions of people had died, planets were destroyed, and he was talking about it as if it was a regular game of cards. But—with some effort—I stayed silent. This was a man known for being a manipulator. He would say anything to get a reaction from me, to put me in a weakened frame of mind. Nobody got to the high rank of Leader-General without playing mind games.

Vutti's lip twitched, as if he sensed my internal struggle. "You've been told about the aftermath of your last card game? How the remaining cards have come to life without the magic of the card arena?"

"Yes."

"Don't you think it's your responsibility to fix?"

"No. I don't."

He paused for a long moment. "What a strange answer. You created the beast after all. How can it not be your responsibility?"

"I created it on the Confederacy orders. Do you hold yourself responsible for the lives of those killed during the wars?"

"Of course. I see each and every face."

That made me pause. I'd imagined him to think of those deaths as collateral damage, as a justified cost in growing the Confederacy's power. Then I realised he was manipulating me again so I sat back in my chair and shrugged. "You're a weaker man than your reputation then. The world knows you as a monster."

"Ah, so you do know me," he said, pleased. He leaned back in his chair too, crossing his long legs. "The world knows you as a monster too, Samus. Possibly even worse than I. After all where I bring war, I also bring the Confederacy, which in itself brings healthcare instead of disease, human rights instead of abuse, order instead of chaos. It seems you bring only death."

A flush crept up my cheeks. "Enough talk, Vutti. You came here because you need something from me. What is it?"

For the first time, Vutti looked caught off guard. He cleared his throat. "We have a . . . situation on Chuni."

"Chuni? The governing planet?"

He dipped his head. "Yes. A harpy has—" another clearing of his throat, "—has taken residence there, and she's not letting anyone come or go until her challenge is met."

"But you're here," I pointed out, "so the harpy must be letting some people out."

"I was commanded to bring you to her. You're the challenge."

My heart stopped. "What?"

"The opponent she has requested—has demanded—for her challenge, is you. No other person will do apparently." He opened his hands wide. "Which is why I'm here. Believe me when I say we've tried to negotiate with her. For many cycles. Nothing will do apart from you, apparently."

I stared at him, horrified. "No," I said, cutting the air with my hand. "No. I won't do it. I did your bidding last time and look where it got me. I'm staying in jail. I won't do it and you can't make me."

Vutti took his glasses off and wiped them on a red silk handkerchief taken from his breast pocket. As he wiped, he appraised me. He placed his glasses back on the end of his nose and refolded the handkerchief, but he didn't return it to his pocket. Instead, he lay it across his knee and rested his hands on them. "We *can* make you, Samus, and we will. *I* will. You see, when we found you on that ruined planet, you were burned almost to death. We gave you the medical care you needed—"

"And threw me in jail despite our arrangement!" I interjected hotly, fear making my stomach churn uncomfortably.

"You are here because we saved you," Vutti continued, ignoring my outburst. "But not without conditions. The Confederacy honoured its promise to you; you defeated the dragon so we let you live. You didn't, however, free the galaxy of the elemental cards, so we cannot let you leave. A half-fulfilled promise for a half-fulfilled prize." He locked eyes with me. "And I believe you're happy with the outcome, so please don't speak to me in that manner."

When I didn't say anything, just looked at him with revulsion, he continued, "There is something you should know; there were internal, ah, *discussions* about whether we should offer you any medical aid at all when we found you. There was an opinion—a rather loud one—that if we did nothing, you would die anyway, which was absolutely true. It came to an internal vote, which was split exactly fifty-fifty. Your life was held in the hands of one person."

I could guess who. "You."

"Yes, I voted to save you. However, I had a price. A caveat, if you will. We would save you, but a chip was inserted into your brain to take away, at any moment, the gift of life we bestowed on you." He leaned forward on his chair to make sure I looked nowhere else but into his eyes. "So, let me be clear; you *will* come with me to Chuni, and you *will* face the harpy. We just want you to finish the agreement you made three cycles ago; to amend your mistake."

"Do I have a choice?"

"No," he said simply. "You have no choice and you have to

beat her. Whatever the cost."

CHUNI WAS KNOWN as a luxury planet, a planet full of oceans, jungles, mountains, and deserts. No piles of stinking garbage or rotting junkers like the planets I grew up on, but meadows that teemed with life, and unpolluted rivers that had fish—*real, live fish*—that could be hunted and eaten without sickness. The cities were huge and sprawling, and the tall glass buildings glinted under the glorious sun. It was a planet that screamed wealth and prosperity and easy life . . . nothing like the outlier planets. Everything was perfect.

Except the winds.

I didn't feel them until our airship touched down. It was a bumpy landing and the airship swung from side to side as we descended, making my stomach roll over. Vutti held his head in his hands, mumbling beneath his breath as the turbulence got worse. He gave out an audible sigh of relief when the wheels of the ship finally touched concrete. "Fucking winds . . ." he muttered.

"Winds? I thought Chuni only had sunshine and blue skies?" I asked, pressing my face to the small circular window. The view wasn't nearly as exciting as a few minutes before. The greenery was gone; now I could only see glass buildings and the grey, soulless concrete of the landing strips.

"It's the harpy," the pilot said, when Vutti didn't answer me. He unsnapped his harness and spun in his chair to face me. He had a smooth plumpness to his face that said he was well-fed. "She's kept the planet in a wild wind—a *storm* wind—ever since she arrived."

We disembarked onto the loading ramp and were greeted by a young boy who snapped a salute to Vutti. He was dressed in the black Confederacy uniform, all starched and crisp and pristine. His baby fine blonde hair whipped around his face. He didn't look my way at all. It was if I didn't exist. "The officers are waiting for you this way, sir," he shouted over the wind.

"Very good. Take Samus to the harpy immediately." Vutti looked at me. "There's no point in waiting. You're rested and fed so you might as well face her now."

"Yeah, I guess so," I answered, and gestured for the boy to lead the way.

"Oh, and Samus?"

I turned back to Vutti. "You can't leave the planet. The winds won't let you, so don't even think about escape. And remember that I have your life in my hands."

I didn't answer because there wasn't anything to say. I gave my own snappy salute—though mine stank of sarcasm—and followed the boy through the expansive city streets, trying not to gawp at the wealth I saw everywhere. The markets at home were just a few mostly-empty tables that displayed chunks of stringy meat or piles of second-hand smelly clothes. Here, there were whole carcases—fat and well-fed—strung up and swinging in the wind. There were stands that had decorated cakes and sweetmeats. People wandered around, laughing with one another, no cares in the world. They didn't have that starving, hollow-eyed look that I was used to seeing, and they didn't scurry from place to place, their heads down, looking to leave the streets as soon as possible.

"Do you want to try a cake?" the boy asked me, following my hungry stare over to the cake stall.

I shook my head quickly. I didn't want to eat. My stomach had that familiar churning feeling, but it was fear I felt. I had none of that excited anticipation burning through me at the prospect of a wager. I used to live for that feeling. That *need* to compete and win. I was about to embark on one of the biggest wagers ever and I felt nothing but fear.

That scared me.

"How far to the harpy?" I asked, turning my mind away from my fear.

"I have no idea."

I stopped and turned to look at him. "What? Then where are you taking me?"

"The harpy comes when she wants. She knows we're looking for her. We just have to walk towards where we think she is and she will summon us."

"That makes no sense."

He shrugged. "It's the way it is."

"For how long?"

The boy considered; his youthful face turned towards the sky. "About four cycles. Maybe a little longer."

Almost since the battle. My actions that night had consequences more far-reaching than I'd realised. "And you just . . . live with it?"

He nodded and continued his walk. I noticed that he had a limp and he leaned to one side ever so slightly with each step. "Yes, we don't really see her much. Just the winds," he said, oblivious to my study. "Well, that, and the occasional tests."

"Test? What's the test? What happens when they fail?"

"The test of knowledge and they die," he answered. He had to raise his voice towards the end as a particularly vicious gust of wind hit us. "She likes to wager. She likes to wager on people's lives."

Does she? I felt a shudder at that.

"How many times—" But I couldn't finish my question because my breath was sucked right out of my throat. The world tilted ten degrees, making my stomach *swoop* unpleasantly, and then spun as wildly as if I was in an airless washing machine. The markets spiralled around and around me, moving further away and spreading out until it was nothing but a thin line of black in a whole load of white. I closed my eyes and gripped my knees, willing for the feeling to end.

"It's the harpy!" I heard the boy yell. He sounded as strangled as I felt, but there was no fear there and I wondered how many times he'd been through this.

I don't know how long passed. It could have been minutes, hours, days, but eventually the spinning world started to slow and it retracted back towards me. The markets were gone. We were now in a luscious green valley, surrounded by the tallest mountains I'd ever seen.

The boy was also gone and I was standing alone, waiting. The wind, whilst a little bit gentler here—and definitely fresher—still whipped at my clothes. It was cold, much colder than anything I'd ever experienced before and it sliced through the thin material of my boiler suit. I was just about to start walking— where, I had no idea—when I heard a voice behind me.

"Mother . . ."

Years of living by myself, either abandoned on the planet Gavala after The Night of the Dragon Cards or in my solitary jail cell, had made me nervous. Jumpy. Usually, I couldn't help but whirl around to face any sudden noise. But not this time. Not with *her* voice. I recognised it immediately though I'd never heard it before. A warmth flooded through me and my hunched shoulders relaxed. The tension in my stomach melted away like snow in the sun. I turned, my entire body softening, and there she was.

The harpy.

She was breathtakingly beautiful. Her long, dark hair hung to her waist in shiny waves. She was wearing a white, floor-length dress that kissed her flawless, soft figure. The silky material fluttered in the wind around her. There was nothing about her that looked like the ugly, haggard harpies on the cards I used to carry. The only magical thing about her were the two huge eagle-like wings that opened up behind her as she walked towards me, barefoot. "Mother," she said again, her small black eyes on mine. "You came to me."

"I didn't have much of a choice," I answered, unable to look away.

"No, I'm sorry about that." She took another step towards me. "I could have brought you here, of course, but I thought it better that you made the journey yourself."

She gestured to the carpet of moss. "Please, sit."

I looked down but didn't move. "Why am I here? What do you want with me?"

"To find out what comes next," she said, as if I was silly child.

"What do you mean?"

"You created the first; the dragon. And afterwards, you created the giant. From him, all of us were birthed. There are thousands of us, all ready to answer the call of the card master. That is you, Mother. We have waited for you. And now, with the choice you make, I will know what comes next for our kind. Your actions have brought us to this pivotal point so far . . . and everything now rests on how you answer my challenge. We cannot move forward until we know."

I swallowed. Despite the calming influence of the harpy, I could feel my heart beating in my chest. "We?"

She smiled and it brought such a beauty to her face that I could barely breathe. "Your sons and daughters, though only I am here right now. We wouldn't want to . . . reawaken your competitive side and pit one against the other, would we?"

"Would you fight if I ordered it?" I asked, curious in spite of myself. A worm of heat wriggled in my stomach and I knew what it was; that familiar *need* to wager was unfurling like a little flag inside me. What would it be like, I wondered, to have the ultimate arena with *all* card creatures fighting each other?

"We would, if the wager was big enough. But that is not why we're here. Sit!" she commanded, and before I knew it, my knees buckled and I crumpled to the floor.

The harpy sat beside me, gracefully tucking her feet beneath her. One wing stroked down the left side of my body and I felt the toughness, the rigidity of her feathers. "See, isn't this nice?"

"What do you want from me?" I asked again.

"I told you. I want to know what comes next."

"I don't know."

She nodded approvingly. "The truth. You tell lies so frequently—a gambler always does—that I wondered if you would be truthful with me."

"I don't lie, I . . . bluff."

"Another lie. Don't lie to me. I can tell."

We sat in silence for a long moment. My hair tickled the skin of my neck and I scratched it away. I realised it was being stirred by the breeze coming directly from her. In that instant I knew she would have been an elemental card. The dragon had been fire incarnate; the giant had been earth and life. The harpy—my daughter—was a creature of air.

"You need to leave this planet," I said after a few moments of silence. "Or at the very least, let those who live here come and go as they please."

"Why should I do that?"

Because they will kill me if you don't. That's why I am here. To save my life. But I couldn't say the words out loud. They were selfish. Self-interested.

"Yes, they will kill you," she agreed, answering my unspoken words anyway. She turned her head to look down on me. She was so much taller than I was. "I know all about Vutti's threat, but he can't harm you here. His mindless magic, his . . ." she snapped her long fingers together, "his electronic chips have no power. Not here."

"But if I leave?"

She smiled at me. It was a shy smile, like a girl flirting with a boy she liked. "I can stop the chip or I can start it. And I can't say that you don't deserve it for you are not a good person. You have killed many, both my kind and yours." She paused, studying my face. "But you cannot stay with me either."

I was surprised to find myself disappointed by her rejection. I'd known her minutes but already I loved her. I wanted to stay with her. "I don't know what happens next. Vutti said you wanted something from me but if it's some sort of plan or direction . . . then I can't help you. Send for someone who can."

I went to climb to my feet but her hand shot out and pulled me back down with tremendous force. Her fingers bit painfully into my shoulder.

"We're not finished," she said, her tone so much harder than it had been moments before.

I gasped. "You're hurting me!"

"You hurt thousands of my brothers and sisters. All but a handful were maimed and killed in those card arenas of yours, brought to life by magic that you didn't understand. If you can't figure out what happens next then I shall tell you; we will have a wager about the future. Just you and I, Mother. It appears the magic of the cards gave me some of your impulses, and the joy of gambling is one of them."

I froze. "What?"

She smiled. "Vutti sent you here to answer my contest. He knows I intend to challenge you to a wager, though I do not think he understands the consequences of giving permission to you as my opponent. You see, me and my kind don't answer to the Confederacy laws, Mother, we answer only to the magic of the contest. Vutti will have no choice but to honour the outcome. The magic binding the challenge is as unbreakable for him as it is for us."

"I don't understand . . ." I said uncertainly.

"It's simple: I fight for the lives of my brothers and sisters, and you fight for yours."

"But you're living now?"

"No, we just haven't been killed yet," she corrected sadly. "Your Confederacy does not want us to live. If it has its way, then we will be hunted down and killed one by one. It will be difficult for them, of course, and they will lose thousands of men for every one of our kind that they kill . . . but they will try. No, I don't want my brothers and sisters to live in fear. This war against us must stop. One way or another it *must* stop.

"So, if I win then we are free. Nobody will hunt us. I will

destroy the Confederacy weapons. I will ground their ships with storms." She met my eyes. "The leaders of the Confederacy will die. The high scoring card players will die—as they should for their crimes against my kind. That means *you* will die, Mother, as you have by far the most points in the universe, thanks to your last two card games. But those that don't oppose us can live."

I rubbed at my mouth. "I die?"

"Yes, though it would sadden me."

"And if I win?"

"If you win then you live. I will kill the man who holds your life in his hands. I will free this planet from the storm. And my kind will cease to be a part of this universe, including me. *That is the power of card magic.*"

I tried to ignore that powerful excitement building in my chest and think rationally. I thought I'd learned my lesson. I thought I'd burned my fingers so badly in the last two challenges that I would never think about placing a bet ever again. But here I was, letting that temptation—that familiar *need*—lead me on once again, and knew I wouldn't be able to resist it. My life was on the table again, yes, but this time the stakes were higher than ever before . . . and that made it interesting.

Could I refuse this?

Was it too . . . tempting?

More importantly, could I make this decision without Confederacy authority? I thought, attempting one last moment of rationality.

"The Confederacy has no choice in this," the harpy said, reading something in my face. "This is between you and I; the creator and the leader of the beasts. You will decide and you will decide *now*. We shall see who is the greater player of the game."

It was her words that decided me. I may be deeply ashamed of my actions that led to this point . . . but I also felt a savage pride that *no one* had yet defeated me. Nobody had beaten me at cards. I lifted my chin and said with as much surety as I could, "Let's do it. Let's play your game," I agreed.

Her smile grew so large it was almost feral. "Good."

"How do we do this?" I asked. "There aren't any arenas left in the galaxy."

"And good riddance!" she snapped, her tone cold. A terrible gust of wind hit me, almost knocking me over. "As I said, no longer will we do your fighting for you."

"Then how . . . ?"

"We will fight with words." When I looked doubtful, she clarified. "With riddles, Mother."

"The test of knowledge," I said, repeating the boy's earlier words.

Another nod of approval. "Yes. I will ask you three riddles. You must answer them all correctly to win the challenge."

I wasn't a wordy type of person, preferring the brute strength of the card arena. In fact, I couldn't recall the last time I was asked a riddle. But a challenge was a challenge, and a bet was a bet.

She watched me considering her proposal with those fierce black eyes of hers. After a few moments she asked, "Do we have a deal?"

"Deal," I whispered, a terrible sense of déjà vu flowing through me.

I FOLLOWED HER down to the river and watched as she stacked freshly split wood into a pile. She scratched her long nail down the bark of one of the smaller pieces and blew softly at the same time. One single flame sparked to life. It quickly grew to a roaring fire. "It seems right that we're surrounded by all the elements, isn't it? Fire," she gestured to the fire she'd just created. "Water," she waved her hand towards the river. "Earth," she plunged her clawed hand into the ground and pulled free a clump of dark, rich soil. "And air." She smiled at me, making it clear she meant herself. "How many times have you played the elements to their strengths during the card game, Mother?"

"Hundreds," I said, my heartbeat now slowed so I could think of something other than the wager again.

"Thousands," she corrected. Her wings slid open, the feathers spreading like coal-stained fingers. She laid a hand on my shoulder and asked formally, "Do you wish to hear the first riddle?"

"Yes," I said, no hesitation. Distantly, I heard—

remembered?

—that familiar *seeeeeeuuuuuutttttt!* ring between my ears. It was the sound of the table-arena locking in the cards pre-fight. I hadn't heard it in many cycles. I guess I'd never hear it again.

The harpy dropped her hand and took a step back. *"Voiceless yet it cries, wingless yet it flutters, toothless yet it bites, mouthless yet it mutters. What am I?"*

I blinked. The words had slipped by me, not sticking in my mind at all. "Again?"

She repeated the riddle, her voice louder as the wind started to rise around us. I ran her words through my mind, puzzling over each word. I had no idea how long I sat there, muttering beneath my breath. The harpy watched me, her face expressionless, her eyes unblinking. "Do you know the answer? Give me an incorrect answer and you lose the challenge."

I felt a jolt of fear at her words when the answer hit me in the face. Literally. I staggered backwards as a sudden gust of wind pushed and pulled at me. "Wind," I said, barely audible. "The answer is wind."

The harpy smiled her beautiful smile again and something inside me relaxed. "Very good," she said. "Do you want to hear the second riddle?"

"Yes."

"Okay. This one is a question. *What flies forever, but rests never?"*

The answer came immediately. I was amazed that I didn't even have to think. "It's wind again, isn't it?"

Her wings stretched, the feathery tips fluttering. Her face darkened briefly. "You win the second round, Mother. Have you heard that riddle before?"

"I don't know," I answered honestly.

"I finally get the truth from you. Do you want to hear the third?"

"Yes. I do," I said quickly, starting to believe that I might actually win.

"Listen carefully, for this one is not as easy as you think." She took a deep breath and stretched out her wings as far as they would go. The wind was vicious now and I struggled to stand. Even so, a panicked sweat trickled down my back. *"Born of Earth, but with none of its strength. Moulded by Flame, but with none of its power. Shaped by Wind, with all of its clarity.*

A holder of Water, with all of its beauty. What am I?"

My stomach clenched unpleasantly and I felt a small spark of fear. Before hearing the riddle, I'd anticipated the answer to be one of the four elements. She'd mentioned them as she built that fire, after all. And something inside me said that the riddles applied to the harpy's original card strengths; clearly, she was an air card. There was no doubt about that in my mind. So, it had made sense that the first two riddles had been about wind. I'd expected the answer to the last riddle to be either fire, earth, or water. But the riddle had already listed those.

"Repeat please?" I asked, my mouth dry.

When she repeated the riddle, speaking slowly and clearly, I made myself concentrate on the words, playing them over and over in my mind. I repeated them so much that they lost all meaning. I couldn't think of anything but the elements, but clearly the answer was not that.

"Fuck," I whispered.

"You can refuse to answer at any time," the harpy called over the wind. Was that triumph in her tone? I looked up sharply to see that the feral smile was back, sliding up her face revealing sharp white teeth. "You will forfeit the challenge, of course, but as you have answered two riddles correctly, I will grant you a partial prize; I will destroy that chip in your head and you can keep your life even though you have the most points in the universe. Forfeit and you partially win."

"That is not winning everything," I whispered, voicing the worst fears of any gambler.

"You win your life. Isn't that enough?"

It should be. For anybody else it would be.

But it wasn't for me. I couldn't walk away from a bet. I never could. Even when the course of action was to fold and back away from the table-arena, I always upped the stakes. That was my strategy. This was no different. I sank to the ground, taking a few deep breaths. I swallowed down the lump of fear in my throat, knowing that I was one wrong word away from mindless panic.

The harpy's smile deepened. She no longer looked beautiful; she looked ferocious. Her hair had curled in the wind, taking on an untamed and wild look. Her long dress was whipping around her body.

I sat there for a long time, so long that my legs went numb and my back ached terribly. Still the answer didn't come. I was about to accept defeat and throw in the towel when a memory suddenly came to me. It was of Flick, my opponent from the Night of the Dragon Cards. He'd goaded me into combining those two cards, sending me down this path. I remembered him sitting back in his chair, the card-table arena between us, a smug smile on his lips. The table-arena had locked in our cards with that distinct *seeeeeeuuuuuuuttttttt* noise.

Flick, so confident in his cards, had raised his glass in a sarcastic salute to me. I could almost taste that pungent, oily drink of his . . . but it was his glass that stuck in my mind. The glass with his thick hands wrapped securely around it.

It was made by sand, taken from the earth.

It was melted in fire and blown into a shape by air.

It could hold water.

"Glass!" I yelled, jumping to my feet so quickly that I almost balled straight into the fire. "It's glass!"

"Your answer is glass?" the harpy asked, her tone both amused and annoyed. She took a step towards me, her bare toes curling in the grass. "You want to bet everything on that answer?"

"Yes! Yes, I do! It's glass. The answer is glass!" I said excitedly, coming to stand before her. The closer I got, the more brutal the wind grew. I held my hand over my eyes to shield them. "Am I correct?"

"Yes." And then for some reason, she grinned.

"So I win?" I asked, uncertain. "I live?"

"You live," she confirmed with a dip of her head.

I should have been excited, but instead I felt like I had somehow lost the game. That I'd failed. Something didn't feel right. "But what about you? What about the other creatures?"

"Do not worry about us, Mother. Vutti will die, the storms will stop, and we will cease to be in this universe, as agreed."

My mouth was dry. "You will cease . . ."

"Yes, as agreed. That is the magic of the cards. We must obey."

"Then I can leave?"

"No." The word was stated matter-of-factly.

"W-what?"

"No, you can't leave," she said simply, gripping me by the wrist so hard I thought my bones might snap. "You won the death of my kind but we never agreed on when. You won your life and the end of the storms, but we never agreed that you would win your freedom. Had I won, the leaders of the Confederacy would have died, but I did not guarantee the safety of anybody else."

Aghast, I stared down to where her fingers were gripping my wrist. It took a long time to understand her softly spoken words. Had I exchanged one jail cell for another? If she was going to cease to be, why should I remain alone in this strange place? If not the leaders, who would die? "What . . . ?"

But before she could answer, there was a sudden roaring of engines and a violent gust of wind—different from the kind that exuded from the harpy. It had an industrial smell to it. A *manmade* stink that didn't belong here. Then there was an incredible explosion that sent me flying backwards like a ragdoll. My head hit something hard on impact and everything went black. When I came around, someone was yanking on my arm.

"Come on, goddamnit! She'll wake up any minute!" someone screamed at me.

My stinging eyes fluttered open and I saw my old friend Poole peering down at me. He looked so much older and wearier than I remembered. There were deep wrinkles etched into his overly tanned face.

"Poole?" I croaked out. I let him pull me to my feet. I was trembling all over. "What are you doing here?"

"Saving your arse. Again. Now, move! She won't stay down forever!" He flapped a hand over to where the harpy lay spread-eagled, her arms flung up overhead. Her hair was perilously close to the fire.

I wiped at my mouth, surprised when my hand came away smeared with blood. "What did you do to her?"

"I dropped a water bomb on her. It's her opposite element. It'll keep her down, but only for a little while. God, it's like playing a real-life game of the cards." He swallowed. "Come on! We need to get back to the ship!"

"How did you know I was here?" We started to run towards his ship, with me less steady on my feet than Poole.

"I knew what was going on as soon as you left the jail planet. I knew they'd try and drag you into the elemental war." He shot me a stern glance over his shoulder. "And I knew you wouldn't be able to resist whatever wager they'd tempt you with."

"I had to save—"

"Mother!" the harpy screamed from behind us. She was on her knees, leaning heavily to one side, and her now-ugly face was twisted with fury. "We had a deal!"

Terror made me move. I lowered my head and pumped my legs harder, feeling the burn almost immediately. We sped towards the ship. Within moments we were on it and away, lifting into the air with speed I never knew Poole's old junker could reach. "Go! Go!" Poole shouted, grabbing hold of the airlock door—the only thing within reach.

We were rocked by a huge wave of turbulence, sending the craft almost vertical. "Storm winds!" Poole cried to his husband Tuttle. "She's awake! Can you outfly it?"

"Fuck. Oh fuck," Tuttle muttered, gripping the controls so hard his knuckles were white.

"Can you outfly it?" Poole screeched as I hung onto the back of Tuttle's seat for dear life. His only answer was to yank down on the controls in front of him. I was slammed with acceleration and thrown to the back of the aircraft. My head smashed into something hard and for the second time that day, I blacked out.

WHEN I NEXT awoke, I was lying down in an old bed, a frayed blanket yanked up beneath my arms. It was mostly dark but there was a spear of light coming through the black curtains hanging at the end of the room. The smell—salamander berries and stale cigarette smoke—hung familiarly in the hair and I breathed it in. After a few minutes, I carefully slipped from the bed, wincing as the mother of all headaches settled between my eyes.

"You want to be careful," Poole said, entering the room carrying a tray. He flipped a switch, turning on a single hanging bulb in the middle of the room. "I think you have a concussion."

I sat back down at the edge of the bed, not entirely confident that my trembling legs could support my weight for long. "You came back for me."

"For some reason, I always do."

I took the glass of water from the tray he carried in and took a sip. It was cool and sweet . . . and reminded me of her riddle. "The harpy? Is she dead?"

He shook his head. "I don't think so. The storms are gone so I'm assuming you won whatever bet you had going?"

"For some reason, I always do," I replied, trying to sound flippant. I failed. "The Confederacy?"

Poole sat down beside me and patted my hand. His warm, sour breath wafted over me but I no longer felt repulsed as I used to; I felt safe. "They either think you're dead or they're happy you won. Either way, there's been no news about your recapture on the 'Fed channels. Besides, I think they have bigger things to worry about right now than some escaped card player."

"The creatures?"

Poole gave me a hard look. A long time ago he would have flinched at such a direct stare, but now it was me who felt unnerved. "What did you bet this time, Samus?"

"Everything . . ." I whispered. "But I won. The creatures should have died."

"You bet against a harpy, you foolish woman! Whatever was promised, she would have made sure it was cleverly ambiguous." He closed his eyes and took a deep breath. I couldn't tell what he was thinking. Then he spoke, his eyes still closed. "The creatures have attacked Chuni. From what I've heard, they've killed Vutti. They've also killed all of the Confederacy pilots."

Vutti, yes. I'd bet his life. But the pilots . . . ? I swallowed. "But I won . . ."

"Yes, you won. Again," Poole confirmed. His tone held no emotion. "But the creatures still live and every Confederacy pilot is dead."

I sank back on the bed, mixed feelings coursing through me. I should have felt joyous hearing my victory said out loud. I should have felt thrilled that—despite everything—I was still the undisputed card player of the galaxy. Nobody could take it from me. Not now. Probably not ever. I should have felt pride, maybe even a little private triumph that, for the third time, I'd bet everything on the ultimate wager and emerged the victor.

But after looking into Poole's face, I felt nothing but a deep sense of shame.

We All Fall Down

Sara C. Walker

WHITE FLAKES OF ash drift from the night sky like falling snow outside your window. The breeze shifts, bringing the sweet scent of singed cedar and maple. A woman's screams puncture the night. You want to close the windows, but you can't. Not yet.

The ash reminds you of a game you used to play with your sisters. You recall holding hands, making a circle, skipping around, and chanting, "Ashes, ashes, we all fall down." You know there was more to the game, but you can't remember. You must have been wearing pretty dresses, but all you can see in the memory is your sisters' feet clad in white stockings and black-strapped shoes. You can't see their dresses or their faces.

Is it a memory or a memory of a dream?

The night sky twinkles behind the upward drifts of smoke. You wish upon a star that the counter-spell will work as the witch promised. You close your eyes and hope you will be able to speak to your sisters again.

Hopes and wishes are all you have left.

You head out into the night to collect the required stinging nettles.

The bonfire wanes, the crowd begins to disperse, dawdling back to their homes. The night air reeks of death—sweet, pungent, sick. The streets take you away from the pyre, to the fields on the edge of town. But when you arrive you remember you've already pulled all the nettles from these fields. There's only one place left.

A wandering mist creeps up from the river, enshrouding the stone markers. There's always mist in the graveyard. Some say it's haunted, filled with restless spirits of the dead. You try not to think of this, try not to wonder who might drift among the graves, as you make your way towards the river, to the weeds growing on the embankment.

You think of your mother. She would tell you that mist is not haunted spirits but elevated droplets of water—or something. You try to remember. You have a warm, loving feeling when you think of the times she took you outside for alchemy lessons and you wonder if she misses you as much as you miss her.

You pluck the stinging nettles—you only need enough for one last shirt—and head for home. A couple on their way to from the witch burning sees you; they stop and whisper to each other when they see you come out of the graveyard.

In this town, they know you only as the mute woman who knits shirts out of weeds. They think you mad but harmless. They burned the witch you lived with; stole her away in the night, and all you could do was stand there, biting your tongue until you swallowed blood. You knew it was only a matter of time before they turned on you.

With a last glance at the graveyard, you shudder, then hurry home.

ONCE, YOU LIVED with your six sisters in a prosperous city with your mother, a brilliant alchemist. You were all so content, until she took a husband.

You and your sisters were all so close to marrying age, and he forecasted the cost of future wedding celebrations would cut too deeply into his political ambitions, so your stepfather hired a witch to make a potion that would rid him of his new step-children.

On the day the witch delivered the potion, your sisters were dutifully attending their needlecraft lessons, while you slipped outside to the park to climb trees and build forts.

As the witch was returning home, she came upon you asleep

under a beechnut tree and offered you a chance to save yourself and your sisters.

Her instructions were very specific: not one word spoken to anyone, and six shirts knit by your own hands from stinging nettles and nothing more. Yes, she said, *the nettles will scratch and blister the skin on your fingers, and your blood will seep into your work. You'll have to work quickly. Your memories will fade along with theirs, until eventually, they will forget they were human at all.*

It is necessary, she said, *for only the blood of one clone can break the spell that binds the others. Oh, didn't you know?*

While you were speaking to the witch in the park, six white swans flew down from the cerulean sky and landed in the pond. The witch pointed out her handiwork.

Your sisters had been a nuisance to you, annoying you with their noise and chatter, bickering and squabbling, raucous laughter and tears at all hours. Why should you care what happened to them?

But they were also your playmates. Your first friends. Your best friends.

You imagined your world without them and found it quiet. Too quiet.

One of the swans waddled across the grass and sat at your feet. As you marvelled at being so close to the majestic bird, the others wandered over and sat down, surrounding you.

You skipped needlecraft lessons so you had no idea how to knit one shirt out of spun wool, let alone six out of plants, but you agreed to the witch's terms with the nod of your head, so the witch took you to her cottage in the countryside, where you learned those needlecraft lessons you'd so badly tried to avoid.

Now here you are: five shirts completed, one to begin.

A FLUTTER OUTSIDE your window signals their arrival. Two of your sisters climb in through the bedroom window. They change into their human form and dress in the clothes you laid out for them before joining you in the front room where you stand at the window.

Outside, the town sets fire to another witch.

Your sisters tell you about her. She was the woman who tended the public gardens. Some accused her of selling potions.

Others claimed she sold only cough syrup and tisanes. You barely knew the woman they speak of, but grief clenches your heart anyway.

Your sisters quibble about the rumours.

Once, all six of your sisters would visit you, but that number has dwindled down to two. Sometimes it comes as a surprise that you miss the chaos and noise of having all of your sisters together.

You return to your knitting. Your sisters continue to natter at each other while going through your pantry and eating what crumbs they find. You have so much you want to say, so much to ask—how are the others, do they remember who they are—but if you utter one word, you will lose them forever.

Eventually your sisters grow bored of bickering and begin to tell stories of the old days, of when you were all children playing together, braiding each other's hair—or pulling it.

This. This is the worst and best part. You need to hear these memories, these family stories. You need to remember why you're making your hands bleed—you need to hear it no matter how much it breaks your heart to remember how life once was, to hear the memories and not be able to share any of your own.

Their time with you is short as always. The spell only allows them to return to human form at midnight for a few hours. They go into your room, place the clothes on the bed and sneak out the window. You hear the flap of wings as they fly away. A distant cry lets you know they've rejoined the others on the river.

They believe they're saving you with their visits.

Maybe they are.

YOU WORKED ALL day to make the final shirt, taking as few breaks as possible to rest your raw, blistered hands. You're knitting faster than ever before, but all you have is a round, shapeless thing. Half a shirt with no sleeves. Even after all this time, your knitting skills are still basic at best.

At midnight, your sisters flutter in through the open window. They burst into the room before they are fully dressed. Something is wrong. The sun is screaming at you. The townspeople saw you in the graveyard. They're going to burn you. Do you see that? They think you're a witch now.

Your sister throws her hands up in frustration, kicks over a chair, slams her fists on the table. Her body rocks with soundless sobs; she throws herself onto the floor and weeps.

The other stands there, staring at you. Her silence is profound, stoic, and pressing against your ears. This sister knew all along this was hopeless.

You want to explain—the words form and re-form on your tongue. You clamp down on your teeth to keep them inside; you clench so hard your jaw aches, a headache forms, tears blur your vision.

It's taking everything you have to remain silent, to not explain. You want so badly to tell them it will be all right, you're nearly finished—

What have you done? What have you done? What have you done?

It should have been you. It should have been you turned to swan, wild child that you are, skipping your lessons, hating your sisters for their noise, for their perfect needlecrafts . . .

Tears run down your face, fall onto your hands, stinging them anew.

One shirt. One last shirt remains. Soon—so close to happily ever after.

It's not too late. It's not too late—

They flap and flutter out the window. You listen for their trumpet when they rejoin the others. You're up all night, knitting, waiting.

THE TOWNSFOLK COME for you in the morning, pulling you from the chair where you fell asleep knitting, waiting to hear the cry from your sisters that never came.

All that knitting. All those days and nights of bleeding, blistered hands. Hands so raw you couldn't sleep, couldn't hold a loaf of bread to feed yourself.

And the witch who saved you, who was stolen in the night from you. In the end, her help didn't matter. Her life didn't matter.

All for nothing.

You feel you owe her at least something, after all she did for you. So before these people lead you away from the cottage, you grab the five completed nettle shirts and the one you're still knitting. The townspeople don't object so long as you go quietly.

They lead you to the town square, and stand you on a platform. You continue to knit furiously while the people pile wood around you and the town crier reads out the laws against witchcraft—laws your stepfather brought to force shortly after you escaped the city with the witch.

The rustle of unfolded wings surrounds you and white feathers drift down like snow from the cerulean sky. One by one, six white swans land on the growing pile of wood, rising up and flapping their great wings, getting in the townspeople's way. The people try to shoo them off, swat them with sticks, but the six swans remain resolutely at their posts.

A swell of emotion rides through your heart. Your nostrils flare. Tears blur your vision. They came. You were so sure you'd never see them again, but here they are. Despite everything, they still believe they're saving you.

A torch is lit.

The shirt isn't quite finished, but you're out of time.

They're about to set all seven of you on fire.

You throw the shirts over your sisters, and one by one, they return to their human shape—the nettle shirt forming a feathery white dress around each of them—all but the last. The shirt you hadn't finished was missing an arm. One sister returns with a wing.

You failed her. This wouldn't have happened if you'd attended your needlecraft lessons. You both know it. You all know it. But no one seems to mind. They all laugh.

For the first time, you notice they all wear the same face. Your face. You don't know why you didn't see that before.

Your sisters wobble under their new legs like newborn fawns, but they stand. They grab you, and hands clasped, together you run.

Finally, with the spell broken, your voice is freed. All you can do is laugh as the wind blows through your hair, your memories return, and you begin to sing, "Ring around the rosy . . ."

The Sky Thief

Elise Forier Edie

YOU'RE RECORDING ALREADY?

Am I speaking too loud? I can never tell how loud I am. I lost my hearing.

Yes, it's about your article on Lori Lockheart. I called you because it was bullshit, and I felt you should know. "A divine and forgotten treasure," you wrote. "The Joan of Arc of feminist music." "There would be no Ani de Franco, Suzanne Vega, no Pink or Lady Gaga, without Lori Lockheart carrying the standard into battle before them."

No, I don't deny she had influence. "Cry in the Sky," was as resonant as Joni Mitchell's "Blue," in its way. And I don't deny Lori made a mark. But, original? Please. Every note she played, every word Lori Lockheart wrote was stolen. I know, because she tried to steal me. In the end, she lost her life. And I lost my voice.

I can see you're quite young. So you've only looked at old footage of Lori, in Monterey, or at Haight-Ashbury, am I right? Well. None of those films do her justice, anyway. No mere camera ever picked up what Lori Lockheart had. She sang, and you knew the meaning of the word "spellbound." I fell to my knees the first time I heard her.

It was in Beaumont, Texas, where I grew up. Not far from Janis Joplin yes, although we didn't know one another. What? Oh, it was utterly ghastly. Oil refineries everywhere. Horrendous, postwar American housing developments. Men with black fingernails, women in smudged aprons and high heels. Laundry hanging under hot skies. Air that always smelled of petrochemicals. So your sheets smelled too, of oily smoke. My earliest memories are of having to do those nuclear attack drills at school. You know, "the Russians are coming?" If you've ever wondered why the Sixties cultural revolution happened, look no further than those drills. You spend your whole childhood worrying about the end of the world, you're taking off all your clothes at Woodstock too, believe me.

By age fifteen, I knew everything about me was wrong. I had no other term for it. I didn't know what a lesbian was. I just knew I was poorly made. I had strange longings and not just to kiss cheerleaders. I was filled to the brim with yearning for adventure, fortune, undiscovered worlds. But I didn't know how to find that. I didn't even know where to begin. As a girl, growing up in the 1950s and early 60s, all I had ever learned to do was as other people told me. And they told me to be a servant and vessel for some man's children. I was groomed to wash some man's clothes and cook his meals. To sew housedresses with McCall patterns, and cut the crusts off of Wonder Bread sandwiches. And all through high school, I dutifully tried to achieve those goals, by wearing girdles and falsies, going to dances with earnest, damp-handed boys. But God!

By my senior year, I was thinking it might be a good idea to kill myself. And can you blame me?

But then I went to a concert at a local college.

In a sweaty hall with a thousand other people pressing elbows, I toppled head over heels for Lori Lockheart. I had never seen a woman—a human being, really—like that in my life. Barefoot, dressed like a gypsy, and hauling around a bone white lyre. She was like something from a book, or a dream.

Look at the skin on my arms. It just went to gooseflesh. That's what she did to me. To everyone. It's funny, isn't it? I had sung in church choirs my whole life, but it had never occurred to me until I heard Lori, that a human voice could inspire feelings of divine inspiration. When she sang "Three Fishers" and

"Lavender's Blue," everything I was and everything I wished for tangled together and trilled.

She finished her set with "The Sky Thief." You know that song? It's based on a myth. The usual story. A virgin goddess is tied up and raped by some selfish, lustful god. She bears him twin sons. But instead of being a good vessel, Aura was defiant. She smashed her children on the sea rocks.

"Never will I walk as myself again. Never will I sing as your leman. For my rage is like a wild, wild wind. And I am a vengeful demon. I will have my succour. And I will make you suffer." I could swear Lori's eyes met mine when she sang that. It was like being pierced by an arrow of pure joy. My legs shook. I crushed my plaid skirt in my fists. I sank to the floor. Well. I was just a girl. I didn't know anything.

Would you mind handing me the Kleenex? That box there. Thank you.

I went home that night, where my father was drinking beer on the couch and watching television, where my mother was hunched over her sewing beside him, and suddenly, suicide was no longer a consideration. Whatever was wrong with me, I felt like Lori's music had blown it away, like a good wind can blow away the stink of a refinery.

I bought a guitar with my babysitting money. I found a chord chart in a music book at school. I spent every hour I could practicing. And two years later, I scandalized the whole town by running away to New York City. What can I say? I was eighteen years old and my heart was on fire.

How many suicidal teenagers have been saved by a song? More than you think. More than you will ever know.

How I revelled in New York! Everything about that crazy city delighted me. Summer cloudbursts, honking horns, war protests, roaring subways. I was free as a lark, singing and playing my guitar at every open mic, in every Village dive that would have me. But I only ever played for an audience of one.

She was in the city somewhere, you see. I had read it in a magazine. So, every time I took a stool and tuned up, I imagined Lori Lockheart out in the shadowy audience, and I sang for her and her alone.

When people talked about those early performances of mine—and they did—everyone said I transported myself and my audience into another world. Well, I wasn't trying for that. I was just calling to Lori, calling for her to find me. I was that much in love.

The night it finally happened.

Excuse me. Something in my throat.

It was autumn. There was a bite to the air. The garbage bags piled up on the sidewalk for pick up all had dead leaves scattered on them. That night, I did a little set at a dive called "Delicate."

On those Village stages back then, the light always shone in my eyes so the audience looked like dark shapes mounded behind a haze of cigarette smoke. But I could feel them listening. And I heard the swell of applause after every song. When I finished my set, and stepped off the platform, passing through a veil of light into darkness, I was met by smiles.

I had to sidle through tables to get to the door, holding my guitar. It took a while. Some people wanted to speak to me. Fellow musicians gave me a wave. Near the back, a woman sat alone. She was dressed in a long black veil, like the old song. Do you know it? It's about a murderer. "She walks these hills in a long black veil. Visits my grave when the night winds wail."

Seeing her, I felt a chill scrabble down my spine. Her skirts must have been full of static electricity, because they reached out and clung to me as I squeezed past. She rose and touched my shoulder with one hand. Sparks popped between us.

"Wherever you're going, let me come with you," the dark lady whispered.

I was terrified. I almost ran out into the night. But once I slipped out the door and up the stairs to the sidewalk, I balled up my tips in my pocket and waited, guitar in hand for her to follow. I had to know. And minute or two later, when she eased up beside me, black skirts floating, I did. She pulled off her veil and it wasn't a gleaming skull, or a black void, like I'd imagined underneath. It was Lori Lockheart. She had finally come to me.

My dear. If something like that's never happened to you, if you've never had a dream come true, then all I can say is, God help you. God help you.

I might be standing there yet today, near Christopher Street, frozen by amazement, but Lori took my hand and everything inside me unlocked.

I could breathe.

I could weep.

I did both.

We walked through damp New York streets together, under golden leafed trees. It was beyond romantic. And when we wound up at her apartment, I put my guitar down in the hallway, and . . . Well.

Let us say at that point, I honestly didn't know two women could be that way. Lori showed me everything. And afterwards, she cooked me food, on a little two-burner stove. Later, sitting up in bed half-dressed, hair, thighs, and silk shawls a-tangle, we played music and sang. I don't know how long that went on. It was as if I fell down a faery tunnel and if someone told me Lori Lockheart had pleasured me for a hundred years and a day, I would have believed them. I would have said, "Yes, I know. We were in each other's arms forever."

But even then, she was laying her plans to destroy me. I should have guessed when I saw the altar. And beside it, Lori's beautiful lyre.

Of course, I didn't know it was an altar at the time. To my ignorant eyes, it looked like a shelf filled with beautiful bones, stones, and flowers, all artfully arranged amidst incense burners and pots of honey. But it was a witch's altar, decorated for Samhain, and ready for a sacrifice. That night, I knelt naked before it and touched the lyre.

Funny, isn't it? A homonym. Liar. Lyre. Even the word itself was trying to warn me.

A lyre's music conjures images of long ago, don't you think? Lords and ladies dancing the pavane perhaps, or peasants feasting by firelight. Lori Lockheart's was Celtic in style, ten-stringed, ivory white. You probably know its sound from her recordings. Unearthly, and with a strange resonance. When the white lyre's strings were plucked, it's almost like you heard another lyre inside it, playing counterpoint.

"What sort of wood is this?" I asked.

"White ironwood. Very old," Lori said.

"It feels more like stone than wood. It's so smooth, like a shell, a big shell." The lyre was so sensitive, it thrummed when I touched it, the strings playing along with the beat of my heart. Even when I drew away from it, it trilled, vibrating with my movements, like it was part of my flesh.

"The first lyre was a turtle shell. The Greek demigod Hermes gave it to his brother Apollo." Lori knelt beside me. Her hands plied my sides. "But leave that old thing alone. Let me make you sing instead, Clarissa." Her tongue circled my ear.

Well, I was young. And she played me very well. So, I let her seduce me in front of the altar, not knowing I was already part of a spell. The pots of honey poured on my body. The incense smoke that circled around us. The way Lori bit me gently in the thigh, causing exquisite pain. Even the lyre, tingling along with my pleasure, was part of Lori's magic. In the end, you couldn't tell the difference between its cries and mine.

You don't believe in witchcraft? It doesn't matter. Lori did. She had charms for everything. Protection, fortune, nourishment, love. And her music. Her music in and of itself was a charm.

But I didn't know that. I only knew I was living in a dream, and Lori was in it. By the following summer, I was part of her band and we were planning a European tour. My music career had begun to soar.

I had sold two songs. One was covered by a psychedelic flash-in-the-pan called The Marvelous Mystics. But the other one Judy Collins recorded, and it made the charts at number sixty-one.

I know, that doesn't sound like much, but for a girl from Beaumont, well! I was walking through the world swathed in a sort of shimmering curtain of wonder and gratitude. I had found my adventure. A gorgeous woman loved me. We sang and played folk music together on stages all over the coast. We went to parties in New York with Cat Stevens and Leonard Cohen. We were writing songs together, and planning to release our first album, "To the Gods of Sunlight and Song."

But there were warning signs. Here, I'll show you one.

This picture was taken when we were recording "Gods." Most of these people are session musicians from the Wrecking Crew. The guitarist is Carole Kaye. There's Hal Blaine by his drum kit. Next to him is me. And there's Lori, looking . . . diminished, yes. Old, really. And one can excuse it by saying we had been working night and day in the studio and practically living on amphetamines. But she looks so much dimmer than the rest of us. And while we're laughing and talking, her eyes are trained on something else. Can you guess what she's looking at? Yes, the lyre. It was propped in the corner, just out of the frame.

We had to stop early that day because Lori's voice had given out. She'd literally lost her breath, right in the middle of a song. It was very scary, the way she faltered and fell down, gasping and turning blue.

She told us not to worry. As a child she'd been asthmatic. The problem had been aggravated by New York pollution, and all those nights in smoke-filled coffee houses. But she was certain it would clear up, once we got to Europe. Fresh air and sunshine, Lori said that was all she needed.

Then shortly after, I heard the name Mar Laine . . .

I want you to picture a typical late Sixties loft party in New York, straight out of Andy Warhol. Music. Psychedelic lighting. Black light posters. Girls with spidery false eyelashes swaying on a dance floor. Boys in paisley shirts and striped pants circling them. Big windows looked out on city streets, all lit up with neon. It's so painful now to think how sophisticated we thought we were. We were children, all of us.

Anyway. I was one of those spider-eyed girls, with straight hair and a see-through blouse. But instead of swaying, I was sitting on the floor—everyone sat on the floor, dear me, we thought we were so anti-Establishment in those days—and I was talking with a nice man named Tom Flatwort. He had rust-coloured sideburns and gold-rimmed John Lennon glasses. He was an old friend of Lori's and one of her favourite beards. I mean he was homosexual too, and needed to hide it. It was illegal back then, did you know? We all had to pretend to be straight to stay out of jail. So, when we went out, Tom would escort Lori. One of his lovers would escort me. And we'd all go home together and pair off the way we wanted. A mutually beneficial arrangement.

Anyway, Tom must have been a little drunk that night, because at one point in the conversation, he started calling me "Mar." And finally I said, "Clarissa! Okay? My name's Clarissa. Who's Mar?"

He blinked and got very apologetic. He told me Mar was a girl Lori had been with, before me. "You remind me of her," he said. "She sang the same way. Clear as a bell. And drew you in, the same way you do. She had a light. A presence."

Well! I barely heard his compliments, because I didn't enjoy being told I was "like" anyone. At that time in my life, I wanted to be unequalled. "Like" another girl? Immediately, I pressed Tom for details. What had happened to Mar Laine? Where was she?

He hedged, but I pried it out eventually. Mar and Lori had begun their love affair in boarding school, while they were still teenagers. After graduation, she and Lori ran away to Europe. And while adventuring there, Mar Laine had drowned in Greece. She was twenty, the exact same age as I.

"Just horrible, right?" Tom's eyes were bloodshot, his head drooped. "But maybe a blessing in disguise. After the accident, that's when Lori got serious about her music. Like she channelled all her grief into art. She came back from Europe with that lyre and . . . well, the rest is history."

Oh, that story made me furious. I was such a jealous idiot. Poor Mar Laine was long gone, but I sulked like I had caught her and Lori in a closet with their hands up each other's skirts. Why had Lori never mentioned her? Did she still love her?

I had to find out. But I didn't ask Lori. Instead, I spent two days at the New York Library uncovering terse newspaper articles, that only answered half my questions. Mar had died on one of those obscure islands in the Mediterranean. A desolate place, where there's nothing at all to see but a ruined temple, dedicated to some long-forgotten Greek deity, crumbling in the dried grass, atop a cliff. Maybe a hundred fisherman and their families. Dozens of cats. That's all. Mar Laine had gone down to the beach one night and poof.

They never found her body. But everyone assumed she went swimming and died.

Yes, I too saw the connection right away. "Carry Me," that first album of Lori's, is full of dying girls, isn't it? And storms, blowing things to pieces. "Zephyr," "The Swan's Mistress," "The Sky Thief." It's all a confession too, every note of it. You just have to listen. The coda to "Carry Me," for instance. "Hark, hark, the dying lark. Fie, fie, her bones do cry. She weeps for thee. While she curses me. Carry me. Carry me. And drop me in the water."

Listen to the album again, and listen to those lyre overtones. You'll hear it, too. There's another song altogether, singing underneath the recording. Like two different meanings, a liar and a lyre. It's the same story told again and again, a woman enraged, a lover murdered, a curse delivered, a baby killed, over and over, like some madwoman's muttering. Once you hear it, it's quite disturbing, like listening to a murderer's confession.

But back then, I was too trusting of Lori—or too jealous of Mar Laine—to see the pattern. The way Lori would get in her cups, and talk about a deal she made with herself, that she would change the world with her singing, that her fame and fortune would know no bounds, that she would do whatever it took to make it. Over and over, she said it. "No price in this world too high for art. I would kill for it, to be just that much better."

Hold on. I'm fine. I'm almost at the end.

Before we left for our European tour, there was one other significant occurrence. One night, I awoke and thought I heard Lori whispering to someone else in the other room. I heard her say, "I don't want to replace you. But I must." She sounded as if she might be crying.

Of course, I rose and ran to her. But I found her alone, curled on the floor with that lyre. "I thought I heard you talking."

"Who would I talk to?" Lori, who could hold thousands of people transfixed by her voice, was speaking so softly, I could barely make out the words. I was suddenly afraid again, like that night I met her in the long black veil.

"Come here." She held out her hand. The lyre chimed with her words, tingling and thrumming, because she was holding it tightly against her breasts. Lori's heart was racing and the lyre was singing with it. I knelt by her side.

"I love music," she whispered.

"I do, too."

"And I love you. I love your voice. It reminds me of someone I knew."

"It does?" Now my heart was racing, too. Two hearts fluttering like birds in the room. Was she finally going to tell me about Mar Laine?

"Yes. She loved life. She loved me." I waited for her to tell me more, but all she said was, "Do you love me, Clarissa?"

"Of course."

"Would you ever leave me?"

209

"Why would I have to?"

"Exactly." The lyre trilled. "You don't. Not ever, darling."

There was a neon sign outside out the window of the apartment, and the light it cast turned her face a deep pink, and then blue. It was beautiful and hallucinatory. And all the time she spoke, or breathed, the lyre played.

When I woke the next day, I thought the whole thing might have been a dream. I remembered a beautiful red-haired girl being with us in that room. And while Lori wept, and asked if I loved her, this girl had sung, "The Sky Thief."

"My name is in the wind's wild cry. The storm that sears down from the sky. Say it, and you'll suffer. But I will have my succour.

"Say my name, Clarissa," the girl had told me in my dream. "Say my name and you won't have to die."

After that, we went to Europe.

I have only two things to say about that tour. One is "amphetamines." I don't know how we would have done it without them. The second is, "remarkable," because, you know, London, Paris, Amsterdam, Brussels, Berlin.

Ancient churches. Real castles. Misty mountains, straight out of Tolkien. The sounds of church bells on Sundays. Footsteps echoing through cobbled streets. Trying to learn "thank you," and "excuse me," in twelve different languages. Eating pasta and pastries and drinking bottles of good wine, from every country.

For a girl from Beaumont Texas, it was nothing short of a miracle.

But all of us were gaunt and exhausted after ten or twelve weeks. Lori began to look positively skeletal. Towards the end, she couldn't sing at all. Her asthma flared along with some kind of respiratory infection. I sang all her numbers the last few weeks of that tour. No, I really did. There's a live recording from Dublin somewhere. You can check if you like. I sang every note. Lori didn't have the strength. And no one complained, by the way. By then, my voice was better than hers, clearer and more powerful.

We finished our tour in Rome. I saw the Coliseum by myself because Lori was too ill. I begged her to go back to the States, hole up in New York, see a doctor, or many doctors. But she said we had earned a holiday. She wanted to go to Greece. There was a little island she knew of, with only a few hundred people and a forgotten shrine. "I'll get better there. I just need fresh air and rest," she told me.

Well, I would do anything she asked. And anyway, I wanted to see the place where Mar Laine had died.

Of course I thought it was strange! Of all the thousands of places in the world where Lori could rest—why would she want to go to the island where her lover had died? But I couldn't separate what I wanted from her wants. Who was I without Lori Lockheart?

So Greece, yes, all lovely, hot, and quiet. White and indigo buildings climbed sheer cliffs. Sagebrush bristled all around brown hills. Silence nestled everywhere, on the beach, and in the blazing white pillars of the ruined shrine. No one on the whole island spoke a word of English. When we wanted food in a restaurant, Lori and I had to go into the steamy kitchens, and point at fish and grape leaves and slabs of white cheese on the countertops.

In the few pubs and groceries we frequented, I would sometimes get sidelong glances and hear whispers from the dark-eyed proprietors. I didn't know what anyone was saying. Still, I'm pretty sure they were whispering about Mar Laine. An American girl disappearing on their island. It must have been a memorable event. Surely they recognized Lori. But if she noticed the whispers, Lori didn't let on. And she never mentioned to me that she'd been on that island before.

It was odd, I agree. But we were making love in the sparkling blue ocean. We lay twined and naked in the sun every afternoon. And at night, after bathing, we saw stars like sand grains, scattered all over the sea and sky. It was beautiful. I could have been so happy.

But Lori still couldn't catch her breath.

We slept, and read and wrote songs. Lori wrote hers in a sheepskin notebook that she tied with twine. One day while she was dozing, I peeked inside. The songs she was writing were gruesome, sad. Orpheus, stopping time with his songs, but left loveless. Leda wishing she could fly. One ballad was based on the Grimms' story, "The Singing Bones."

Do you know it? It's about a man who killed his brother to

win a princess. But when the dead boy's bones were made into a horn, it trumpeted the song of his death and the bad brother was executed for his crimes.

While I was reading that one, a little breeze blew up and the lyre's strings vibrated and sang. Lori awoke.

"What are you doing?" She snatched at the notebook.

"I was curious is all. Will you play them for me?"

She looked at the lyre, still shrilling. "I was waiting. What day is it?"

When I told her, she said, "Then it's time."

"Time for what?"

"Time for music, Clarissa."

Lori told me she wanted to play her songs at the ruined temple, at the top of the cliffs. I thought it a strange idea. She was still weak, and the hike to the temple was not easy. But Lori thought it would be fun. She wanted to debut her new ballads in a rustic setting, she said. The moonlight would give an aspect to the stones that the light of day did not offer. The stars and wind would be her first audience. As always, I did as she asked.

If you've ever seen Apollo's temple in Delphi, you have an idea of what this ruin was like. Tumbled white rocks, pale, broken pillars thrusting up out of the earth, and golden grasses all around. Everything there was somehow more lovely, more sacred because of its decay.

In the daytime, there were birdsongs and insects on those cliffs. But at night, the ruin was like a church, solemn and silent. We walked up the hill slowly. Lori carried her lyre. How the sky sparkled above! And the ocean thrummed distant below. When we reached the shrine and stepped together onto some whitened remnants of old stone wall, the hairs on the back of my neck rose.

Lori turned to me. Wind caught her skirts. She had the white lyre slung on her shoulder. "Did I ever tell you I found my lyre here, in this very place?" She hadn't, of course. Lori had told me nothing of Mar Laine, or of Greece. She had only ever lied about the lyre. Now she strummed it and said, "It was like it was waiting for me. Here on these rocks. This sweet sound."

I looked at the lovely desolation all around. There were no trees from which to make a lyre. "Someone left it behind? Another musician?"

"You could say that."

My heart began to hammer. "Who? Who left it?"

"You shall meet her soon. Listen, Clarissa." There was a sound pulsing, pulsing. Because Lori was holding the lyre and the lyre was singing. Breezes blew through its strings. Lori's heartbeat made a bell-like rhythm. "Do you love me?" she asked.

"You know I do."

"And will you always make music with me?"

"If you wish it, until the world ends."

"I wish it. I want you to never leave me. I want your voice with me forever."

Her hair streamed in the wind as she bent her head and whispered something. And that's when the sky cracked to pieces behind her.

Well, I have no other way to put it. It was like a big rock had been flung through a giant window glass that broke the very stars. And out of the void left behind, she came.

I was an ignorant girl. You understand? I had barely finished high school. I had grown up in Beaumont, Texas. I knew nothing. Still, even if I'd been thoroughly grounded in Greek mythology and history, I wouldn't have recognized that thing for what it was.

In the fifty years since, I've looked at statues, paintings, reliefs, mosaics. Artists who depict the goddess of breezes always show a glorious woman of great beauty. And perhaps you could call that creature beautiful, if a hurricane or a tornado is beautiful. You see a hundred-foot high spiral of wind churning above a cornfield, maybe you think, "That's gorgeous. Nature surging in all its wild strength." Maybe. But more likely you are running for your life. Because that tornado is going to kill you. And up close, it won't be beautiful at all. It will be mindless and merciless, and filled with corpses. It will engulf you, strip you and grind you to powder while you scream.

Aura was angry. Aura was hungry. And Aura was coming for me.

There was no time to ask any questions. How Lori knew she was there. How Lori knew how to call her. I've thought about it since, endlessly. Who knows? It might have even been an accident with Mar. Two girls went to a deserted temple for a night of moonlit sacrilege. They stripped and sported and afterwards sang to the stars. Perhaps the echoes of ancient rites accidentally awakened a goddess. Aura appeared, ravenous for a sacrifice. A life was demanded. A blessing was given in return. A blessing of breath. A voice to charm the world.

But I suspect Lori knew all along about magic. And what sort of sacrifices Aura might demand.

The goddess's mouth was like a giant hole in the sky, full of razor-sharp teeth, bright as icicles. Around those teeth, great, midnight wings flapped, freezing the air down to the ground. Pinned by her gaze, I fell back and beat my hands and feet on the ground, in some horrid parody of ecstasy. I could feel my life streaming out of my body as the goddess sucked away my very breath.

I could not speak, or swallow. And through it all, Lori sang, her voice growing stronger and stronger. She sang while Aura lifted me in the air, high above the cliffs. In her arms of splintering cold, I still heard Lori singing. And her bone white lyre sang counterpoint.

"For my rage is like a wild, wild wind. And I am the vengeful demon."

What we do to one another. What we do. You called Lori Lockheart "the Joan of Arc of feminist music." A standard bearer for sisterhood. But she would sell her sisters, I tell you, before she would stand with them. She was no better than those shitty old gods, who snuck behind their wives and raped defiant women. Took their succour, then sprouted wings and flew away, free as birds.

Aura pressed her icicle teeth to my body and still Lori sang, urging her to destroy me, so she could live longer with the blessings of a goddess, so she could sing and bring the multitudes to their knees.

Look. Here is the scar. Right over my womb. It looks like an appendix scar, but it isn't. That's her teeth in my belly. I would be eaten and dashed on the cliff rocks like a wingless bird, except as Aura pierced me, I remembered my dream. The redheaded girl with the neon-lit face. I realized Mar Laine had tried to warn me. She had told me to say her name. And so, as Aura prepared to smash me to pieces, I screamed so loud my throat bled. And Mar answered me with her bones.

Yes. The lyre. Not made from white ironwood, or even a shell. The lyre had been fashioned from Mar Laine's bones. It sang with Mar Laine's sweet, sweet voice. It stayed with Lori forever, and thrummed with her heart.

At the sound of Mar's scream, the goddess dropped me. I fell on the grass, instead of the cliff's rocks.

Hard earth drove into me and I felt things break inside.

Just before I lost consciousness, I thought I saw Aura reach with her night clad arms and pick up Lori. She hovered, while Lori thrashed like a bird in a net. As blackness engulfed me, I heard her flesh spatter, her spine snap. Those were the last sounds I ever heard.

The hearing loss, yes. Doctors say it was a blow to the head. From the sudden tornado on those cliffs in Greece. A wind picked us both up and slammed us down. One of us died and one of us lived. Neither of us ever sang again.

The lyre? I don't know what happened to it. Maybe it was crushed along with Lori. Maybe Aura took it, when she stormed back out of this world having taken her succour. Maybe it is propped in the corner of a Greek fisherman's hut. I went back to look for it, when I healed enough to walk again. But I never found it. So I can't prove it was made from the bones of Mar Laine. But I believe Aura took Mar's life and breath. I believe, she gave Lori something in return. A magic lyre and a blessing, perhaps. A voice to hold the world transfixed. But it didn't last. And when Lori started to lose her voice, she thought she'd repeat the spell and maybe take mine, too.

Come now. You know perfectly well people sell their souls, their love, their integrity, all to make things of great beauty. Why did you think Lori was any different? There's a price for fame and fortune, my dear. She was willing to pay it with blood. My blood. Mar's blood. So none of that music was hers! Lori built her fame on strings fretted on her lover's bones. Sisterhood, my ass. She would have sold her sisters in a minute. And I would, too. After all, I offered up Lori to save my own skin.

What we do to one another. What we do.

I suppose if I'd died that night, she would have kept on singing. Yes. Who knows what other remarkable things she might have played? But I loved my life. And even voiceless, I have loved it. I robbed the world of Lori Lockheart.

We take and we give, even as we breathe don't we? You say that's a shame, my dear, and maybe it is. But would you kill me for more of her music? Would you have me dead for one more song?

Late Tuesday

Oliver Smith

The forecast said 'weather fair and sunny',
so my Aunt served tea to the self-made widows
among potted palm trees on the balcony,
where they sheltered beneath umbrellas
debating the finer points of necromancy.

In her cup she stirred a whirlpool of Earl Grey
and cast her evil eye over prophetic leaves.
She called "get up Nephew—we need more tea."
Outside I found another season haunting
what should be a sky-blue summer-Thursday.

I feared a grimmer day had come undone:
its stars unfinished, its sunset a poor thing,
or it had committed some deadlier sin,
and so been condemned to walk again beyond
the grave, not knowing the rest of better days.

In the corner store I asked my friend, Mr K,
who said "the old times are dead and gone."
A thorough materialist, he did not believe
that time could hold spirits like a bottle.
"You cannot decant the past into the future."

Spectral drizzle fell on the canned goods
contradicting him. This was similar
in texture to the rain of Tuesday-last;
it poured in thin streams wetting the beans
and Full-English-Breakfasts-in-a-Tin.

K was wrong: the past is a leaky barrel
of Malmsey tainted by an essence
disturbingly reminiscent of the corpse
of my Aunt's dead lover hidden three years
earlier in the cellar by my late Uncle.

The ghost of Tuesday's smile played
across K's face while an insubstantial
customer idly browsed the spectral wine.
Outside, a ghostly number twelve bus met itself
(running late) halfway down the high street.

It stopped and disgorged my Uncle in a winding sheet.
Back home, this untimely manifestation waited
with an ostentatious hatpin impaling his heart
and groaned showily among the potted plants.
But even in death he was ignored by my Aunt.

Wind Song

Sarah Van Goethem

A Smudge of Something in the Air

Letty Ashdown plucked off one of her lace gloves and attacked a fingernail with her teeth. She could barely breathe she was so taut with anticipation, though to be fair, that could've been partially due to her too-tightly laced whale-bone corset, an irony that didn't escape her.

The driveway to Stone Sparrow Inn was studded with carriages, including their own, carrying her father, her stepmother, and herself. Everything was wrapped in an eerie mist that had descended with dusk, and Letty peered through it, searching under the gas lamps for a familiar face. Every crinoline and top hat for twenty miles was surely here, all clamouring toward a memorable evening of folk music, lobster, and bittersweet farewells to the sailors.

If Letty had her way, she would not be saying good-bye, not this time. She would disappear into the fog, leaving behind scandalous whispers on lips, all surely instigated by her stepmother. It'd started already; the critical looks, the pressed lips, the muttered word, *siren*.

Her stepmother made a sound of disgust, and then, "Violetta, for heaven's sakes, stop chewing your nails. It's unsightly, and incredibly nauseating."

Heat prickled along Letty's collarbone, but she did her best to ignore the woman and instead ripped off a hangnail with fervour, tasting blood. Another minute, that was all, and she could escape the stifling carriage and her stepmother's disapproval.

Harriet Ashdown nudged her husband in the ribs, unwilling to let it go. "Tell your daughter, no gentleman likes a woman who chews her nails to the quick."

Letty didn't often respond to the criticisms; she didn't think Harriet worth her time, and besides, she'd found other more productive ways to deal with her stepmother's constant attacks. But her own impatience combined with Harriet's scowl proved to loosen her tongue this evening. "It hardly matters what my hands look like if they are to be covered in ridiculous gloves every waking moment."

Harriet, quite unused to being opposed openly, gasped. "Did you hear that, Arthur? The impertinence . . . and after I had those gloves especially made."

For yourself, Letty thought. *But your fingers were too pudgy.*

Letty often wished her inside voice was more outside when it came to Harriet. But there was only one person she could talk freely with, and that person was not in the carriage.

Reluctantly, Letty slid her glove back on, slowly and with purpose. She hated the way it itched her inner arm and especially loathed the embroidered spray of flowers in coloured silk that adorned the backside. Flowers were a reminder of her stepmother's nitpicking, and worse, of the things she left unsaid, if it was even plausible to believe that anything in the woman's head could remain unspoken. Letty knew first-hand though; Harriet was fluent in a whole other language of silent disapproval. A nosegay of yellow carnations left on Letty's vanity meant disdain and a tussie-mussie of soft pink peonies at the dinner table meant anger. Letty knew all the meanings, straight from Harriet's floriography book in the parlour. There was no mistaking her stepmother's intent.

Determined to even the score, Letty had recently left her own not-so-discreet messages: drawings of ships, stormy oceans, and rugged bluffs with pointed, dangerous edges. And always the faint smudge of something in the air, something wild and dancing in the wind, with hair the colour of rust, unmistakably like her own, and wings, a blur of downy feathers, just barely seen.

Even now, Letty could feel Harriet's shrewd eyes on her as Letty continued to fuss with the detestable glove, and Letty knew her stepmother's mind was turning, wondering. Questioning everything she thought she knew about her stepdaughter. Going over everything that had transpired in the past few months.

Letty fanned herself; it was far too hot in the carriage for gloves, not to mention corsets and crinolines and layers of petticoats and stepmothers who could make you sweat in the cold of winter. *What conclusion have you come to, stepmother?* Letty thought, and she had the distinct impression she was fanning not herself, but a fire.

The rumours and gossip and old legends weren't enough. Letty wanted more. Letty wanted Harriet to actually believe her own gossip, to *know* it in her bones.

Letty cast a coy glance at her father, making sure Harriet saw it. Then, she hummed a little under her breath, a quiet lullaby, one she often sung under her own window at night, while the waves lapped gently against the shore. It was an old folksong her mother had taught her. It caught her father's attention, softening the lines in his face.

Harriet pursed her lips, latching onto her husband's arm. "You did hear what your daughter said to me, right Arthur? You haven't gone deaf, have you?"

Her father blinked, dazed, and Letty swallowed down a giggle at how perfectly his response suited her needs. "Indeed, I did, dear." Her father paused, drawing out the moment, searching, Letty knew, for the conversation that he'd dismissed. Finally, it came to him. "Letty makes a good point. No one will see her hands,"—her father winked at her over Harriet's head—"after all, she's a proper lady, *with gloves.*"

Letty was glad of the dark to hide the pink bloom in her cheeks.

Harriet's nostrils flared as their carriage pulled up to the front of the inn. "So, you're *not* going to do anything about your daughter's dreadful behaviour?"

The door swung open and Letty sucked greedily at the damp air that rolled in from the ocean. It was considerably cooler outside and she could practically taste the saltwater, and a new life, already.

"Of course I am, dear." Arthur Ashdown got out first and helped his wife down from the carriage. "In fact, I intend to find her a respectable husband this very evening."

Letty stiffened.

Harriet craned her neck around to look at Letty, a smug smile plastered on her face. "How wonderful. I do believe that's exactly what she needs."

Letty knew what Harriet meant. She'd heard Harriet's voice echoing through the plaster walls, night after night. *Letty needs to settle. Letty needs to be tamed. Letty is flighty, given over to her whims. Young single women are not to be trusted on their own. It's dangerous, Arthur. Scandalous.*

For Harriet's benefit, Letty flapped her arms a little as she got out, as if she may fly away into the inky sky instead of enter the inn. She was half-bird, after all, wasn't she? She jumped down from the carriage without waiting for her father's hand, and for a moment she remembered when she was little, when she'd swung out above the water on a rope swing and let go. The delicious feeling of being airborne, of flying.

Sometimes, in her sleep, she flew. Arms like wings. Long and feathered. She skimmed the land and then zoomed out over the wide blue stretch of water, as far as she could go. As far as her voice would carry.

She landed with a jolt on the ground, her boots pinching her feet. For good measure, she gave her head an extra jerk sideways, knowing full well it would cause Harriet to fret.

And right on cue, "Oh, for heaven's sakes." Harriet reached over and fiddled with the yellow rosebuds that trimmed the rolls of Letty's coiffure. "Your flowers are wilting. How you manage to ruin everything—"

Harriet sucked in a breath, pulling back. Pinched between her fingers was a small white feather, the very thing Letty had intended for her to find.

Letty feigned interest in smoothing her skirts, pretending she hadn't seen, and her father was oblivious, in conversation with the carriage driver. Harriet spun around abruptly, as if giving up altogether on Letty, and shook the feather away, trembling. It twisted and caught in the light breeze and drifted away into the dark. Letty patted her handbag; she had plenty more. *Plenty*.

"Shall we?" her father asked, finally, as the carriage creaked away.

Harriet linked her arm through Arthur's, shoulders tight, lips drawn into a thin line. She made no attempt to shield her voice, though Letty thought she could hear a discernible difference in Harriet's tone. Less steady than before, less sure of herself. "You mark my words, Arthur, that daughter of yours will spoil any marriage match you attempt to make."

Letty trailed them to the double front doors, somewhat satisfied; she'd seen the fear in Harriet's eyes when she'd plucked out the feather. The shudder that had run through her.

Harriet had something right, at least. Letty would indeed ruin any marriage prospect her father suggested, unless it was Jack Hawk, whaler aboard the *Orca*.

DREDGING UP OF the Past

The *Orca* had returned to the cove in July, a few months past. Letty had been traipsing along the hilltop, the sun hot on her shoulders, singing to herself, when she'd spied it in the distance. She'd quickly run inside of the house and claimed her father's oldest instrument—the lute—and hurried down the sloping hillside.

What had made her do it? The thought still came to her often, unbidden. *What had possessed her that day?*

Townsfolk were gathering on the beach, Letty remembered it clearly. They were whooping and shouting, excited by the returning ship. Letty hadn't joined them. Instead she'd quietly arranged herself on an outcropping of jagged rock, meticulously tucking seagull feathers into her hair. When she was ready, she had picked up the lute and played another of the songs her mother had taught her. Her favourite one. The Wind Song.

She'd sung.
I'll sing you a song,
I'll lure you home,
I'll bring you back from the sea.
My voice in the air,

Is all that is fair,
It'll bring you back to me.

THE TOWNSFOLK HAD gone quiet, Letty recalled. The men dreamy-eyed. The women crossing themselves and hiding their children behind their skirts. Harriet Ashdown had stood at the front of the crowd, arms crossed over her ample bosom, slack-jawed.

That had been the start of it, Letty acknowledged. The dredging up of the past, the uncovering of the old stories that had simmered just beneath the surface. That had been the day she'd given her stepmother cause, for once.

But Letty had sung on, welcoming the *Orca* into the harbour. She'd had to; there was something inside of her, something that had sparked and flickered and then blazed into existence. Her voice had carried on the wind, echoing out across the water in a way that made her feel powerful. Alive.

That night, the stories had begun to circulate around the celebration fire, when they thought Letty had gone. When they thought she couldn't hear or see. When they thought the dark hid their faces and their words.

Violetta Ashdown, my stepdaughter, a harpy, Harriet had whispered, starting it, and it had flowed through the crowd like the moonshine.

No, a siren, a young man corrected, swaying a little, a goofy smile on his face. *Beautiful. Seductive.*

Maybe both, people had said. *Maybe both.*

In the end, after a debate, they'd settled on siren.

There'd been signs before, hadn't there? a widow had asked, her face more radiant, younger, in the firelight. *Have you seen her feet? Always barefoot, and scaly. No lie. And why doesn't she play the piano or the violin or the flute like the other girls? Why an old lute, a relic from days bygone?*

A precocious little girl had peeked out from her mother's skirts, mouth working, unable to stay silent, unable to sleep. *And why all the feathers always caught in her hair?*

She has a point. She has a point.

And the elders, when finally asked, when poked and prodded for their wisdom, had spun a tale of yesterday. *Her mother was the same you know. The songs. Her voice over the water.* Then, a pause, a lowering of voices. A secret, forgotten, uprooted from the grave. *That's what happened to the* Wind Song, *you know. Crashed herself into the rocks, and not a thing to blame . . . except the singing.*

And then someone younger had asked, *Was that the ship's name? Truly? The* Wind Song?

A flutter of a bony hand in dismissal. *Oh, well no, it was something else,* The Red Swan, *or* Red Raven, *yes that was it.* Red Raven. *But . . . The* Wind Song, *now that's poetic, isn't it?*

Yes, yes, so romantic, so much better, the townsfolk had all agreed. And then, more solemn, a wife of one of the men recently returned, *At least* The Orca *made it to shore safely. That's something.*

Thank God it didn't perish on the jagged rocks.

Yes, or become beached on a non-existent sandbar.

An old man had agreed, puffing on his pipe, his voice guttural. *Yes, that's something all right.*

And the sailors, all of them unharmed, a plain-faced young woman had said, hands placed haughtily on her hips. *Not a one lured in by her song.*

Yes, yes, everyone had murmured. *Not a one. Not a one.*

MEET ME ON **the Widow's Walk**

Well maybe just one, Letty thought, scanning the crowd in the gleaming foyer. People were mingling everywhere in the inn, both those who were travelling guests and those who had lived in the cove their whole pathetic lives, like herself, and were only here for dinner. The chandeliers sparkled overhead, reflecting off the gilded mirrors and the shining damask-carved wood and, Letty noted with a wry smile, her father's bald head.

All around, Letty drew curious looks. *Siren,* she imagined the women were saying behind their fans and gloves. *Siren,* the men murmured, sipping their scotch.

Siren, siren, siren.

A prim-looking waiter ushered her father and Harriet into the dining room, but Letty hung back, hot and distracted.

"I need to use the powder room," she said.

The waiter pointed. "Far side of the lobby, to the right of the second staircase."

"Thank you."

Her father's brows furrowed. "Don't be long, I'd like you to meet someone."

How incredibly unlikely, Letty thought. *Poor Father, trying so hard.* Out loud, she promised, "No more than a few minutes, Papa."

A lie.

Harriet eyed the clock on the far wall, waggling her fingers in greeting to another woman whose gaze burned into Letty. "Three minutes, Violetta," she warned. "No more."

Oh, do just be quiet for once, you old Church Bell, Letty thought. *You can shove your three minutes straight up your bustle.*

When they disappeared into the ambience of the gaslit dining room, Letty ignored the stares she continued to gather and headed to the front windows. Pushing aside the lace curtains that hung beside the heavy brocade, she peered into the drive. Carriages were still arriving, along with a slew of sailors on foot, but she didn't see Jack.

Where was he?

There was a tap on her shoulder, and Letty jumped. "Mistress Ashdown?" The young messenger was all knees and elbows and business, practically shaking with nerves (at being this close to a *real siren*, she could only assume) and was unaware that he'd startled her.

Letty recovered quickly. "What is it then?"

"Delivery, miss." The boy held out a lanky arm, clutching a bouquet of deep red roses.

Letty was momentarily stunned, and gaped at the crimson flowers. *What was the meaning of this?* Letty cast a glance at the dining room, but quickly realized it wasn't Harriet. Harriet would send delphiniums, hydrangeas, or oleander, messages that said *beware.* Not messages of love. If Harriet sent red roses, she'd send them upside down, to mean the opposite, to imply Letty would never find love. If it wasn't her stepmother, it had to be—

"Jack." Letty ripped the roses from the boy's hand, only realizing after she'd done so, that it was the right hand the boy had extended, right for *yes.*

Jack was saying yes!

Letty bounced on her toes.

She sent the boy away with two lines of a song sung into his ear alone, that left him bewildered and grinning, and then searched the bouquet, finding what she wanted. A small note was tucked into the centre.

Meet me on the widow's walk.
J.

SING FOR ME Again, Siren Girl

Letty had first met Jack the night the *Orca* had docked.

While the townsfolk had hooted and danced and drunk themselves stupid, and finally turned to another topic other than Letty being a siren, Letty had dragged herself to the mouth of a small cave, and listened to them from afar. She'd never fit in, with her flaming hair and her uninhibited ways, and she'd sung softly to herself, thinking of the mother she'd never known.

Fools, she'd thought again later, still thinking of the story of the doomed ship, of the woman who'd single-handedly entangled it with her magical song. They'd mixed it all up, giving the ship the name of her mother's song. How their stories were stretched and altered, distorted to suit themselves. How they loved a good story, no matter how it was attained. No matter how much it needed twisting.

Perhaps I should change my own story, Letty had thought quite suddenly, and she'd found the idea to be so tempting, she'd started with the song. The words had come easily, and she'd sung them with an intensity she hadn't known herself to possess before.

I'll sing you a song,
And you'll take me away,
You'll take me out to sea.
My voice in the air,
Is a beautiful prayer,
As I sail away with thee.

NO ONE COULD hear her, or so Letty had thought.

Until a shadow had darkened the cave entrance not long after. She'd never forget that first glimpse of Jack, a dark silhouette against the stark white of the moon.

He'd plunked himself down beside her, without invitation,

and his features had eventually materialized as her eyes adjusted. His sinewy arms, the sharp angle of his cheekbones, his wide mouth.

Oh, how many times she'd kissed that mouth since.

Letty had known from the first words he'd said to her, *well, hello there, siren girl,* that she had to make him hers. It was the way he'd laughed, straight from his belly, mocking not her, but them, the townsfolk, the tales they had told on the beach. *Sing for me again, Siren girl, won't you?*

Siren girl.

It had a nice ring to it, like the *Wind Song.*

Maybe I will, she'd said. *Or maybe I won't.*

Oh you will, Siren girl.

He'd been so sure of himself, of her, of the two of them together. It had become her pet name by which he called her, first teased and tested, then petted, and finally breathed into her ear for the rest of the summer as she'd soared above him.

Her Beautiful Bittersweet Song

Letty hurried up the right side of the two massive curved staircases and stood at the top, three stories later, panting. When she caught her breath, she swept down the dim hall, leaving the drone of the guests, all lemmings headed to dinner, behind her. Finally, she found what she wanted—another narrow winding staircase leading to the roof.

At the top, she pushed open the door and stepped into the cupola.

Arms encircled her from behind and there was the smell of rum and something woody and spicy. "There's my siren girl."

Letty spun around, dropping the bouquet of roses beside the satchel on the floor. She wrapped her arms around Jack's neck. "You said yes."

"Of course, I did." Jack cocked his head, listening to the sounds below, then directed her toward the door and out onto the railed platform, where they were completely alone, shrouded in the fog. The air was cool, raising gooseflesh on her arms. "It's not customary for a woman to propose to a man," he murmured, pulling her close again, into his warmth. "And really? A formal message on parchment with your father's seal? Shameful. Whatever shall I do with you, Violetta Ashdown?"

"Marry me?" Letty suggested, feigning innocence.

Waves licked the shore, a soft sound, and the moon was high in the sky, giving the mist in the air an ethereal quality. It was the perfect night to sail away with Jack Hawk, just like in her song. The way she'd attracted him in the first place.

Letty inhaled. "What is it you smell like?"

"It's from the West Indies, bay leaf and spices." Jack nuzzled her neck, hands roaming.

Letty leaned her head back, with a contented sigh. "I cannot wait to leave."

Jack paused, a hand hovering over her bodice. "Leave?"

"Yes, tonight," Letty said slowly. "Together."

Jack pulled away, studying her. "*I* will be leaving tonight. We will be married when I return."

Letty shook her head, brushing a thumb over Jack's bottom lip. She'd known she'd have to explain. It was hard to get things through men's thick skulls sometimes, especially when it was out of the ordinary. "No . . . we will be married *tonight* darling . . . and I will accompany you. At sea."

Jack laughed nervously, shook her off, then moved to stand by the railing as if it were somehow safer there. "Certainly not. No women aboard. The *Orca* is not a hen frigate, Letty."

"There are *already* women aboard." Letty had prepared herself with facts, and she was ready to list them, quite calmly. "There's Eleanor Mayhew."

"The Captain's wife!"

"And Caroline Abbey, on the *Narwhal*."

"Again—a Captain's daughter. This is not happening, Letty."

Jack was so resolute, so unyielding.

Letty's composure buckled. Her temper flared. She ripped the dreadful gloves off and tossed them over the balcony, watching them flutter and disappear. Then, she attacked the roses in her hair, ripping at them. "I will disguise myself as a boy, then. Is that preferable to you?"

"You will do no such thing." Jack snatched her hands, holding her still. "You will be my wife—when I return."

Letty raised her chin, determined. "I will not be your wife, unless you take me *with* you."

"You don't mean that."

No, dammit. She didn't. But she said, "I do."

They locked eyes.

A cloud moved across the moon and Jack's face dimmed like the first time she'd laid eyes on him, only the whites of his eyes shining in the dark. If there was one match for Letty Ashdown, one opponent who could match her fire and toss it back, it was Jack Hawk. "There are fleas onboard. We only eat greasy salted pork and hard biscuits and cockroach-laden molasses. And what of storms, or worse, mutiny?"

This is mutiny, Letty thought, forcing out a solitary tear. Nothing could be worse than another day with Harriet. "I will die here, Jack, always waiting for you." She gestured toward the sea, though she could barely make it out in the fog. If only she could command the weather like her mother had in their stories, whip up a tornado, or better yet, a tsunami, with a great wall of water. Take down ships in her wake.

But all she had was her song. Her beautiful bittersweet song.

Unlike with Harriet, Letty did not hold her tongue. She said everything she meant. And more. "I will sit on the rocks and sing for you until I die. You'll return eventually, and they'll tell you, Jack, they'll say, *she sung herself to death. Poor girl.*"

"That's very dramatic." Jack wiped the lone tear away with a raised brow, unmoved. "*Or* you could die out there, you know, on the ocean. It's *actually* dangerous. I will not bring you. I *cannot.*"

Letty turned her back on him. "Then, I *cannot* marry you, Jack Hawk."

Jack groaned. "You're the one who proposed to me, if you recall."

"Well, I withdraw the offer."

Jack began pacing, back and forth, across the balcony, his hand raking through his hair. "You drive me to insanity. You are *so* unreasonably stubborn."

"And you're a coward," Letty returned. "You would've never proposed to me at all had I left it in your hands."

Jack came to a stop in front of her, gripping her by the shoulders. "If you thought that, why would you ask me, then? Why would you want someone if you thought they didn't want you?"

What a ridiculous conversation this had become. Jack had always wanted Letty and she knew it. They both wanted only each other. From the first moment. The first song. The first kiss. They burned for each other.

A new thought occurred to her. "I'm with child."

Jack narrowed his eyes. "You're not."

Letty inspected her now naked and ravaged nails. "What if I am?"

"All the more reason *not* to take you," Jack growled.

Letty smirked. "Good news then, we're in the clear. I can go."

Jack kissed her hard then, his lips smashed into hers, teeth crashing together. He came away breathless. "You're impossible."

Letty studied him most seriously, then let her eyelashes graze her cheeks. "Impossible to leave, you mean?"

"Violetta!" a voice called, from somewhere far below. "Where have you wandered off to, girl? I know you're out here and I intend to find you."

"It's my stepmother," Letty mouthed, with a roll of her eyes, and yet a sharp pang of fear deep in her gut. She sank her ragged nails into the flesh of Jack's upper arm. "I *will* perish if you leave me with her." Letty was serious this time; Jack was her only hope of escape. "I will jump,"—Letty motioned to the railing—"I swear to you, I will. I would rather die than spend another moment with that woman. And with everyone else in this town . . ."

Letty trailed off, choked on her own words. She didn't cry this time, not on purpose, because it was too real. Too raw. A life with Harriet, and without Jack, was no life at all.

Letty saw the way Jack's shoulders slumped, his surrender. He knew. He saw inside of her when no one else did. She'd fed the fire with the townsfolk and her stepmother certainly, there was no doubt about that. But what difference did it make? She'd always been a little different, and people didn't much like different.

It was easier to put a name to different. In this case, *siren.*

Jack blinked several times, as if deciding something, then groaned. "God save me." He began unbuttoning her heavy dress.

"Not that I'm complaining," Letty said, "but what are you doing?"

"We'll have to go with the disguise." Jack had her dress

undone quickly and Letty shrugged out of it, giddy.

"I'll be a boy, then?" Letty clasped her hands together and dropped her petticoats, while Jack unlaced her corset.

Jack's breath was a hiss in her ear. "Not to me, you won't."

Letty shivered, shedding the rest of her attire. "I'll need a boy's name. How about Lenny?" She clapped a hand over her mouth, to stifle a giggle. How easy it was to change a few letters, a song, a name, a life.

Jack retrieved clothing from his bag and began to dress her in his slops. "This is only until we get to Hawaii, then you will stay there with the community of American women." He added, pointedly, "As a woman."

Letty squinted at the *Orca* at port in the distance as Jack dressed her, just able to make out the sails glinting in the moonlight. If she played her cards right, no one would ever know where she had gone.

"Violetta!" Harriet's voice below was teetering on rage. "I have found your gloves, you cannot hide from me."

Watch me, Letty thought.

She should probably leave Harriet a message, that would be the nice thing to do. Like all the messages Harriet had left Letty with the flowers.

Letty plucked the remainder of yellow roses from her hair and sprinkled them around her dress, adding a slew of feathers from the stash in her handbag. "Did you ever hear the legend of the woman who haunts the widow's walk?" she asked Jack, retrieving the bouquet of red roses from the cupola and setting them upside down beside the dress.

"No." Jack eyed her warily, and Letty swallowed down her laughter.

"Story has it she was a siren, like her mother before her. But unlike her mother, she didn't lure the sailors to their deaths. Instead . . . she fell in love with one of them."

"Did she?" Jack asked, head cocked to the side, a giant grin on his face. Despite everything, they'd never said those words to each other yet. *I love you.*

"She did. She really did. And then, on his last night ashore, she simply disappeared." Letty lowered her voice to a whisper. "Vanished into thin air, pining away for her love. The body was never found, though all her clothing was. Sometimes people see her perched as a bird on a branch, a sparrow they say, staring out at the sea, and often, they even smell roses. And always, yes *always*, they hear her song on the wind, floating out above the inn."

Jack reached out uncertainly and dislodged one last feather from her hair before plopping a cap atop her head. He brushed the feather over his lips, kissing it. "Maybe you really are a siren," he mused.

"Maybe I am," Letty agreed, "maybe I am."

Before Jack whisked her away into the night, she sang her revised version of the Wind Song one last time, for her stepmother's benefit, and maybe her own. It was such a haunting melody, even more so in the dark, and it drifted and floated through the mist, eventually settling on the wet sand and rocks below.

I'll sing you a song,
And you'll take me away,
You'll take me out to sea.
My voice in the air,
Is a beautiful prayer,
As I sail away with thee.

Letty could still hear it when the ship pulled away from the harbour at dawn the next morning. She knew the song was a part of this place now, a piece of it, no different than the rocks and the sand and the water. It was what legends were made of. It was a thing to be unearthed when the breeze blew just the right way, a gentle puff or perhaps a raging squall. And sometimes maybe even in the motionless air, in the calm before a storm.

Biographies

Rhonda Parrish
Editor

Like a magpie, Rhonda Parrish is constantly distracted by shiny things. She's the editor of many anthologies and author of plenty of books, stories and poems. She lives with her husband and three cats in Edmonton, Alberta, and she can often be found there playing Dungeons and Dragons, bingeing crime dramas or cheering on the Oilers.

Her website, updated regularly, is at rhondaparrish.com and her Patreon, updated even more regularly, is at patreon.com/RhondaParrish.

Rose Strickman
The Snow Wife

Rose Strickman is a fantasy, science fiction, and horror writer living in Seattle, Washington. Her work has appeared in anthologies such as *After Lines, Sword and Sorceress 32,* and *Earth: Giants, Golems, & Gargoyles,* as well as online e-zines such as *Aurora Wolf* and *Luna Station Quarterly.* Check out her website at aqua-wombat-29pf.squarespace.com/ or connect on Facebook at facebook.com/rose.strickman.3

Davin Aw
Into Thick Air

Davian Aw is a Rhysling Award nominee whose poetry has appeared in *Strange Horizons, Abyss & Apex, Star*Line, NewMyths.com,* and *Not One of Us,* among others. He lives in Singapore with his family.

Mark Bruce
Faery Dust

Mark Bruce is a family law/criminal law attorney in San Bernardino. He worked for seventeen years as a public defender and has been a lawyer since 1987. He won the 2018 Black Orchid Novella Award and has been published in Alfred Hitchcock Mystery Magazine and other publications. He is also a disabled Vietnam-era veteran (US Air Force). His son is getting a PhD at Michigan University, Ann Arbor in Aerospace Engineering. He is unmarried though not unscarred: His second wife has admitted to trying to kill him twice. They're still friends. But he keeps her at arms' length.

Alexandra Seidel
Of White Cranes and Blue Stars

Alexandra Seidel spent many a night stargazing when she was a child. These days, she writes stories and poems, and drinks a lot of coffee (too much, some say). Alexa's writing has appeared in Future SF, Uncanny Magazine, Fireside Magazine, and elsewhere. You can follow her on Twitter @Alexa_Seidel, like her Facebook page (www.facebook.com/AlexaSeidelWrites/), and find out what she's up to at alexandraseidel.com.

Damascus Mincemeyer
Dead Man's Hustle

Exposed to the weird worlds of horror, science fiction, and comics as a boy, Damascus Mincemeyer has been ruined ever since. He's now an artist and writer of various strangeness who's had stories published in the anthologies *Fire: Demons, Dragons, & Djinns, Earth: Giants, Golems & Gargoyles, Hear Me Roar, Bikers Vs the Undead, Psycho Holiday, Monsters Vs Nazis, Mr Deadman Made Me Do It, Satan Is Your Friend, Monster Party, Wolfwinter, Appalachain Horror, Hell's Empire, Crash Code,* the *Sirens Call* ezine, and the magazines *Aphotic Realm, Gallows Hill* and *StoryHack.* He lives near St. Louis, Missouri, USA, and can usually be found lurking about on Twitter @DamascusUndead

Cherry Potts
Final Flight

Cherry Potts is an author, publisher, and creative writing tutor. Publications include a lesbian fantasy epic, two collections of short stories, and numerous short stories published in anthologies and magazines in print and on-line, and performed at Liars' League in the UK and Hong Kong.

She has completed her second novel and is currently working on three more.

Cherry is visiting lecturer in creative writing at City University of London. She runs Arachne Press and is the founder of literature festival, Solstice Shorts.

Cherry sings in choirs for fun and lives with her wife and a very spoilt cat.

Ellen Haung
The Ravens, Before Returning.

Ellen Huang is here for the dragons, unicorns, and changelings of this world. She holds a BA in Writing and a minor in Theatre from Point Loma Nazarene University. The retired Managing Editor of *Whale Road Review,* she is published in *Moonchild Magazine, Prismatica, peculiars, Vamp Cat, Elephants Never, Quail Bell Magazine, Bleached Butterfly, South Broadway Ghost Society, Ghost City, Ink & Nebula,* and *Enchanted Conversation,* among others. She runs a blog in which she connects nostalgic or underrated films to her spirituality. Follow if you wanna! worrydollsandfloatinglights.wordpress.com

Giselle Leeb
Their Disappearing Edges

Giselle Leeb grew up in South Africa and lives in Nottingham. Her short stories have appeared in *Best British Short Stories 2017 (Salt)*, *Lady Churchill's Rosebud Wristlet*, *Black Static*, *Mslexia*, *Litro*, and other places. She is a Word Factory Apprentice Award 2019 winner and an assistant editor at *Reckoning Journal*.

http://giselleleeb.com
Twitter: @gisellekleeb

Bronwynn Erskine
Swanmaid

Bronwynn is a Newfoundlander-by-choice, a payroll professional, and definitely not three cats in a trench coat. She writes primarily fantasy with occasional forays into horror and soft science fiction, and threatens to write a western one of these days. When not writing, she enjoys dabbling in acrylic and watercolour painting, costume sewing, and embroidery art.

Kevin Cockle
The Whippoorwill

Kevin Cockle is the author of over thirty short stories appearing in a variety of anthologies and magazines. His novel *Spawning Ground* is narrowly believed to have invented the micro-genre of "occult game theory", and was published by Tyche Books in 2016. In 2019, Kevin alongside co-writer Mike Peterson won AMPIA's Rosie award for the feature-film screenplay "Knuckleball", breaking a persistent streak of long-list nominations, honourable mention citations, and other close-but-no-cigar metrics.

Elizabeth R. McClellan
Nephele, On Friday

Elizabeth R. McClellan is a domestic and sexual violence attorney by day and a poet in the margins. Their work has appeared in *Chrome Baby, Star*Line, Dreams and*

Nightmares, Apex Magazine, and many others including the *Moment of Change* anthology. They are a multiple-time Rhysling nominee and past winner of the Naked Girls Reading Literary Honours Award. They dream of maenads in silk, bad girl, jackets and monsters dancing the tarantella. They can be found on Twitter @popelizbet.

Chadwick Ginther
Golden Goose

Chadwick Ginther is the Prix Aurora Award nominated author of *Graveyard Mind* and the Thunder Road Trilogy. His short fiction has appeared in many magazines and anthologies. He lives and writes in Winnipeg, spinning sagas set in the wild spaces of Canada's western wilderness where surely monsters must exist.

Christa Hogan
The House with a Pond with a Girl in It

Christa Hogan studied writing and editing at North Carolina State University and is a recovering freelance writer. She's written volumes of magazine articles, corporate newsletters, and blog posts, and more than a dozen educational non-fiction books, all of which have been published and have earned enough income to pay for childcare so she can keep writing. She's also written three novels, which have not (yet) been published (or earned her a dime). She loves them anyway. Her first published short story, "Elma Honey", appeared in the Bronzeville Bee. When not writing, trail running, biking, and chasing three boys, she teaches yoga and meditation. Keep up with Christa on Twitter @christachogan and in opinionated fits and spurts on Medium at medium.com/@cchogan1.

Rowena McGowan
Research Log ~~33

Rowena McGowan has lived in more Canadian provinces than most people have visited. As a child, she won a writing contest with a story about a unicorn that murders someone, which rather set the tone for the rest of her life. She has had short stories in several collections and is hoping to publish her first novel soon.

You can find her @rowena_mcgowan on Twitter. You can also try whispering her name into the ear of the nearest white horse. It won't get a message to her or anything, but she thinks it would be neat if people did it.

Laura VanArendonk Baugh
Eiyri

Laura VanArendonk Baugh writes fantasy of many flavours and non-fiction. She lives in Indiana and enjoys Dobermans, travel, chocolate, and making her imaginary friends fight one another for imaginary reasons. Find her award-winning work at www.LauraVAB.com.

Alyson Faye
Raven Girl

Alyson lives in the UK; her fiction has been published widely both in print anthologies—*DeadCades*, *Women in Horror Annual 2, Colp, Strange Girls* and *Stories from Stone*—and on sites like The Horror Tree and The Casket. Her Gothic story, *Night of the Rider,* is published by Demain in their Short Sharp Shocks! Series, along with her crime novella, *Maggie of my Heart.*

Her work has been placed in several competitions, read in podcasts, and is available as downloads. She performs at open mics, teaches, edits, and attends horror conventions.

https://alysonfayewordpress.wordpress.com/
@AlysonFaye2

Mara Malins
Time to Fold

Mara Malins battles spreadsheets by day and fiction by night. She lives in Manchester, England, with her menagerie of two cats, two turtles, an aquarium that always needs cleaning, a social media loving partner, and a disobedient garden. If you want to know when her next fiction is released, or see thousands of pictures of her cats, find her on Twitter at @maramalins, Goodreads on Mara_Malins, or check out her website at www.maramalins.com

Sara C. Walker
We All Fall Down
Sara C. Walker writes urban fantasy novels and speculative fiction and poetry. Her work has appeared in anthologies published by Exile Editions, Dark Dragon Press, and GallyCat. When not writing she enjoys hiking through the forests of Central Ontario. Find out more about her forthcoming works at www.sarawalker.ca.

Elise Forier Edie
The Sky Thief
Elise Forier Edie is an author and playwright based in Los Angeles. Her hit play "The Pink Unicorn," opened Off Broadway in 2019, and has been seen all over the U.S. and Canada. Her speculative fiction has appeared most recently in Mysterion Magazine and The Young Explorer's Adventure Guide. You can learn more about her—and read more of her stories—at her website eliseforieredie.com

Oliver Smith
Late Tuesday
Oliver Smith is a writer from Cheltenham, UK.

He is inspired by the landscapes of Max Ernst, by frenzied rocks towering in the air above the silent swamp, by the strange poetry of machines, by something hidden in the nothing.

His prose has been published by Ex Occidente Press, Flame Tree Publishing, and Broken Eye Books.

Oliver was awarded first place in the BSFS 2019 competition for his poem "Better Living through Witchcraft" and his poem "Lost Palace, Lighted Tracks" was nominated for the 2020 Pushcart Prize. He holds a PhD in Literary and Critical Studies.

Oliver's website is at oliversimonsmithwriter.wordpress.com/

Sarah Van Goethem
Wind Song
Sarah Van Goethem is a Canadian Author. Her novels have been in PitchWars and longlisted for the 2018 Bath Children's Novel Award as well as CANSCAIP'S 2019 Writing for Children Competition.

Sarah also writes short stories, some of the most recent being: "Accidents are not Possible" for *Grimm, Grit, & Gasoline*, (nominated for a Pushcart) and "Maggie of the Moss" in *Earth: Giants, Golems, & Gargoyles*.

Sarah is a nature lover, a wanderer of dark forests, and a gatherer of vintage. You can find her at auctions, thrift stores, and most definitely trespassing at anything abandoned.

Follow her on Twitter: @sairdysue